Washington Square Secrets
Book 3:
LOYALTY

By

Carrie Dalby

Book designed and published by Olive Kent Publishing
Mobile, Alabama

Cover art by Amanda Manley
Title and chapter fonts in Yataghan—Regular
carriedalby.com

*In memory of
Jay Dalby, Rebecca Jett,
and the members
of the Mobile Police Department
lost in the line of duty*

One

At least the smell of blood was fresh. Thanks to the neighbors on George Street who had heard yelling and then gunshots, the victims had been found before their blood could congeal. Officer Jim Abbott had responded to the flashing light on the call box as soon as he saw it, but the detective and reinforcements had already arrived by the time he got to the house.

"I'm glad there's no decomposition to deal with," Detective Callaghan remarked as the officers gathered outside the kitchen door.

The sight of the woman's bloody chest wound amid her khaki dress and the husband's brains splattered on the kitchen wall turned Jim's stomach with the remembrance of his fellow soldiers. The carnage of the trenches in France seemed like eons ago until something like this brought it to the forefront of his mind. Jim shuddered and rested his hand on the doorframe against the threat of blacking out.

"Abbott," Detective Callaghan barked, "get out front to control the spectators."

Officer Keegan caught Jim's eye and motioned him down the back stoop.

Once they were in the darkness of the back yard, Officer Keegan clapped Jim's shoulder. "Is it your first murder scene?"

He swallowed hard, tasting bile. "Yeah."

Keegan nodded in sympathy. "Give it another five years. By the time you're thirty, your stomach won't churn. Take a smoke if you need it. I can watch the street."

"I'm all right, but thanks." Jim lifted his uniform hat and ran his blue sleeve over his damp forehead. "I'll get out there before Callaghan has my hide."

Jim savored the cool October night as he slowly rounded the house. As soon as the crowd saw him, they stepped away from the lawn.

"What's the word, officer?" a man called from the street.

"I'll leave that to the higher-ups to announce." Jim stopped on the front walk, his hand smoothing over his holster hidden beneath his coat.

When the coroner wagon arrived, the crowd got antsy.

"What about the Harts' boy?"

"I saw him go next door. Fran is always watching out for the neighborhood kids."

"Is the boy hurt, officer?"

"There's nothing I can say, ladies and gentlemen." Jim motioned the neighbors back as an empty gurney was carried into the clapboard house.

When a second stretcher was brought in, a handful of newspaper reporters arrived from the direction of Government Street, including Nathan Paterson, Jim's downstairs neighbor. The reporters sized up the crowd and went for those most willing to talk. Nathan did so while opening the stiff notebook hanging by a strap around his neck. It unfolded like a little desk, allowing him to take notes with only one hand. The amputee had lost his right arm during his service in the Army Signal Corp, but he had found ways to keep doing the job he loved.

By the time Detective Callaghan followed out the first gurney with a shrouded Mr. Hart, the reporters had filled several pages with notes.

"Detective!" Nathan called out. "Washington Square is typically a quiet area. Was this a robbery turned sour?"

"How will these concerned neighbors sleep tonight?" another reporter questioned.

Detective Callaghan straightened his tie. "It appears to have been a domestic dispute. Nothing that would concern anyone else, though we would like to speak to those with adjoining properties that might have heard or seen anything out of the ordinary at the Harts' residence this evening."

"Hart was a hothead," a man said. "We could hear him at our house across the street whenever he complained about the yard, his supper, or his kid."

"I think he was a drunk," a lady said. "A no-good drunkard."

"Mrs. Hart always looked worn out."

"With a man like that, who wouldn't?"

"All right, all right," Callaghan said. "If you have something of importance—directly relating to the screaming many of you heard—I'll talk to you one at a time."

There was a grumble, then silence as the second stretcher exited. Even draped it was obviously a woman.

Blood had seeped through the white sheet from the slight form beneath.

"Abbott." Detective Callaghan caught Jim's elbow and leaned close enough for him to smell the tobacco on his breath. "Go next door and check on the kid. Someone will be here for him before long."

Jim nodded and went across the lawn to the other single-story house. After knocking on the front door, he stood back on the small porch, hat in hand. The interior door opened, but little could be seen of the dim house through the screen.

"Hello, officer. Are you here for Ernest? I just got him settled with a glass of milk." The woman opened the screen door. Her eyes were dark and her brunette hair was in a tidy bun. "Do come in."

"Detective Callaghan wanted me to check on the boy." Jim followed her down the unlit hall.

In the soft glow of the electric kitchen lights, she seemed about the same age as him.

"Ernest," she said as she approached the blond boy slouched at the table for three nestled against the wall. "You have a visitor. Officer…"

"Abbott," Jim finished. "Hello, Ernest."

"Hi." He stared at the hat in Jim's hand rather than make eye contact.

"Did you get enough to drink?" the lady asked.

"Yes, Miss Wilton."

"Would you like something, Officer Abbott?"

He wanted something strong, but politely declined.

"Please join us," she said.

Jim pulled out the chair she motioned to, with the boy to his left and the woman to the right.

Ernest Hart's blue gaze was still locked on Jim's hat so he offered it to him. "Here, Ernest. Give it a go."

He reverently set it on his head. The brim slipped over his brow, but it didn't hide the grin on his face.

Miss Wilton laughed. "You look sharp, Ernest. With a little bit more growing, you'd fill it out nicely."

Smile fading, he tilted the hat back and met Jim's eyes for the first time. "Are my parents gone?"

Jim glanced at Miss Wilton and swallowed. "Yes, Ernest. Some special people came and took them away."

"Then I'll be safe tonight." He looked at the hostess. "I can stay here, right, Miss Wilton?"

Jim saw the concern in her countenance.

"That's not how situations like this work, Ernest," Jim interjected. "Do you have grandparents or an aunt and uncle?"

"Aunt Narcissa is the only one I know. She lives in Florida now because her and my dad fought too much."

"They're brother and sister?" Jim pulled out his pocket notebook. When Ernest nodded, he asked another question. "Is she married?"

"No."

Jim jotted down the name.

"Miss Wilton always gives me cookies when Mommy sends me over and waves when I pass her house."

"Some people are extra friendly. Do you know where in Florida Aunt Narcissa Hart lives?"

"Talla…Tallahapsie."

"Tallahassee," Jim said and wrote it down. "It's the capitol. It will take a while for her to get here at any rate. Fortunately, there's a special home for boys in situations like yours. You could put up there a day or two."

"Miss Wilton let me come here, and the detective said I could."

"But that was just for a little while, Ernest," Miss Wilton said in a kind voice.

"You don't want me? Dad didn't want me either." Ernest squeezed his eyes closed and began rocking, causing the table to shake. The hat slid over his face again and a tear slipped off his chin.

"I'd just gotten him calm, Officer Abbott," Miss Wilton whispered. "I don't like to think of him being shuffled off to a boys' home in the state he's in."

"Could you keep him here if it were allowed?" When she nodded, he continued. "Do you have a telephone I could use?"

"It's in the dining room."

Miss Wilton took him to the other room and hurried back to the boy. Jim asked the operator for Judge Spunner's house and hoped for the best.

When Jim rejoined Miss Wilton and Ernest in the kitchen, he noticed the matronly hand she had on the boy's shoulder. Ernest's head was buried in his arms, resting on the table and covered with Jim's hat. Jim motioned Miss Wilton to him.

"I need to wait for someone. I'll be out front if you need me. Is it all right if I bring the gentleman inside when he arrives?"

"Straight to the kitchen."

"Yes, ma'am."

There were still several reporters on the street but most of the neighbors appeared to have retired for the night. Jim took his station on the Harts' front walk, halfway between the house and the street, and nodded at Nathan. He latched his travel desk shut, knowing Jim would tell him all he could once they were both home.

A few minutes later, Judge Spunner parked his Cadillac Victoria along the curb beneath the large oak tree at the front of the Wiltons' property. When the headlights cut off, it seemed darker than ever.

"What are you doing here, Judge Spunner?" a reporter called. "There's been a crime, but this would be the speediest trial ever."

A few people laughed and the judge flashed his disarming smile.

"I'm here on a personal matter, gentlemen." When he strutted toward the front walk, he nodded at Nathan, but knew better than to call to him even though he was old friends with his wife's family. The newspaper wanted to look impartial, but that was like trying to stop sea turtles from returning to their nesting grounds.

"Thank you for coming, Judge." Jim offered his hand. On the front steps of the Harts' house, he whispered a brief description of the murder-suicide and the kid wishing to stay with the neighbor.

Detective Callaghan joined them. "Abbott, you've got a lot of nerve consulting with a judge on my case."

"I'd call it initiative," Judge Spunner said. "Officer Abbott sees an issue and is bright enough to solve it without worrying the higher-ups. That's something to appreciate. I personally don't settle for less than the best, even in my tenants."

"What's this about?"

"Ernest Hart," Jim said. "He's upset, naturally, but Miss Wilton can calm him. He'd rather stay with her than go to the boys' home while we contact his aunt in Florida. I think that would be—"

"You've been interrogating my witness, Abbott?"

Jim pulled out his pocket notebook. "I was invited to sit with him when you told me to check on the boy. I used the opportunity when it presented itself. His closest kin is an aunt in Tallahassee. It will take a while for her to arrive, so why not keep the boy comfortable where he's familiar? The neighbor is willing to watch him, and I brought in the judge to get his legal opinion on the matter."

Judge Spunner grinned. "You'd make a damn good lawyer, Jim. Bring me to the Wiltons. I haven't spoken to the ladies since Mr. Wilton died."

"Ladies? I've only seen Miss Wilton."

Detective Callaghan followed them next door.

"Mrs. Wilton is an invalid," the judge explained. "I don't think she's been out of her house since her husband died a decade ago. My uncle handles their estate at our firm. It will be nice to see them. Miss Wilton was always a pretty thing."

Two

The tread of heavy footsteps came down the hall, followed by three men entering the kitchen. The detective Francesca Wilton had spoken to earlier came last, but sandwiched between him and Officer Abbott in the lead was a former neighbor she hadn't seen in years.

"Francesca, darling, you haven't changed a bit." Sean Spunner took her hands and kissed her cheek. "It's good to see you."

"Hello, Judge Spunner."

"None of that. Call me Sean as you did when we were even younger." He winked.

Before she took ill, Francesca's mother's favorite topic of conversation was men. She warned her daughter away from those like Sean Spunner—deadly as molasses to flies, luring girls with their sweetness only to drown them. But Francesca already knew all about Sean from her friend Josephine's dealings with him.

Francesca gave him a reserved smile. "All right, Sean, though I do believe I always referred to you as Mr. Spunner."

Sean chuckled. "How's your mother?"

"Not well, but not any worse than she has been the past few years."

"Yet you wish to bring another soul in need into your care." He lifted her chin so she looked into his golden eyes. "Is there enough of you to extend yourself even more?"

"It would do my heart good to look after Ernest."

"You've always been a dear." He grinned and turned to the others. "I was fortunate enough to waltz with Francesca at her first ball. I bet she's still graceful on the dance floor."

"Enough of the good old days, Judge." Detective Callaghan stepped forward. "We need to concern ourselves with 1920. Will Miss Wilton be able to keep the kid, or do I need to contact the boys' home?"

"I'll personally vouch for Francesca's good character and will argue the point that keeping Ernest in familiar surroundings during this time is the best option to anyone seeking to follow regulations."

"That's good enough for me," Detective Callaghan said. "I'll put my time into contacting the next of kin. Abbott, I'll ask the chief for you to be the liaison in this matter. Come with me while I explain a few things." The detective nodded at Sean, then Francesca. "Good night, Judge. Miss Wilton."

After the police left, Sean claimed the seat Officer Abbott previously used. He leaned close to Ernest and took his elbow. Not used to the touch of a loving father, Ernest flinched away. Sean settled back to give him space.

"I just want to tell you, Ernest, that Miss Wilton is your temporary guardian. That means you need to listen to her and make sure you behave with respect while you're here. Will you do that?"

Ernest nodded.

"Good. I've got three children at home—a boy and two girls. My son is six, but I think you've got a couple years on him."

"I'm seven."

"You're big for your age. I'm sure you'll be a great help to Miss Wilton. I want you to stay home from school for a week. Play in the yard, read, and whatever else Miss Wilton thinks is a good way for you to spend your time, all right?"

He nodded again.

"And Officer Abbott is an equally fine person to be looking in on you. He was a soldier during the war and a security guard at a bank before he became a policeman." Sean gently tapped the uniform hat still on Ernest's head. "You talk to him if you're ever worried. Officer Abbott will help you—and you too, Francesca."

"Thank you, Sean."

"I'll inform my uncle of the situation. Do you still have hired help?"

"During the day."

"Send word to me or my uncle if you require more. We'll see to it." He stood and offered his hand to Ernest. "You're the man of the house here, Ernest. I know you'll do well."

Francesca walked Sean to the front door. "I appreciate everything."

"I'm happy to help." He motioned next door. "That's the old Barnes house, isn't it?"

"Mrs. Barnes moved in with one of her sons after her husband died. None of the siblings wanted it, so it was sold. The Harts moved in this summer, and the street hasn't been the same since."

"That's a shame, but I'm glad the boy has you, even if it's just for a few days." Sean kissed her cheek. "Take care, Francesca."

Upon returning to the kitchen, she rinsed the milk glass. "I'm going to make up the guest room bed. Would you help me, Ernest?"

"Yes, Miss Wilton."

He carried the blankets from the linen closet and followed her to the room.

"I hope you'll be comfortable here."

"I will, Miss Wilton."

"Call me Fran, Ernest." She finished with the bedding preparations and straightened. "I suppose I could loan you a shirt to sleep in."

There was a soft rap on the front door. Officer Abbott was on the porch, arms filled with items for Ernest and a friendly smile on his handsome face.

"I was just lamenting about what Ernest could change into for bed," Francesca said as she motioned him inside.

"I thought it best to get a few supplies. There will be an officer on duty next door until the investigation is officially over should you need to collect anything else."

"Thank you." She turned to Ernest. "Office Abbott brought some of your clothes and even your toothbrush."

"Your mother kept a tidy house so it was easy for me to find everything." He handed the pile to the boy.

"Thank you, Officer Abbott. I guess you'll want your hat back."

"You can keep it until tomorrow. I'll be stopping by in the morning. Keep it safe for me." Officer Abbott's smile was reflected in Ernest's huge grin. "Goodnight, Ernest."

Francesca walked the officer to the front door. "I can't thank you enough."

"I'm glad my idea to involve the judge worked out. I didn't know he personally knew you, but Judge Spunner seems to know everyone in Mobile. How early is too early to stop by in the morning?"

"After eight o'clock would be fine. Come to the kitchen door."

Officer Abbott nodded. "I wish you the best with the boy."

A quarter of an hour later, Ernest was washed, brushed, and in his pajamas.

Francesca walked him to bed. "Would you like me to sit with you tonight?"

Blue eyes wide and shoulders tight, Ernest nodded.

"I need to wash up, but I'll leave the corner lamp on."

His shoulders lowered slightly.

"It can stay on all night if you'd like. Shall I tuck you in or are you beyond that?"

"Mommy always tucked me in."

"I'll happily do that for you, Ernest."

He slipped between the blankets and smiled at her. "Goodnight, Miss Fran."

"Goodnight, Ernest. I'll be back soon."

***

Friday morning, October eighth, Francesca woke as the sun began glowing through the guest room curtains. Amazed she had managed a few hours of sleep in the chair, she rubbed her neck and slowly stood.

Ernest slept curled on his side, the blanket bunched around his neck so only his angelic face and mop of blond hair showed. Francesca sank back into the chair, the weight of her lost decade threatening to strangle her. If her father hadn't died and her mother been bedridden, she could have had a child of her own—maybe even several. But Francesca was a fixture in the house as much as the hideous parlor couch from the previous century.

She quietly dressed, choosing clothing with more care than she had the day before. An ecru blouse and tapered blue plaid skirt she had mail-ordered the month before made her appear fashionable along with low-heeled shoes. But her hair was another story. Francesca had the cook trim it straight across at her waistband every month. A bun was the only option though it was antiquated. Francesca knew she was in danger of becoming a spinster, but felt like it for the first time in her thirty-one years.

Mrs. Wilton rang the silver bell when Francesca exited her room. She hurried to check that Ernest was still sleeping before opening her mother's door.

"Good morning, Mother." Francesca kissed her cheek, smooth from the lack of sun and stress.

"Franny dear, how is everything? I thought I heard something last night."

"You know how noisy the neighbors can get." She clicked on the side table lamp and reached for a medicine bottle.

"I miss Dolores Barnes since she moved."

"We all do." Francesca missed the whole family, especially the youngest two—Cordelia and Tristan, though they hadn't lived there for years. Tristan had been her beau once upon a time. He was married now with two children. Cordelia was married as well, but would never be a mother. She visited Francesca at least monthly, but it used to be weekly when her mother lived next door.

"It was noisier than usual last night."

"Mr. Hart won't bother us anymore." Francesca paused. "There was a worse fight than usual. He shot Mrs. Hart and then himself. At least, that's what the police are saying, but I wouldn't wonder if she pulled the trigger first."

"How horrible."

"Ernest is staying in the guest room. He's comfortable with me after all the times his mother sent him over when Mr. Hart would come home drunk. But a policeman is tasked with checking Ernest while he's here since I'm not an official guardian."

"That good for Ernest, but why is he allowed to stay here rather than be sent to the boys' home?"

"Judge Spunner told the police it was okay."

"Solicitor Finnigan's nephew has been as brazen as a peacock since he was a boy."

Francesca would have laughed if she wasn't worried about her mother's agitation. "He was elected just before the armistice, Mother. He's been a judge for nearly two years, and the city hasn't fallen apart. He stopped by last night and told me to send word to him or his uncle if we ever need anything."

"Is his smile still devilish?"

"He oozes sweetness as he always has."

Her shoulders rose with a weak shrug. "I told your father that night Mr. Spunner danced with you that I'd rather go blind than see my daughter with a scoundrel like him. Ruth Melling admitted on a few occasions that the one solace of her daughter dying was that it broke her engagement to the man."

Francesca didn't think Sean was as terrible as that, but she offered her mother a smile rather than argue. "If you're settled, I need to check on Ernest."

"Franny," Mrs. Wilton said. "A boy is no substitute for a man."

"But a child fills another void." Francesca spooned her mother's morning medicine into her mouth.

Mrs. Wilton swallowed and sighed. "You're as stubborn as your father was. I don't want breakfast today. Tell Becca to cook brunch instead."

"Yes, Mother."

"And go for a walk, Franny. You're looking pale. There's no need to hover when the nurse is here. You need to care for yourself, dear."

Francesca smiled. "Yes, Mother."

Pleased to have an excuse to take Ernest outside without worrying her mother, Francesca hurried to check on him. He was still in peaceful oblivion, so she waited in the kitchen for Becca to arrive.

The Wiltons' cook for two decades bustled in, her arms full of the dairy delivery off the back porch. As she packed the ice box, Francesca whispered about the Harts' murder-suicide and Ernest staying with them.

"He's very quiet," Francesca said. "But he'll make a little more work for you."

"I know how to feed a growing boy, Miss Fran."

"Thank you. Mother wishes brunch today—nothing beforehand—and a policeman will be coming to the kitchen door sometime after eight. Please let him in and offer him coffee or whatever else might be on hand."

Feeling she had everything under control, Francesca sat in the guest room to wait for Ernest to wake. He didn't stir until almost eight, eyes wide with fright.

"It's all right, Ernest." She perched on the edge of the bed. "You're with me, remember?"

"I had a bad dream." He threw his arms around her. "But I feel safe here."

Francesca quickly kissed the top of his head. "Good, because you are safe. Get dressed and then we'll go to the kitchen for breakfast."

Becca had pancakes frying when they entered the kitchen.

"Ernest, you remember Becca, don't you? Whenever you get hungry during the day, ask her for assistance."

"I'm pleased to have a young man in the house, Ernest."

They settled at the table across from each other as they had the night before, Francesca with coffee and Ernest with milk. Officer Abbott's hat was on the table between them.

The nurse arrived to prepare Mrs. Wilton's sponge bath while they continued breakfast.

Ernest was polishing off his fourth pancake and Francesca her second when a deep voice called "good morning" from the back stoop.

Officer Abbott wore his thick, brown hair slicked back, highlighting a widow's peak hairline. His grin was that of a man barely old enough to serve his country, though

Sean had said he was a veteran of the Great War. But his haunted green eyes displayed he had seen much in his life, no matter how short.

"Good morning, Officer Abbott." Francesca opened the screen for him. "Please join us. Would you like coffee or pancakes or both?"

"Both, thank you, Miss Wilton."

Becca added more batter into the frying pan, and Francesca brought a cup to the table to pour coffee for the policeman and more for herself.

"Well, Ernest, how did you do last night?" Officer Abbott asked as he took the empty chair.

"Good, Officer Abbott. Miss Fran keeps me safe."

"And you kept my hat protected. Thank you. The detective couldn't reach your aunt last night, so he'll try again today."

Ernest grinned before shoving in another forkful of pancakes.

"We'll be going for a walk to Washington Square Park after breakfast," Francesca announced.

"I'd be happy to accompany you there," Officer Abbott said. "I typically walk that way as part of my morning patrol."

"Could you help me climb the trees?" Ernest asked.

"I'll teach you everything I know," he assured him.

When they left, Ernest held Francesca's hand as they made their way down the road. The dappled sunlight through the oaks was nothing compared to the warmth of the child's touch. When the park came into view, Ernest ran across the corner of Chatham and Palmetto Streets to the park. A dog barked at Francesca as they passed the Graves' house.

Merritt Graves opened the iron gate, keeping her dog behind the fence. "Hello, Fran, and Officer Abbott."

"Hello, Merritt," Francesca said to the neighbor who visited her mother each week.

"Chat as long as you wish, ladies. I'll watch Ernest. Have a good day, Mrs. Graves." Touching his hat, Officer Abbott nodded before crossing to the park in pursuit of Ernest.

Not until he was in the grassy area did Merritt speak. "That's the Harts' boy, isn't it? I read Nathan's article over breakfast."

"Yes, and the whole block heard the horrid event." Francesca shivered. "Ernest asked to stay with me until his aunt comes for him."

"But you have no experience with children."

Merritt only had a decade on Francesca, but was already a grandmother. Knowing she didn't mean to sound critical, Francesca explained. "I couldn't send him to strangers after all he's been through. Officer Abbot called Judge Spunner, and he approved the temporary custody idea. It's not official, but between the judge and the police, I'm sure things will work out until Ernest's aunt arrives from Florida."

"Sean could talk anyone into anything, all while keeping himself out of hot water. I fear Officer Abbott is of similar stock."

Francesca watched the man hoist Ernest onto a low oak branch. "He's tasked with checking on us twice a day, but he's going beyond a physical check-in, making sure Ernest is comfortable with the situation." Francesca turned back to Merritt. "How do you know Officer Abbott?"

"He's one of Sean's tenants in the apartment building Winnie oversees. He lives upstairs from her and Nathan. He's proven helpful to them but...." she shook her head at whatever memories of her daughter and son-in-law concerned her regarding the police officer. "It's that dimpled grin—quick to grab at hearts. How is your mother managing the news?"

"Concerned, as I figured she would be. I should go to the park now."

"Telephone if you have any questions, Fran. I'll be over to see your mother on Monday, as usual."

"Thank you, Merritt. I appreciate it."

Across the road, Ernest was sitting at least five feet up one of the trees. Officer Abbott stood within catching distance should Ernest lose his balance, but he didn't draw attention to his safety stance.

"Could we have a picnic here?" Ernest asked when Francesca joined them.

"I didn't bring any food, and that's the most important part of a picnic."

His eyes brightened. "What about later?"

"I think we should stay at home the rest of the day in case Detective Callaghan has news about your aunt, but we could picnic in the yard."

He looked at Officer Abbott. "Could you join us?"

"I have to keep to my patrol, Ernest, but I'll be back to check on you this evening." He looked at his wristwatch. "I better get going. Show me how you can climb down."

Ernest edged himself to the trunk and scrambled down. On his feet, he looked up at the policeman for several seconds.

"Thank you for helping, Officer Abbott."

He ruffled Ernest's hair and smiled. "And thank you for being a quick learner. Keep Miss Wilton safe, and I'll see you later."

If Officer Abbott had winked at her before turning away, Francesca would have believed Merritt's opinion of him. But true to her own thoughts of the man, he merely nodded respectfully and whistled his way down the sidewalk.

"Officer Abbott," Francesca called. "If you can make it in time for supper, you're welcome to join us."

"I appreciate it, Miss Wilton." He lifted his cap and strolled away.

When Francesca and Ernest returned to her house, Josephine Harrington was waiting for Francesca in her mother's room, who was fussing at their guest. Ever since Josephine's mother passed away over two decades ago, Mrs. Wilton felt the need to try to teach her decorum and the finer things a true lady should do—not that Josephine paid a lick of attention to it.

"Really, Josephine, a woman your age in trousers is an abomination. Cutting off your hair was one thing, but showing your shape as you do is scandalous."

"I see no reason to adjust my comfort to the world's opinions. But be assured that Cyrus loves me in trousers almost as much as he loves me in nothing."

"For shame, Josephine!" Mrs. Wilton said with a frown. "There's a child present."

After quickly hugging her oldest friend, Francesca took Ernest's hand. "Mother, I'm sorry we left for a walk before Ernest could say hello, but I didn't want to interrupt your bath."

"That's all right, Franny. Ernest can sit with me while you and Josephine talk." Mrs. Wilton patted the edge of the bed and Ernest hopped up. "Tell me about your walk."

Josephine linked her arm through Francesca's and led her to the parlor, where they settled side-by-side on the sofa.

"I came as soon as I could get away." Josephine's hazel eyes were on her friend, her hand clasping Francesca's. "I wanted to check on you after the horror next door. Your mother told me the boy is staying with you temporarily. Is there anything you need?"

"I don't think so, but thank you. There's a policeman who's supposed to check in with us twice a day, and Judge Spunner said I could call on him or his uncle for anything."

Josephine rolled her eyes. "Sean Spunner will say anything to gain a woman's favor. Come to me, Fran. I'll help without a nauseating display of chivalrous pomp."

Francesca laughed, causing Joephine to grin.

"Your house feels mostly settled, but do you need Deborah's mediumship skills?"

"No, we're all fine. Ernest is resilient. I'm glad he's been here enough times to be comfortable with me, even if the reasons he was here were troublesome."

Josephine nodded in understanding because Francesca had previously shared about Ernest taking refuge at her house from his raging father. "Spring Hill isn't too far for me to arrive within the hour if you call."

Francesca stood with her. "I know. And I appreciate it, Jo. I'll be in touch."

Three

Jim arrived at the Wiltons' house at six o'clock, stopping on the screened back porch as he had that morning.

"Evening, Officer Abbott," the cook said. "Come right in."

"Thank you, Miss Becca." Jim removed his hat. "Where would the best place be for me to wash up?"

"You can use my sink. I'm fixing Mrs. Wilton's supper plate, then Miss Fran will be in to serve while I sit with her mother."

Jim unbuttoned his uniform jacket, setting it and his hat on one of the dining chairs so he could roll up his sleeves before he washed.

"Mrs. Wilton might want to meet you—if she's in the mood for more company. She had Miss Jo this morning, which set her off a bit, and then Ernest stayed with her for a while." Becca poured a glass of iced tea. "But she likes to know who's paying calls at her house, even if it isn't for her."

"I'd be happy to see her whenever she's ready for me." Jim lathered his hands and forearms with a lemon-scented bar of speckled soap. "I've never seen soap like this."

"That's one of Miss Jo's recipes. Miss Fran refuses to use anything but her friend's tea and soap blends."

Jim wasn't sure he liked how soft it made his hands feel when he was drying them on the towel Becca handed him, but he enjoyed the citrus smell. He reset his sleeves and jacket before tucking his hat under his arm as the cook left the kitchen with a tray.

A moment later, Miss Wilton entered. "I'm glad you could join us, Officer Abbott. Ernest went to wash. I'll have supper on the table in a minute."

"Is there anything you need help with?"

"No, thank you." She tied a pink flowered apron over her slim blue skirt and turned to the stove.

Jim stood awkwardly in the corner—trying not to stare at the way Miss Wilton moved around the kitchen with graceful ease.

Ernest hurried in. "Officer Abbott!"

"Hey, Ernest." He plopped his hat on the boy's head and grinned in return. "Did you have a good day?"

"Yes, sir." Ernest kept a hand on the eight-point hat to keep it from sliding off as he looked up at Jim. "Miss Fran and I played checkers this afternoon."

"Come pour your glass of milk, Ernest," Miss Wilton said from across the room. "Officer Abbott, would you prefer something hot or cold to drink?"

"Whatever you're having is fine."

She fixed two glasses of tap water, which Jim took from the counter before she could bring them across the kitchen. Not until the food was on the table and he had pulled out Miss Wilton's chair so she could sit did Jim take his own place. Ernest hung Jim's hat on the right finial of the back of his chair.

Miss Wilton gave a simple prayer over the food and then crossed herself. Jim followed her lead and Ernest copied him. Then they took turns dishing up from the stuffed flounder, greens, and cornbread platters in the middle of their three-person table setting.

"Where do you usually eat supper?" Ernest asked Jim while they were eating.

"At home or with neighbors. Sometimes at a restaurant if I'm working late or headed out somewhere."

"Mommy used to take me to a restaurant once a month. I liked to get pot roast and potatoes."

"I'll have to ask Miss Becca about fixing that next week," Miss Wilton said.

Blue eyes lighting up, Ernest smiled. "And chocolate ice cream?"

Miss Wilton's generous lips pulled into a smile. "That might need a special trip to an ice cream parlor."

As they were finishing the meal, Becca returned. "Mrs. Wilton will see you now, Officer Abbott. It's the first open door in the hall."

"Do you need your hat?" Ernest asked.

"No, keep watching it for me." Jim ruffled the boy's hair.

Ernest pointed to the number under the eagle medallion on the front of it. "What's the ninety-six for?"

"It's my identification number." Jim touched the badge on his chest with the same information. "It's as good as my name if you called into the station and needed to get in touch with me."

"Officer ninety-six!"

Jim saluted and went for the hall.

Only a side table lamp with a rosy shade on it burned in the bedroom. Propped on a wedge of lacy pillows, Mrs. Wilton looked like a shrunken version of her daughter but with glossy hair streaked with white done in two braids that lay over her shoulders like a mantle.

"Good evening, Mrs. Wilton," he said as he stopped at the foot of the bed.

"Come here, officer. Let me get a good look at you. It's been ages since I've seen a man around here besides Dr. Moore or Father Quinn. Franny and Becca get to see the grocery delivery boys, but they never come to my room." Her smile was as broad as her daughter's, and though she looked tired, there was a spark in her dark eyes. "Why you're a fine sight! I wonder why neither of them mentioned that to me."

Jim grinned at the compliment.

"Yes, a handsome figure. I'd be pleased to have you stop in when you can spare the time."

"Of course, Mrs. Wilton. I'll be here twice a day, so send word if you feel up to a visit."

"Very good." She sighed as she looked him over. "Please ask Franny to play a hymn or two on the piano for me. I like to listen while I go through my magazines before bed."

"I'd be happy to pass the word, Mrs. Wilton."

While Miss Wilton took the piano bench before the upright grand, Jim sat on the parlor floor with Ernest, the checkerboard between them. They must have played a dozen games before he said goodnight. It was going on nine when Jim finally walked home. As much as he enjoyed his evening, he knew he needed to drop by the Wiltons' house during non-mealtimes in the future so he wouldn't make a nuisance of himself.

Across Government Street and onto Hallett—only a few blocks separated him from the scene of the crime. His thoughts stayed on Ernest and his guardian as Jim approached the apartment house. Strains of Chopin spilled from the downstairs unit. Winnie Paterson enjoyed playing dreamy piano tunes while her son fell asleep, and Jim enjoyed the calming effects as well. Nathan was on the front porch smoking. The lone light between the doors leading to the Patersons' ground-floor apartment and the Williams' unit in the front of the second floor backlit his head. The glow of Nathan's cigarette deftly moved between his lips as he snatched the pack of Lucky Strikes off the table and tossed it at Jim.

"Join me." He handed him his lighter when Jim reached his side.

"Thanks." He lit one, placed the items on the table, and took the solo chair across from the wicker loveseat.

"Your check-ins with the Hart boy go all right?" Nathan asked.

"Ernest is doing well and lamenting the day when his aunt arrives. Fortunately for him, that won't be until sometime next week."

"What's wrong with the aunt?"

"She's related to his father for one thing, but said she couldn't take off work on the weekend because she's on the housekeeping staff at a hotel. But he's enjoying his time with Miss Wilton. He really likes her."

Nathan ran his hand through his hair and chuckled. "You better watch out with all this checking in on single ladies."

"I doubt I have what a classy woman like Miss Wilton wants."

"You've got *something* the ladies want. Marie Marley still asks Winnie about you, and there was that redhead you brought to the broil this summer that couldn't keep her hands off you."

Jim laughed at the memories of his last two attempts at relationships. "Marie is sweet, but you know I'd never be good enough in her father's eyes. He wants all his girls to marry up and won't allow the youngest the likes of me when the others have snagged a doctor and an old Mobile name. And it was a blessing when the redhead moved to New Orleans. She was downright crazy!"

The piano score ended and the screen door opened. Winnie came to the seating arrangement looking fresh in a simple cotton smock that draped her slight pregnancy belly. Nathan was lucky to have his pretty high school sweetheart and a solid marriage at the age of twenty-one. Their heartaches helped forge their bonds stronger though it had been hell in the moment.

"Do you need anything, Nathan?" Winnie asked as she placed her hand on his shoulder.

"Just you. Your concert was lovely."

Her dark locks swung above her shoulders as she sat close beside him. After kissing her husband's cheek, she looked at Jim through her wire-framed glasses. "Hey, Jim. I hear you've got a full plate with work right now. How's Miss Wilton doing with the neighbor boy?"

"Great. He really likes her."

"She's kept an eye on the neighborhood kids ever since I can remember." Winnie's hand went to Nathan's forearm. "When we stopped by to see her on the way home from my parents on Easter, she had Percy laughing and playing within seconds."

"She sure did." He ground out his cigarette in the ashtray and rested against his wife's side.

"Judge Spunner told me he danced with her the year she debuted. How old is she?" Jim asked.

"She's a decade older than me, and about that much younger than Sean," Winnie said. "I'm not sure of her birthday, but she's at least thirty by now."

"She's very young-looking."

"But still a spinster," Nathan remarked.

"Miss Wilton hardly had a chance with the death of her father and a sick mother," Winnie said in the woman's defense. "She did lose at least one admirer though. Tristan Barnes courted her on the front porch for a couple years but gave up waiting and married another soon after."

"The judge still admires her," Jim said. "You should have seen him calling her *Francesca* and fawning over the memory of dancing with her."

"Poor Hattie," Winnie said. "Sean loves her to distraction, but I do believe there's a pang of regret that she isn't a graceful dancer. Sean has always loved to dance. He taught me when I was twelve."

"Not all women are fully accomplished like you." Nathan's lips went to her neck. "Intelligent, a skilled pianist, beauty on the dance floor, a fabulous cook, and a devil in bed."

Jim couldn't help watching the way Winnie smiled as she arched into her husband's touch. He wanted the same thing—a sweet woman to love at the end of the day, the comforts of home and family.

Putting out his smoke, Jim stood. "Try to keep the noise down when you go inside."

Nathan pulled away from Winnie. "Don't be jealous. Have dinner or supper with us tomorrow."

"Thanks, but I'm going fishing after I check in with Miss Wilton and then out to the dancehall tomorrow night. Goodnight, Nathan. Winnie."

She stood and gave him a hug. "Stop in whenever you want, Jim."

Jim squeezed her tight in return. "Thanks, Winnie."

"Hey now," Nathan said playfully, "I can't have you doing more to her with those two arms of yours than I can."

He dropped one, but kept Winnie close to his side with an arm around her shoulders as he turned to Nathan. "I hope I don't need to remind you how blessed you are, Paterson. See y'all later."

Jim went down the side steps and around the corner of the house to the wooden stairs in the back that led to his studio apartment. It usually felt cozy, but an air of emptiness permeated the space so much he opened all the windows to try to air it out.

After a hot shower, he pulled open the cabinet with his Murphy bed to cool the sheets. Jim collapsed on the couch and tried to forget the feel of Winnie's hug. She meant well, but it made his situation even more pathetic. Rather than remember the solace of his friend's arms, he recalled the joy on Miss Wilton's face when Ernest asked for ice cream. Her unguarded smile was wide and welcoming. Hopefully it wouldn't haunt his dreams because at that moment, he'd give anything to kiss her.

***

The one Saturday Jim got off work per month was a morning that made Octobers in Alabama proud. The azure sky rose above him as he shouldered his pack, creel, and fishing poles and descended the back steps. It would be a bright one, but not too hot.

Protection duty was pulled from the Harts' house after the body matter had been scrubbed from the kitchen the day before, but the sergeant warned Jim about going inside unnecessarily. The department feared a foundation issue because the house had felt like it was shaking when the first officers arrived on the scene.

At the Wiltons', he went through the side gate, leaving his gear and wide-brimmed straw hat at the back corner of the house before going up the kitchen steps. The cook waved him in.

"Good morning, Miss Becca," he said.

"Morning, Officer Abbott. As nice as you look in uniform, it's good to see you in regular stitches."

Francesca Wilton entered the room. "Hello, Officer Abbott."

"Good morning, Miss Wilton. Was everything all right last night?"

"Ernest is settled in wonderfully, but he did wake up once with a nightmare." Eyes flickering over his khaki pants and pale blue button up shirt, she frowned. "I didn't think of you having to come on your day off. Don't feel you have to stop in later."

"It's my pleasure, Miss Wilton. I'm just on the other side of Government. It isn't an inconvenience, and the company is nice."

She nodded and shyly turned away.

"Do you need breakfast, Officer Abbott?" Becca asked.

"No, thank you. I had grits and coffee before leaving for the express purpose of not over-stepping the gracious hospitality offered here."

"It's no trouble," Becca insisted.

"As long as this house is part of your assignment," Miss Wilton said, "the kitchen is always open to you."

"I appreciate it, ladies. If you don't need anything, I'll be off."

Ernest hurried in from the hall, face glistening pink from a recent scrubbing. "Hi, Officer Abbott! You're not a policeman today?"

"I'm always a policeman, but I don't have to report to the station until tomorrow." Jim ruffled his hair and then smoothed it back down. "Take care of Miss Wilton, and I'll check in later."

Ernest grabbed his hand, a look of expectation on his face. "I could watch your hat for you."

"It's at home, Ernest, but I'll see you this evening."

He shuffled backward, discouragement pulling down his face.

Miss Wilton waved Jim away and went to comfort the boy.

With guilt tugging at Jim, he collected his things and hurried to the streetcar on Government. After switching tracks, he took the southbound line to Monroe Park.

Jim walked down the bay until he found a quiet spot. The gentle lap of the water was his focus as he waited for something to tug the line. It was slow going, but he wasn't there for the chase.

Hours later, when his creel was half full and the stash of food and drink close to gone, Jim started his trek north. Skirting the edge of Monroe Park, he caught a streetcar and stayed to the side, aware of his undesirability with a basket of fish and sweat-stained clothes.

Jim exited on the south side of downtown near the neighborhood he'd grown up in, hoping to catch up with a lady on her daily route. She didn't come into sight until he was nearing St. Emanuel and Elmira Streets. Her full, black skirt was dusty from her journey and her white-blonde hair tousled beneath the small hat perched on her head. A train rumbled nearby and the smell of low tide from the river beyond mingled with the lingering odor from the multitude of cats she kept in her once tidy yard.

Smelling Jim's catch, a dozen felines surrounded him, yowling for scraps.

"Miss Eilands!" he called, not wishing to approach unannounced.

She stopped after crossing through her gate, shading her pale eyes with a wrinkled hand to peer at him. "Is that you, Jimmy?"

"Yes, Miss Eilands." He carefully took his final steps without treading on the cats.

One jumped onto the rickety fence between them. The lady stroked its back, her frame no more than a skeleton with skin. "You ain't much without that uniform, Jimmy."

He laughed. "So they say, ma'am. I went down the bay for some fishing on my day off."

"You're too late. I already got the scraps from the wharves for my cats."

"This is for you, Miss Eilands, though there's enough to share. It's a special treat for… your birthday."

"You're a month early, Jimmy. I won't accept it. And if you ask me my age, I'll strike you."

"Then take it in celebration of me."

"What are you celebrating?"

"The fact that you haven't cursed me with the evil eye."

Miss Eilands giggled. She had to be around seventy, but there was an air of innocence beneath her rough façade. The root of the genteel lady she was raised to be. After being left alone for decades, she did what she needed to survive and protect her beloved pets while the neighborhood fell to ruin around her.

"Will you allow me to deliver this load so I can go home, Miss Eilands?"

She nodded and Jim went into the house like a pied piper leading a trail of cats.

"You need somewhere safe for the redfish, Miss Eilands. The cats can have the mullet. How are the kittens doing?"

She pursed her lips as though about to defy him, then stoked the fire in her old stove and held out a pan. "Those kittens are snug in the parlor. Bless you, Jimmy, for your kindness."

Four

At eight o'clock Saturday night, Francesca heard a light knock on the back door. Leaving teary-eyed Ernest in the parlor, she hurried to the kitchen. Officer Abbott stood on the back porch in a dark suit and blue bowtie. He stepped into the house holding his fedora and filled the room with the scent of aftershave.

"He's been distraught all evening," Francesca said in a hurried whisper. "This morning was one thing, but tonight Ernest fears you've abandoned him."

Officer Abbott moved toward the hall. She grabbed his hand, then hastily dropped back at the warm feel of him. His green eyes were intense as he stared into her soul.

"I don't know if my keeping him was the right thing to do," Francesca whispered. "Is it fair to allow him to attach to me—to you—when his aunt is going to take him away?"

"You've been family to him these past days. All children need that security, even if it's temporary." His hands captured hers, and his intimate voice dropped lower. "You've done the right thing, Miss Wilton, but sometimes the correct course is painfully hard."

Tears pricking at the corner of her eyes, she swallowed. "Offi—"

"Please call me Jim. I'd like for you to think of me as a friend." He squeezed her hand before slowly releasing it. "May I go to him?"

Francesca nodded and tried not to notice how his suit jacket accented his broad shoulders as she followed Jim to the front of the house.

Ernest bounded off the sofa, jumping at the visitor. "You came back, Officer Abbott!"

Jim tossed his fedora onto the coffee table. "I strive to be truthful in all I do, and I told you this morning I'd be back."

"But you didn't come for supper like you did yesterday."

Jim perched himself on the edge of a chair so they were eye-level. "Miss Wilton and Miss Becca are generous with sharing their food, but I don't wish to intrude too often. I made a point to come today after breakfast and supper times so I could focus on my responsibilities rather than having fun because it was my day off."

"You don't have fun on your day off?"

He laughed. "I have lots of fun on my day off, but I wanted to be sure I did my assignment properly amid my amusements."

Jim Abbott had been dressed for the outdoors that morning and now looked ready for a night around town— probably with a lady.

"You're going to leave?" The boy put his hand on Jim's sleeve.

"Yes, but Miss Wilton has you well-looked after."

"But you could stay."

"What do you need from me, Ernest?" Jim asked.

Francesca approached them. "Officer Ab—"

"Jim," he interrupted.

She gave an exasperated sigh. "*Jim* looks to be on his way to a dance or something, Ernest. We need to wish him goodnight."

"But he could dance here. We have a piano and a gramophone."

"Don't be silly," she said. "There's no one for him to dance with."

"You're here, Miss Fran." Ernest, wide-eyed and smiling, took all the annoyance out of her.

"I'm sure Jim wouldn't be interested in—"

"I'd be honored if you'd dance with me, Miss Wilton."

"I'll get the music!" Ernest hurried to the gramophone they had been listening to that afternoon and cranked the handle.

Before Francesca could stop him, Ernest lowered the arm. The doily she'd had in the horn earlier to muffle the sound was back on the side chair. She hastily shoved it inside to lower the blast of the waltz.

When she turned back, Jim's hand was outstretched. Francesca accepted him with a touch of hesitation. Jim's left arm was high with her right, and his other hand slipped sensually to her waist. It had been years, but she settled her hand on his shoulder and followed his lead with precision. Before she realized it, the song ended. Francesca found herself smiling at Jim.

Ernest clapped. "You're beautiful, Miss Fran!"

Her cheeks flushed with his words and Jim's rapt attention as the next song began. Lowering her eyes, she stepped away, but Jim didn't release her hand.

"I'm terribly out of practice," she said. "But at least I didn't tread on your feet."

"You were magnificent, Miss Wilton. It's no wonder Judge Spunner raved about dancing with you. Might I claim one more?"

"Won't you be late to—"

"There's no place I'd rather be than right here, right now."

And with the flood of warmth his words created, she believed him.

Francesca felt Jim's closeness even more. His hot, minty breath. The flex of his fingers at her hip. The strength of his arm supporting hers. At the end of the song, he dipped her back and held her in the pose for what felt like hours as he stared into her eyes. Once she was upright, his lips went to her ear.

"You're spectacular, Francesca," he whispered before turning his grin on Ernest. "Isn't it past your bedtime, young man?"

"Yes, but I need to wash."

"Check with Miss Wilton." When Ernest refused to move, Jim spoke again. "I'll stop by in the morning on my way to Mass. I work the afternoon shift, and depending on my workload, I might not make it by until you're in bed, but I will stop in."

Ernest hesitated a moment, then flung his arms around Jim's legs. "Goodnight, Officer Abbott."

When the boy turned to Francesca, she smiled. "You know how to wash and dress for bed. Don't forget to brush your teeth."

"Yes, ma'am." Ernest scampered off.

Francesca sighed and tucked a strand of hair behind her ear that had come loose from her bun.

"Is there anything I could do before I leave?" Officer Abbott asked in a soft voice.

"No, thank you…Jim." His name felt forbidden on her lips.

He flashed a smile, as though he knew how she felt. On his way to the door, he paused and looked back. "I meant what I said, Miss Wilton."

"That you'll come back tomorrow?"

Jim chuckled. "That too, but I was referring to you being spectacular. Have a good night."

Once Ernest was tucked into bed, Francesca went to her mother's room.

Francesca found her leaning forward in bed at an awkward angle. "I hope the music didn't disturb you."

"It was startling. You haven't played the gramophone at night since the days Cordelia and Tristan would visit."

She blushed and nodded as she helped her mother reposition in bed.

"Franny, if you want to go out, go. I wouldn't even know you left."

"I could never leave you alone, Mother." Francesca kissed her cheek.

"Then hire a nurse to sit with me. There's one in the mornings, plus Becca, but you hardly leave." Her cool palm rubbed the back of Francesca's hand. "I've felt guilty all these years—my only child. People will think I trapped you here."

Francesca swallowed the lump in her throat. "No one thinks poorly of you, Mother."

"You're still beautiful. You could catch the heart of a man—maybe even that handsome police officer." She smiled as though she knew they had danced together. "You don't have to deny everything else to care for me."

"Miss Fran?" Ernest called.

Francesca waved him over. "Did you need something, Ernest?"

"I just want to be sure Officer Abbott will come tomorrow."

"He will, I promise." She kissed his forehead. "I'll check on you in a few minutes."

***

Jim Abbott came to the door while Francesca rinsed her breakfast dishes. In his Sunday best suit and an emerald tie almost the same color as his eyes, he looked even nicer than he had the night before.

He crossed to the table where Ernest ate. "Good morning, Ernest."

"Hello, Officer Abbott. Miss Fran and I are going to do Bible stories this morning."

"But first you need to finish breakfast and wash up," Francesca said as she approached the table. "Could I get you a plate, Jim?"

"No thank you, Miss Wilton. I'll just take the last piece of bacon if no one else wants it."

"Help yourself." She took the now empty platter from the table. "Coffee?"

"Yes, please."

By the time she returned with a steaming cup, Ernest had carried his dishes to the sink and hurried down the hall.

"Becca has Sundays off," Francesca said as she slipped into her chair. "I typically do cold cereal these days, but I know Ernest enjoys a hot meal."

"Is your mother awake?" Jim asked.

"Not yet."

"Did she hear the music last night?" He brought the cup to his lips.

Francesca nodded. "I assume she thinks it was Ernest's idea."

"It was," Jim said with a grin. "And I thank him for it."

"How was the dance you attended?"

"I didn't go." When Francesca narrowed her eyes, he continued. "I knew no one would be as perfect a partner as you, so I went straight home."

She snorted back a laugh and stood. "I appreciate the flattery though I'm too old for games."

"It's the truth."

Ernest ran in. "Are you leaving, Officer Abbott?"

"Yes, he is," Francesca said. "I'll meet you in the parlor in a minute, Ernest."

Jim set his cup in the sink and turned to her. "I don't believe you're too old for anything, Miss Wilton, but I'm not one to play games at any rate."

The crisp manner in which he walked out the door made Francesca think she had hurt his feelings. She pushed all thoughts of Jim Abbott from her mind as she went for her mother's room.

Mrs. Wilton lay lifeless, the skin around her lips blueish and her chest barely moving.

"Mother!" Francesca took her cold hands. Her eyes fluttered open, but her head lolled to the side.

The nurse didn't come until noon on Sundays, so Francesca dashed to the telephone to call Dr. Moore. She then rang Merritt Graves, hoping to catch their neighbor before she left for church.

Five minutes later, Merritt and her husband were there. Francesca asked Bartholomew to keep Ernest occupied, but the boy wasn't in the frame of mind to accept a stranger. He huddled in the corner beyond the piano.

Merritt stayed with Francesca in her mother's room, sitting on opposites sides of the bed with one of her hands in each of theirs. The bottles on the table rattled as though a train were passing. Ernest stood in the doorway, blue eyes frighteningly large as he gripped the doorframe.

"Ernest," Francesca said, "it's okay. Everything will be all right."

Two huge tears rolled down his cheeks before he ran away. The bottle on the edge of the table fell onto the rug with a *thunk*.

"What do you suppose—" Merritt began, but Francesca dashed after the boy.

"Ernest!" She caught him on the front porch.

"Go away!" Fear quivered his voice as he clutched his arms around the square column.

"I don't want to go away, Ernest. I'm here because I care about you."

"But your mother's gonna die, like my parents."

"My mother has a weak heart and has been sick longer than you've been alive. It's nothing to do with you, I promise." She rubbed his back. "Will you come inside and sit with Mr. Graves in the parlor? That would be a tremendous help to me while I see to my mother."

Ernest nodded and slowly released his hold on the post. Francesca escorted him to the sofa, then hurried back to the bedroom where she waited for the doctor to arrive.

After an examination of her mother, Dr. Moore whispered to Francesca in the hall that Mrs. Wilton was in her final hours. She and Merritt stayed at the bedside until the last shallow breath was released.

Five

"Jim!" Winnie hollered from her back porch.

He paused fastening his belt and went to the nearest window. "Yeah?"

"There's a message for you that's important."

"Thanks! I'll be down in a minute."

Their building had one telephone number, though each apartment had an extension. Winnie, the only one who didn't leave for work, ended up being secretary not only for her husband, but all the tenants. Jim straightened his holster, buttoned his uniform jacket, and ran a comb through his oiled hair once more before stuffing his billfold into a pocket and grabbing his hat.

He hurried down the back stairs and let himself in the utility porch, stopping in the open kitchen door. Winnie was basting a roast at the counter.

"That smells wonderful."

"It needs another hour to cook." She paused to wipe steam off her eyeglasses.

"Allow me to get it back into the oven for you." Jim took the hot pads and lifted the heavy pan into the oven Winnie had opened.

"Thank you, Jim. I'll put a plate in your icebox this afternoon."

"I'll happily dine on cold roast beef tonight."

"And I'll have several loaves of bread ready in a couple hours if you think Miss Eilands would like one." She pointed to the towel-covered pans of rising dough on the far counter.

"She'd love that. Thank you. What's my message?"

"My father telephoned. He and my mother were called to the Wiltons—that's why I'm cooking today instead of Mama. Mrs. Wilton died this morning. Papa thought you should know since you've been checking in on Fran and the Hart boy."

"Miss Wilton doesn't need to deal with that on top of everything else. I was supposed to go to the station first, but if I could use your telephone, I'll call in."

"Of course, Jim." Winnie patted his arm and went to the front of the house to give him privacy.

The sergeant listened to the news about the Wilton household. "All right, Abbott. Find me when you get here. I want a report about the Hart boy."

Jim agreed and hung the receiver on the wall box.

Towheaded Percy tottered in. "Jim!"

"Hey, Percy." Jim lifted him for a hug. "I hope you're giving your old man trouble today."

Nathan entered the kitchen. "So I can blame you for his antics?"

"It wouldn't be the first time I was blamed for other people's shenanigans." Jim ruffled Percy's blond hair and passed him to his father. "Keep your parents out of trouble, little man."

One good thing about hoofing it around town in uniform was that traffic stopped for Jim. He easily crossed busy Government Street. Under the circumstances, he felt the Wiltons' front door was the best option.

The slightly stooped, graying form of Judge Spunner's uncle answered his knock.

He looked Jim over and smiled. "Officer Abbott, come in."

"Thank you, Mr. Finnigan." Jim removed his hat and shook hands.

For the first time in all Jim's visits, the hallway was bright, every door leading into it open as well as the curtains beyond.

In the parlor, Ernest jumped at him. Jim smiled and dropped his hat on Ernest's head.

"Come sit with me, Officer Abbott."

Jim nodded to Mr. Graves who sat by the piano.

"Thank you for coming, Jim," Bartholomew Graves said.

"I'm sorry to hear the news, but I'm here to be of service."

The lawyer went to Mr. Graves. "Now that we have Officer Abbott, you can go home, Bart."

"I'll wait for Merri."

"You know how women are. Why do you think I left Cecelia at home? Merritt is liable to be weeping with Miss Wilton for hours."

Mr. Graves smiled but held his ground. Mr. Finnigan took an armchair near the front window in resignation.

"Do you know these men?" Ernest whispered.

Jim nodded. "That's my neighbor's father, and that's the uncle of the judge who gave you permission to stay with Miss Wilton."

"So they're friends?"

"Yes, Ernest. Both men are our friends."

"Good." He swung his legs, his heels kicking the skirting of the couch. A moment later, he slumped against Jim as though needing the comfort of a familiar figure.

Francesca entered the parlor with Mrs. Graves. After having held her in his arms while dancing, she would always be Francesca in his mind.

"Miss Wilton," Mr. Finnigan said as he took her hand. "I came as quickly as I heard. You're blessed to have an experienced friend like Merritt Graves at your side."

Lips tight, she nodded and accepted a kiss on her cheek from the old man.

"Bart told me Dr. Moore and the undertaker have already come and gone. What can I do for you today to be of assistance?"

"I'm really not sure, Mr. Finnigan." The uncertainty in her typically confident tone unnerved Jim. "Mother has had things planned for years. I sent her chosen clothes with the undertaker, and he assured me he would pull her file and send word to Magnolia Cemetery."

"Then all is under control. I'll contact you tomorrow. We can read the will as soon after the funeral as you wish. For now, my cook will send supper to you this evening."

"Thank you, Mr. Finnigan."

When she returned from seeing Mr. Finnigan out, she took Mrs. Graves's hand. "Thank you, Merritt. I couldn't have done it without you these past few hours. And thank you too, Mr. Graves."

Jim and Ernest watched their goodbyes.

As though she had forgotten about them, Francesca slumped into an armchair. One of her slender hands went to her face and she cried.

The boy leapt from his perch and threw his arms around her, knocking the hat off his own head in the process. "Now you're an orphan too, Miss Fran, but we'll take care of each other."

That made her sob. Several minutes later, her eyes rested on the fallen police hat. Her gaze found Jim and softened. Then it was as if a veil dropped in front of her aching heart. Her jaw tightened, and she steeled her posture as she stood, a hand gently resting on Ernest's shoulder.

"Forgive me, Officer Abbott. I wasn't expecting you so early."

"There's nothing to forgive, Miss Wilton," he said as he stood. "Mr. Graves telephoned his daughter to leave word for me. Winnie told me after I returned from Mass. I could stay or bring Ernest with me if you need time alone. Today is all about making sure you feel secure, whatever that requires."

"We'll be fine, Officer Abbott, but I appreciate the offer."

Ernest retrieved Jim's hat from the floor and returned it.

"I'll see you later, Ernest. And I'm sorry for your loss, Miss Wilton."

Jim walked to Government Street and took the streetcar downtown. Officers in uniform rode for free, but he never sat, even when there were plenty of open benches. When he entered the station on St. Emanuel, he could only think about getting back to Washington Square as quickly as possible.

***

Two hours later, Jim walked up George Street. A handful of boys barely in double digits and younger paused from their baseball game at the intersection of Church Street and waved hello.

"Hey boys. Y'all live on this block or nearby, right?"

They nodded and one pointed to the house across from Francesca's. "My brother and I live there."

"I bet you know Ernest Hart."

They exchanged leery looks and a couple of them nodded.

The tallest one spoke up. "No one liked Mr. Hart when they moved in. Our mother told us not to play with Ernest because she didn't want Mr. Hart noticing us."

"I promise you Ernest isn't like his father. Don't let anyone give him a hard time about what happened with his parents, okay?"

"Yes, sir." They all agreed.

"I appreciate it, boys."

Jim mounted the front steps at the Wilton house and knocked softly. Francesca opened the door, dewy brown eyes red-rimmed.

"I thought you and Ernest would enjoy an outing this afternoon."

"He's napping, but please come in."

Once the door shut, he placed a gentle hand above her elbow and squeezed her arm. "Don't feel like you have to be strong around me, Miss Wilton. I'll not judge you for grieving."

"Thank you, Off—"

His finger went to her lips. "Jim," he managed to speak while fighting the urge to press his mouth to hers.

She almost smiled, but then her limbs trembled. Wrapping her in a hug, he held her to his chest as her tears erupted. Keeping his arms around her shoulders, he focused on the heady scent, like magnolia blossoms, that clung to her lithe figure. The crown of her head tucked perfectly into the curve where Jim's shoulder turned into his neck.

"I'll help you however I can," he whispered. "Please allow me that honor, Francesca."

As she gained control of her breathing, he felt her tense as though awakening to the position she was in. Jim loosened his arms so she could easily free herself.

To his surprise, she hugged him around the waist. "Thank you, Jim."

When she stepped away, Jim handed her his handkerchief. She dabbed her face.

"I thought you and Ernest might enjoy a walk with me."

"Aren't you supposed to be working?"

"My sergeant has told me my most important assignment each day is the welfare of Ernest. Besides, Sunday afternoons are typically quiet."

"I suppose it would be all right."

The patter of Ernest in the hall was followed by the bathroom door closing.

"It sounds like he's up. Should I wait outside to surprise him?"

Francesca nodded, a smile momentarily brightening her face.

Jim waited under the canopy of the massive oak on the edge of the yard, drawing the attention of the boys playing at corner. They gathered around him as Francesca and Ernest exited the house. She wore a jaunty hat and Ernest a freshly pressed playsuit.

"Afternoon, Miss Wilton," the tallest boy said.

"Hello, Tommy. How are your parents?"

"Fine. They send their condolences over your mother's passing." His eyes dropped to Ernest. "And your parents too."

"Thank you, Tommy." Francesca switched her attention to Jim. "Hello, Officer Abbott. Thank you for inviting us on your patrol."

"You sure are lucky!" Tommy's little brother said to Ernest as they turned toward Government Street.

"I have one stop to make before we begin the patrol."

"Where's that?" Ernest asked.

"My apartment. I need to pick up something from my downstairs neighbor."

Francesca held Ernest's hand as they crossed Government, but then he walked beside Jim up the block and a half on Hallett.

Nathan and Percy were on the front porch.

"I'm here to collect bread," Jim told Nathan as he came up the front steps.

"Go on in." Nathan nodded toward the door.

Winnie looked up from where she sat on the piano bench. "There are two wrapped loaves on the counter, one for Miss Eilands and one for Miss Wilton."

"You could deliver Francesca's yourself. She's outside."

When Jim returned to the front room with the loaves wrapped in cheesecloth and twine, Winnie took one and went out the door he held open.

Ernest was on the front lawn with Percy, Francesca standing with Nathan. Jim wanted to watch her exchange with Winnie, but Ernest tugged on his free hand.

"Will you show me your house, Officer Abbott?"

"Sure, Ernest." Jim placed the bread for Miss Eilands on the side of the porch. "We're going upstairs for a minute if anyone wants to join us."

Jim had left his Murphy bed open that morning, so he let Ernest lift it back into its cabinet. He opened and shut it three times.

"When I grow up, I want to have a bed like this."

"A bed like this means you have a small home."

"But it's a happy one." His bright eyes looked around the space and fell upon the side table topped with war mementos—the safe souvenirs, that was. He fingered Jim's medals and then picked up the small, framed photograph. "Is this your family?"

Jim felt the presence of someone in the doorway but didn't look before answering. "It's a family in the French countryside I lived near for a while. They often invited a few soldiers to participate in their festivities and meals. This photograph was taken on Anna's twentieth birthday."

"Is that why your arm is around her, because she was the birthday girl?"

"Something like that."

"Do you love her?" the boy asked.

"No," Jim said with a bittersweet smile. "I was fond of Anna and appreciated her family, but I never loved her."

"And this?" Ernest came with the spent bullet from a German rifle, forcing Jim to look at it.

"That shot passed an inch in front of my nose and imbedded itself in a trench board next to me. I dug it out to remind myself how blessed I am."

Ernest skipped back to the table, replaced the casing, and pointed to the bottom shelf. "And all the books?"

"I read when I can't sleep. Half of those are borrowed from the Patersons downstairs." Jim turned to the door and met Francesca's soulful brown eyes. "Are you ready to go?"

She nodded, but her gaze swept the room as she went for the open door.

"It's not much, but it's been a good fit for me."

"You keep it well," she remarked.

Ernest held the loaf of bread for Miss Eilands as they walked back to George Street to drop Francesca's loaf at the house before going east. Jim chatted about his duties—how he looked out for everyone, stopped if someone was in need, and inspected anything that looked suspicious. They crossed Broad Street and continued their trek toward the river.

"We're headed to the area I grew up in," Jim told Ernest and Francesca. "The woman we're going to visit is kind but often misunderstood. Most days she walks to morning Mass at the cathedral, then to the bakery for free day-old bread, and finally to the docks to collect what fish she can. As you'll see, she has a lot of mouths to feed."

When they crossed the railroad tracks, Francesca looked around nervously at the sagging houses. Jim slowed to keep pace with her and brushed her hand. "There's nothing to worry about. I think you'll like Miss Eilands."

"The floating island woman?" she asked in surprise. "I had no idea she was still around. She always scared me when I was little. She used to chatter about people's certain doom when she passed them in the street."

"She stays silent more often than not these days, and is completely harmless to those who mean her no ill."

"Just look at those cats there on the roof!" Ernest pointed beyond the wooden fence.

"That's just the beginning of them. Miss Eilands!" Jim called from the gate.

Ernest was too busy counting cats to see the old woman approach.

"Jimmy?"

"It's me," he said with a grin.

"Who's that with you?"

"These are my friends."

She peered over the fence at Ernest. "Don't set your sights on one of my cats, little mister. None of these are up for grabs, but I've got a box of kittens in the parlor you're welcome to shop."

"Could I really?"

Jim laughed. "That would be up to Miss Fran, and then your aunt when she arrives."

His shoulders fell. "Aunt Narcissa is allergic to cats."

"Miss Eilands, this is Miss Francesca Wilton, and her neighbor, Ernest Hart. She's looking out for him, and I'm looking out for both."

Mary Eilands nodded, brow raised. "You're keeping a close eye on them, I can tell. Jimmy is a sweetheart, isn't he, Miss Wilton?"

"Yes, ma'am," Francesca said. "He's a very kind young man."

"Y'all come see the kittens."

Jim handed Miss Eilands the loaf when they passed into the weed-choked yard. "Winnie Paterson baked too much bread. She said it would do her a great favor if I found a home for this."

"Does that girl not know how to measure by now?" Her voice was harsh, but there was a hint of a smile on her face. "The fish yesterday was enjoyed, Jimmy. Go on, y'all. Just because I'm old doesn't mean I'm slow."

Ernest and Francesca were soon on their knees in the dusty parlor, up to their elbows in kittens. Orange, white, black, gray—there were three litters to choose from, their mothers lying exhausted nearby.

"Does anything need fixing today?" Jim asked Miss Eilands where they stood in the doorway.

"Besides that girl's heart?" She nodded toward Francesca. "You're going to break her into a hundred pieces if you ain't careful, Jimmy."

He shrugged. "We've only known each other a few days."

"Troublesome days link people quicker, and your bond with her is already strong. I know what happened at the Hart house. Nathan Paterson writes a good piece, even if his wife can't measure."

Jim laughed, temporarily pulling Ernest's attention away from the kittens.

"Come see, Officer Abbott! This orange and white one is fluffy!"

"And playful, but he's a sweet boy, like you," Miss Eilands said.

Jim crouched beside Ernest and rubbed the kitten's neck. "He sure is soft."

Francesca cradled a gray, a finger rubbing behind its ears. There wasn't a hint of tension in her posture as she looked at Ernest with his favorite, and her smile brought a grin to Jim's face.

Six

When Francesca caught Jim watching her, she reflexively smiled. The tenderness in his eyes was almost as moving as the purr rumbling from the kitten in her arms.

"That gray is typically nervous, never straying from its mother," Miss Eilands said.

"Rochester." Francesca held the old woman's milky blue gaze. "I would name him Rochester if I could take him home."

Ernest held up the orange one. "I'd call him Sunny."

Jim's grin was huge. "What do you require of the adopters, Miss Eilands?"

"That Jimmy checks on them as well as he does everyone else on his patrol and delivers fresh fish at least twice a month."

Francesca turned to Ernest. "Do you understand that you might not be able to keep Sunny when your aunt arrives?"

"But I know you'd take good care of him for me, Miss Fran."

Miss Eilands clapped. "I'll find a box for you to transport them in."

A quarter of an hour later, they headed back to Washington Square. Ernest wore Jim's hat and Jim carried a small crate with the kittens as they curled together.

"So you're a Brontë fan." Jim glanced at Francesca as they walked.

"And you're familiar with *Jane Eyre*?"

"All those books I read when I can't sleep. Winnie is fond of Gothic romances."

"I'm surprised she reads them. Her mother is so proper."

"From what I've been told, Judge Spunner has loaned and gifted her books since she was old enough to read, feeding her a healthy dose of Gothic novels."

Francesca laughed. "Now that you mention it, I recall overhearing Merritt Graves complain to my mother about inappropriate books her daughter was getting ahold of years back."

Jim laughed. "That's our Judge Spunner."

"Does he wear a robe?" Ernest asked. "He didn't have one on when he came to the house the other night."

"Only when he's in court," Jim answered. "Hey, look at the power pole over there. That's one of the police call boxes on it. If the light on top of it was flashing, I'd have to use my key to unlock the box and use the telephone inside to talk to the station."

"Could we look inside it?"

"Not right now, Ernest. We need to get the kittens home, but I'll show you another time. There's one closer to your street."

Francesca enjoyed listening to Jim and Ernest, but her smile faded the closer they got to George Street. The doctor, the undertaker, and Mr. Finnigan seemed like weeks ago as despair unfurled inside her.

At the house, Ernest ran ahead to open the door while Francesca stared blankly at an automobile parked beside the oak tree.

Jim gently nudged her arm with his elbow to get her attention. "Francesca, I know it's overwhelming. Try to focus on Ernest and the kittens this evening. Take things one hour at a time."

She nodded and the kittens meowed in their scratchy high voices as Jim carried the crate inside.

"Bring it to the kitchen, please," Francesca said. "We'll get them a saucer of milk."

"How old are they? They might not require milk," Josephine said from the parlor.

"Jo!" Francesca rushed to her friend for a hug. "That must be your car outside, but I didn't realize it."

"I'm sorry about your mother, and that it took me so long to get here. Cyrus took us all out to the country for a picnic. I drove over as soon as we got home. You really need to lock your door when you're gone."

Francesca laughed. "I'm not used to leaving, but I'm glad you're not a robber."

"Still, you're prepared for one since you brought a police officer home with you." Josephine smiled and offered Jim a hand. "I'm Jo Harrington."

He set the crate on the floor, and Ernest immediately sat beside it to pet the kittens. Jim shook Josephine's hand. "Pleased to meet you, Mrs. Harrington. I'm Jim Abbott."

"Jo." She looked over the rim of the box and smiled. "How many times have I told you that you needed a cat, Fran?"

"I never thought I did, but the gray one spoke to me."

"And I bet you named him something silly on the spot."

"Rochester."

Josephine rolled her eyes and looked at Francesca with a raised eyebrow. "How could you be such a romantic fool? I've taught you better."

Francesca's face heated. "I need to get the kittens something to drink."

"Water," Josephine stated. "And they're big enough to manage a bit of canned fish or unseasoned meat twice a day."

"I'd be happy to help Ernest see to it so you can visit," Jim told Francesca.

"Thank you."

When the boys went to the kitchen, Josephine cornered Francesca. "He's very attentive to you."

"He's just doing his job."

Josephine smirked. "Keep telling yourself that if it makes you feel safer. Now, what can I do for you?"

"Nothing. Merritt was here when it happened, and the doctor. Bartholomew telephoned Jim and—"

"Jim is it?" Josephine teased.

"He asked me to call him that."

"I bet he did."

"Anyway, the undertaker and Mr. Finnigan have all been here. I'll set the funeral details tomorrow."

"You know I'll be there for you, Fran." Josephine hugged her. "Do I need to stay and play chaperone?"

"No, and I don't want you here at all if you're going to tease me. Besides, he's too young."

"What's age to mature adults?"

"Let me know when you find some."

Josephine laughed and hugged her again. "I'll stop by in the morning with Del to cheer you up. That's your warning."

Francesca saw her out and joined the others in the kitchen. Ernest was busy overseeing the kitten's dinner, so Jim caught her eye and motioned her into the parlor.

"Thank you for this afternoon, Jim. I haven't been that far from home in years."

"I'll take you out whenever you wish. Do you need anything brought when I come tonight?"

"You don't have to return."

"I want to." Jim stepped closer, their bodies only inches apart. "Please allow me to see you through the heartache, Francesca."

She thought he would kiss her but he merely squeezed her hand before releasing it.

"I'll leave the door unlocked for you." She watched him descend the steps.

***

The supper delivery from the Finnigans' house arrived at six o'clock. Ernest, too busy playing with the kittens and already having eaten two pieces of buttered bread, didn't eat much more than Francesca's tiny portions. She put the leftovers in the icebox, thinking Jim might want them when he arrived.

After supper, they took the kittens to the back porch to show them the shallow sandbox they had set up a few hours earlier to remind them of their space to relieve themselves when they weren't outdoors. Then Ernest brought the kittens in the bathroom to play on the tile floor while he bathed, allowing Francesca to freshen the guest room.

Ernest soon carried the kittens in. After a few minutes of them chasing Ernest's hand under the blanket while Francesca read an old nursery rhyme book, Sunny and Rochester yawned and circled in on each other beside him.

"I think y'all will sleep well," she whispered.

"I love you, Miss Fran. I wish I could stay here always."

Tears glistening in her eyes, she kissed his forehead. "I love you too, Ernest. I'm glad we got the kittens today. I'll leave my door open but keep yours shut so Rochester and Sunny don't get loose. Goodnight."

She clicked the door closed. Without thinking, she turned for her mother's room. Merritt had stripped the linens off the bed. Francesca had no doubt she would wash them thoroughly, but she would tell Merritt to donate them. Her Baptist congregation was always good about helping others while Francesca was so far removed from the cathedral parish, she couldn't remember the last time she'd attended Confession. No, that wasn't true. Gazing at the crucifix over her mother's bed, she blushed at the memory of her heated words within the confessional more than a decade ago.

Francesca and Tristan Barnes had gone for a walk the day after her father's funeral. They ended up within Riley's Wood in an old trench built during the Civil War. It was so deep Tristan had to help her climb down into it. After an hour, he swore they'd have to find a priest to marry them if they didn't leave. He said that while one hand was palming a breast and the other was under Francesca's skirt. It shook reason into her because her mother would never allow a wedding during their mourning time. She had attended confession the following week. But here she was, once again dealing with the death of a parent while a young man paid her attentions. There was no stopping the feelings that grew within her each time she saw Jim Abbott. Her body craved his touch and her soul yearned for the comfort of his arms—Josephine had seen that in an instant.

Francesca paced the empty room, then the hall. The mantel clock struck nine. She put the kettle on, hoping some tea would calm her. It was an herbal blend from Josephine that aided her on sleepless nights. When it was ready, Francesca brought the cup into the parlor, put on a long Beethoven recording, slipped off her shoes, and curled in the corner chair.

Listening to the tune, Francesca closed her eyes and held the tea below her nose. The lavender aroma was soothing. Soon, she was breathing slower. Then she drank.

The tea was gone and she was in a haze of drowsiness when the front screen door opened.

Her heart quickened at the scent of Jim when he entered the dim room. Instead of repelling her, the faint odor of sweat made her yearn even more for his strong arms. His work was physical, mental, and emotional. He probably needed personal connection as much as she did.

"Francesca," he whispered.

"I'm awake, Jimmy."

"I only allow my granny and Miss Eilands to call me that." His face was in shadow, but she heard the smile in his voice.

"I'm an old woman too."

"No you're not." He pulled her to her feet, standing a respectable distance away. "You're in your prime, Francesca."

He released her hands, and she raised them to his broad shoulders.

"Prime is *you*, Officer Abbott. I wanted you to kiss me before you left this afternoon."

His Adam's apple bobbed above his collar with a hard swallow. "I have no problem comforting you and Ernest while on the clock, but kissing you would have been more for me."

She swayed toward him as she stared at the dimple on his right cheek. The lopsidedness of his smile is what painted him even younger than he was. Francesca cupped his cheek to hide the dent with her thumb.

"What about right now?" she whispered.

"I'm off duty, but I'm not in the proper state to—"

Francesca broke his excuses with a simple kiss, then quickly crossed the room, embarrassed at her boldness.

"Francesca." He caught her wrist. "If you want my company, I can go home after work, wash, and walk over in regular clothes."

Touching the buttons, she lifted her gaze. "I like your uniform."

"And you'll continue to see me in it on my official visits."

She nodded and hugged him.

Jim hugged her back before releasing the embrace. "How was Ernest tonight?"

"He brought the kittens to bed with him after playing with them all evening."

Jim's hand went to her shoulder. "And supper?"

"It arrived from the Finnigan house. There's plenty leftover if you'd like to eat."

"I'd love to, but I need to leave."

"But—"

"I'll see you, Ernest, and the kittens in the morning."

Hot and near trembling from the excitement of their contact, Francesca locked the door and leaned against it. She closed her eyes and relived the feeling of being in Jim's arms. As the fantasy continued, quaking vibrated her body.

"Miss Fran!" Ernest cried. "Where are you?"

She hurried past the swaying picture frames in the hall. "I'm right here."

"I thought you left me." His body shivered with the words.

"Never, Ernest. I was only in the front room. Officer Abbott stopped by on his way home to check on us."

"I thought I heard something."

"You heard Officer Abbott coming and going. Would you like me to sit with you for a while?"

Ernest nodded.

Francesca urged him back to his room and helped the kittens settle at his side before taking the armchair.

Sitting there for a half hour helped her clear her head of Jim, but thoughts of Ernest's agitation were too troubling to dismiss.

In the morning while Francesca was getting dressed, a scream pierced the early morning quiet. Running from her room in her silk slip, she took Erenst into her arms.

"It's all right, Ernest." She kissed his hair while she hugged him. "What it another dream?"

He sniffed, arms tight around her waist. "My father came for me in the dark. He said it was supposed to have been me, not my mother. If it had been me, they would still be alive."

Francesca rocked him, making hushing sounds. "You're safe, Ernest. The sun is up and the kittens are ready to play. How about I make eggs and sausage today?"

Ernest nodded.

"All right then. Let's finish getting dressed, then you can take the kittens in the yard while I cook."

After Ernest was outside, Francesca telephoned the Farleys' house on Rapier Avenue to speak with Deborah.

"I'm sorry to bother you so early in the morning, Deborah, but I'm hoping you could help me. This is Francesca Wilton on George Street."

"Of course, Fran. I remember you."

"I live next to the Hart house and have Ernest Hart with me until his aunt arrives in town."

"How very kind of you. I'm sure the boy is unsettled after all that went on at his house."

"Yes, exactly. I have a few other friends stopping by in the eight o'clock hour, and I was hoping you could join us and see if we can figure something out to help Ernest."

"I'll come as soon as I get my family off for the day, but will have my youngest with me."

"That's fine. I appreciate it."

The sense of calm that a medium known for helping clear ghosts from houses in the neighborhood was coming gave Francesca the energy she needed to meet the day. She had Ernest at the table for breakfast at eight o'clock while she finished preparing a tea tray for her company.

She welcomed Josephine and Cordelia first. Sage, Josephine's youngest, looked like her father with her fair curls and blue eyes but she was impishness unbottled like her mother. Josephine set her daughter near the closed upright piano with a rag doll and tin car she produced from her large handbag.

"Whatever did you do to your hair?" Francesca asked Cordelia as they hugged.

"I bleached it." Cordelia's rainbow dress fanned out when she sat on the sofa. "Why shouldn't we change our hair like we change our clothes?"

Josephine laughed. "More like Mathias grew tired of looking at you and wanted a change of scenery."

"He's easily bored, but we agreed to be ornamentations for each other before we married. I happily comply to keep company with his gorgeous face and our outrageous friends."

Deborah Farley joined them with her toddler and infant. Once Cordelia finished cooing over them, Francesca explained her dilemma with Ernest's troubled sleep and emotions that seemed to shake the house.

"He was always agitated when I saw him before because it was when his father was drunk or belligerent or both," Francesca explained. "His fists were often tight when his mother sent him over, but not in a combative pose, more like he was trying to hold something in."

"Fear?" Cordelia asked.

"More likely his response to the situation," Josephine said as her daughter climbed onto her lap. "He might subconsciously be afraid that the qualities allowing his father to behave as he did are in him as well."

"He's just a little boy," Cordelia said with a shrug. "I don't see how he could believe such deep psychological principles."

"Not on an academic level," Josephine explained, "but in his soul."

Francesca nodded. "He is intelligent and intuitive."

"That all is well for the internal," Deborah said, "but don't forget possible exterior forces. There's something wrong in the air surrounding the house next door."

Seven

Monday morning, Jim woke over-heated well before sunrise though he was only in his underdrawers. Kicking the sheet off, he rolled onto his back. The vision that woke him was Francesca in a dress that showed a good bit of her legs and arms, dancing provocatively. Her brown eyes were warm, her broad smile teasing as they communed over a sexy beat. It would have been heavenly upon waking to reach out and touch her. Feel her lips like when she surprised him with a show of boldness the previous night. Jim wanted nothing more than to hold her again. Taste her. If she were here right now…

With a groan, he rolled to his side before sitting up. He showered to clear his head, then hastily dressed and slicked his hair. Jim took a streetcar downtown to a bakery serving coffee and breakfast, allowing him to eat before stopping at the station.

Detective Callaghan was the first person he saw. "Abbott, how's that boy doing?"

"Ernest is doing well." Jim leaned against the counter.

"And the lady? I heard her mother passed."

"They're helping each other through their losses." He crossed his arms and tried to focus on the detective rather than images of Francesca that danced through his head.

"The aunt should be on her way today. At least we can hope."

Jim nodded. "I need to check in with the sergeant."

By the time Jim got to Francesca's house, it was going on nine. He paused at the back stoop to watch Ernest playing with the kittens on the kitchen floor before opening the screen door.

"Good morning."

"Officer Abbott!" Ernest gathered Sunny into his arms and met him as he came through the porch. "See how good I'm doing with him?"

"Yeah, Ernest." Jim ruffled his hair then stroked the kitten's neck. "He looks bigger already."

"Miss Becca isn't coming for breakfasts anymore since Mrs. Wilton passed, but Miss Fran made eggs and sausage this morning. She left some for you on the stove. She's in the front room with company. I'm supposed to wait here with the kittens."

Jim wanted nothing more than to go to Francesca, but dished up a plate of food and poured coffee. He hung his hat on the back of a chair when he sat. He ate slowly, partly because it was his second breakfast, but also because he was stalling for time.

Halfway through the meal, Ernest brought him Rochester. The gray kitten pawed at Jim's thigh as his finger rubbed around the cat's ears while he ate with his free hand.

"It's a bit early for company, isn't it?" Jim asked.

"She had tea for the ladies." Ernest trailed a ribbon across the floor for Sunny to pounce.

The brief squall of a baby came from the front room. Before Jim could ask, Ernest spoke.

"Two of the guests brought babies with them."

"Two? How many ladies are here?"

"Three. One of them used to live in my house."

Jim took another bite of eggs—all thoughts on Winnie's story about Francesca having been courted by the next-door neighbor.

A curly blonde-haired girl toddled into the kitchen and squealed with excitement at seeing Sunny.

Jim immediately put down Rochester and dropped to a knee in front of the child. "Hey there."

She waved her dimpled hand and smiled before pointing. "Kitties!"

"Yeah, those are fun, aren't they?"

Trouser-clad legs stopped behind the girl, causing Jim's gaze to rise. Above the black boots and charcoal pants was a ruffled white blouse. Piercing hazel eyes looked out from beneath brunette bangs that framed a freckle-dusted complexion along with sleek bobbed hair. Even though he'd met Jo Harrington the day before, the sight of her struck him anew because the woman was always talked about as being a witch.

"Is there a problem, Officer Abbott?" Jo asked as Jim continued to stare.

He slowly stood and rubbed his forehead. "No, ma'am. It's good to see you again."

The little girl plopped onto the floor next to Ernest and Jo looked at Jim.

"It's been a long time since Fran had a man concerned with the goings on in this house besides Dr. Moore. I'm glad you're looking out for her, Officer Abbott."

Jim's face heated as he grinned. "I'm pleased to be the one."

"*That* remains to be seen." She scooped up her child before the girl could grab Rochester's tail. "Come on, Sage. It's time to go."

"You're leaving so soon?"

"I came to learn what was needed of me. I have a few things to see to at home before I can complete my task for Fran and—" She nodded toward Ernest.

Annoyed that something was going on with Ernest that he wasn't notified of, Jim followed Jo to the front of the house and found himself staring at the grouping of women in the parlor.

Francesca rose from her seat. "I hope Ernest told you about breakfast." Her voice was low, but all her guests were leaning toward them as though to catch their exchange.

He nodded and rested a hand on her arm for a moment. "Thank you."

"Don't keep that handsome officer to yourself, Fran," a voice said from the couch. "We'd all like an introduction."

Blushing three shades of red by the time she turned to her guests, Francesca motioned for him to follow. "Ladies, this is Officer Jim Abbott. He's tasked with checking on Ernest. Jim, this is Cordelia Barnes-Wolf, my friend and former neighbor, and a neighbor from Rapier Avenue, Deborah Farley. And Jo you met yesterday."

Cordelia—the one who wanted an introduction—wore an outlandish dress of rainbow colors. Her hair was strikingly pale, like it came from a bottle. "Jim Abbott, you've inspired me! I need to paint the uniformed men in our city. Have you ever modeled?"

"I think they used my photo during the war in a Red Cross campaign, but it wasn't anything planned on my end."

"That smile would earn them thousands, I'm sure."

Deborah Farley laughed as she bounced a baby on her knee. What looked to be a three-year-old boy sat quietly beside her. "It's good to meet you, officer. I've seen you patrolling Washington Square many times. You have a calming presence."

"Thank you, Mrs. Farley. It was nice to meet all of you, but I'll get back to Ernest." Jim brushed Francesca's hand with his when he turned for the doorway, hoping she felt his affection.

A quarter of an hour later, Francesca carried the used tea service into the kitchen. "Company is gone, Ernest. You can play with the kittens in the yard."

Jim and Francesca watched the back porch screen snap shut and turned to each other at the same moment. Grinning as he closed the distance, Jim hugged her.

"Jim, don't be upset with me, but Ernest needs help. I thought quick action the best course so I didn't wait to talk it over with you."

"What's wrong? He seems as good as ever."

She held him a moment longer, then stepped back. "I don't want Ernest to hear, and Mr. Finnigan and the undertaker are supposed to be here at ten to go over my mother's funeral arrangements. No offense, Jim, but I'd rather you weren't here when they arrive."

He glanced at his watch and out the back door. "We have a couple minutes, and you know I want nothing more than to help you."

She took a breath. "Earnest is having nightmares and becomes highly agitated when upset. The walls shake and the floors tremble. The first time I noticed it for sure was after my mother died, and then it happened last night when I wasn't in my room like he expected. I know he's causing it."

When he didn't reply, she hurried on.

"I'm not crazy," she whispered as they watched Ernest crawling across the grass.

"I know you aren't, Francesca. I hadn't thought of it in days, but the first responding officers reported the Harts' house was shaking when they arrived. We were told not to hang around if we didn't need to because it might be structurally unsafe."

"It's Ernest," she whispered. "I know it is."

"But what can those ladies do for him?"

"Jo is creating a calming blend of herbs for him and—"

"Is she a witch? Knowing what people say about Miss Eilands, I'll give her the benefit of the doubt."

"It's not a cure, just something to soothe him. I purchase a blend for myself. I wouldn't say it's magical, but there's something otherworldly about Jo—there has been since we were children. Deborah Farley is a medium. She doesn't advertise, but word gets around. She's helped a lot of people in the neighborhood over the past decade."

"And Cordelia Barnes-Wolf?"

"She's a friend, plus a sister-in-law to Jo and used to live in Ernest's house."

"The sister of your old beau."

"You questioned people about me?"

"It's Mobile," Jim said with a smile. "Everyone knows everything about their neighbors."

She huffed in exasperation. "Especially in Washington Square. I'll see you this evening, Jim."

He grinned and grabbed his hat. Outside, he dropped to his haunches beside Ernest.

"When are you coming back, Officer Abbott?"

"Later today, but I can't promise it will be before your bedtime. Make sure you go to sleep without giving Miss Fran any trouble. I'll check in on you."

"Promise?"

He grinned and ruffled the mop of hair above his shining blue eyes. "I promise, Ernest Hart."

Jim tipped his hat to Francesca in the doorway before leaving the yard.

Eight

Becca's supper of redfish, cornbread, and greens was wonderful, but Francesca was too busy fretting to enjoy it. Worries over the help that would be coming that night for Ernest, her mother's funeral, and her growing feelings for Jim kept her distracted. There was no denying Francesca wanted Jim physically, but she wanted his company and conversation too. As Deborah had said that morning, his presence was calming.

After supper, Francesca and Ernest took the kittens into the yard. Rochester stayed near her feet by the back steps, but Sunny bounded after a cricket under the dusky sky. When Rochester meowed, Francesca picked him up. The calming purr that rumbled against her chest reminded her of Jim's caring ways. The forethought he showed in bringing them to Miss Eilands's house was surprising. He was tender and kind—attributes she had always admired in a man.

"Another minute, Ernest, then you need to get ready for bed so you're cleaned up when my friends arrive."

When they went inside, Francesca sent Ernest to bathe while she oversaw the kittens.

"Officer Abbott is a good man," Becca said over the sink of dishes she was washing. "Don't be stubborn about him, Miss Fran."

"I'm trying not to be, Becca."

"I'm glad he's keeping tabs on you during this difficult time. Please know it's a joy to cook for extra mouths, not a burden."

Francesca nodded and gathered the kittens.

"Shall I lock up on my way out?" Becca asked.

"Not tonight," Francesca replied from the hall, hoping Jim would arrive before Deborah and Josephine did.

Ernest bathed and donned pajamas without complaint. He eagerly collected a book, snatched Sunny from his play, and dashed for the parlor to wait for their guests. Francesca followed with Rochester, who perched on her shoulder when she settled in an armchair. She read Hansel and Gretel's story out loud until there was a knock on the front door. Francesca stayed in the chair but set the book aside and moved the sleeping Rochester to her lap.

Ernest brought Deborah, Josephine, and Cordelia into the room, leading them to the sofa. The three took their seats in a row, Cordelia on the far end opening a sketchbook. Josephine took the middle and set a bag between them, and Deborah settled on the far side.

"Please stay, Ernest." Deborah said. "Do you think Miss Jo could hold your kitten a minute?"

Ernest nodded and handed Sunny to Josephine. Then he took Deborah's offered hand, standing before her.

Closing her eyes, she smiled. "You are brave and your mother loves you."

"She's gone."

"She's watching over you, Ernest. You'll never be without guardian angels, whether on this side of life or the other."

"Miss Fran is my angel."

Francesca felt a prickle in her throat. Then Jim's large hand squeezed her shoulder. Freshly showered and wearing a basic suit, he looked too attractive to be sneaking in the backdoor.

Josephine smiled at Francesca and Jim while Cordelia's pencil scratched across the page.

Deborah continued her spiritual reading. "You've often been upset, but that's normal, Ernest. It's okay to be scared, angry, or sad. You've felt a lot of those things recently, haven't you?"

He nodded and brought his hands to her cheeks. "Where are your babies, Miss Deborah?"

"All four of them are at home with their father."

Ernest lowered his hands to his sides. "Is he nice to them?"

Deborah nodded. "Very nice. He plays games and takes them on walks and automobile rides."

"My father never did any of that. He said I wasn't good enough to spend his time with." His hands clenched and his arms began to tremble.

Jim shifted to go to him but Josephine shook her head. Francesca grabbed Jim's hand to keep him by her side.

"He beat Mommy because of me."

"No, Ernest. He beat her because he was broken. It was nothing you did. Not ever." Ernest tremored, but Deborah acted as though she felt nothing. "I know you're upset, Ernest, but your mother is safe now. You don't need to give your father any more power."

"Power?"

"When you allow fear and anger to govern your body, you're giving him power to control you. You need to keep your power, Ernest. Harness your energy."

"Like a horse?" His countenance brightened.

Deborah nodded. "Like a cowboy with a lasso and turn that anger and fear into goodness. Let it out into the world as love, not hate."

"How, Miss Deborah?"

"Breathe, Ernest." She blew out her breath like she was scattering thistledown.

He copied her. On his second exhalation, the floor stopped shaking. Francesca shifted her attention to Jim and watched his wide-eyed gaze.

"Good, Ernest. Do it again." Deborah slipped off her pointed shoes, stood, and motioned to his bare feet. "Feel the strength beneath your feet—that you're connected to this place. This is a house of love. You belong here."

Ernest copied her pose by stretching out his arms which had stopped trembling. He wiggled his fingers and toes, wonder filling his face. Then he threw himself at Francesca for a hug that threatened to squish Rochester.

"I love you, Miss Fran!" He released her and clung to Jim's middle. "I love you, Officer Abbott!"

Ernest then hugged all three ladies, going to Deborah last and holding her the longest. "Teach me more!"

Deborah laughed. "I think that's enough for tonight, but I'll visit again soon. Practice breathing and feeling the connection to where you are."

Ernest nodded, then lovingly took Sunny from Josephine.

"I brought something for you, Ernest." Josephine pulled a small tin box decorated with camellias from her bag. "Did your mother ever let you drink hot tea or cocoa?"

"When Daddy was gone at night."

"This is a special blend of tea I make to be used before bedtime. You can add a bit of honey to it if Miss Fran says it's okay."

"I love honey!"

"I'll show her how to prepare it. Let's go to the kitchen." Josephine stood.

As soon as Josephine and Ernest were in the hall, Deborah advanced. "I sealed your home before entering, but there's something looming outside, Fran. It's in the air so heavy I can almost smell the rot. I need to go next door to investigate the spiritual residue."

"Is it safe?" Francesca asked.

"That's what I need to check."

Jim rubbed his chin. "It's been cleaned."

"Physically, maybe." Deborah clasped her hands and exhaled one of her long breaths. "The key please."

"I'll go with you, Mrs. Farley," Jim said. "Where's the key Detective Callaghan gave you, Fran?"

"In the kitchen, but I need to stay with Jo and Ernest."

"I'll go with you two," Cordelia offered.

"No," Deborah said with conviction. "I don't want to be responsible for anyone beyond Officer Abbot. It's distracting, and I don't know what we'll be walking into."

In the kitchen, Francesca fetched the key from a hook on the far wall while Jim focused on Josephine at the stove. Josephine had attracted attention when they were girls, but it wasn't always a good thing. She bewitched people, drawing out the best or worst in them.

Francesca set Rochester on the floor near Sunny and handed the key to Jim.

He squeezed her hand and gave a nervous smile. "I have no idea what I'm getting into, but I'm doing it for you and Ernest."

Nine

"I've never seen anything like what you did with Ernest," Jim told Deborah Farley as they walked across the lawn between the houses.

She stopped in the dark, leaning close to his shoulder. "That was just a bit of what I've picked up from my experiences over the years, but I'm not an expert on telekinetic activity."

"Did his parents' deaths cause his ability to make things shake?"

"It's probably more of the straw that broke the camel's back. Ernest most likely has been holding back all this energy during his emotional moments and it's finally finding an outlet." She paused a moment and held his gaze. "My specialty is mediumship. I can often see, or at least hear and sense, spirits. They communicate with me."

"You can't mean ghosts."

She nodded.

"How did you learn to do that?"

"I've done it without realizing it since I was a child, but once I moved to Mobile and Sean Spunner learned what

I could do, he loaned me literature on how to best utilize my gift. I suppose you'd say I'm self-taught through Allan Kardec books. I hope that not disconcerting to you."

"I have no idea who that is, but I've heard stories about your work and they've all been favorable, even if I didn't believe them."

Rather than take offense, Deborah smiled in understanding. "I'll warn you as I did Cordelia, I don't know what we're going to face inside the Harts' house. It could be as simple as energy residue from the violent acts or as oppressive as a lingering spirit." She shivered though the night was far from chilly.

"Should I get your husband?"

"No, he has the most important job—watching our children. He's more than happy to put them to bed the nights I'm helping someone, Officer Abbott."

"Call me Jim."

She patted his arm. "I will. And I'm glad it's you with me. What I said this morning about you having a calming presence is true. Your aura is strong, your heart pure. That makes you a perfect companion in dealing with the spirit world."

Jim shook his head. "I have no idea what you mean, or even if I believe this sort of thing. What do I need to do?"

"Much of what I told Ernest—stay grounded if I tell you the house is safe. Otherwise, keep your breathing calm and focus on goodness. What's your faith?"

"Roman Catholic."

"Do you have a cross with you?"

"Unfortunately not. I have plenty of room for improvement."

"We all do, but that doesn't mean we can't be perfect for someone. Having your support during her time of loss means the world to Fran. Not to mention Ernest's predicament."

"Helping them both has been a joy."

"I can see it in your aura."

Jim took the lead up the steps and turned the key in the lock.

"The house is unsettled. Don't ground yourself here. Allow me to go through first. If I tell you to touch me, do it quickly on my skin. It will help me find my center if I get lost." When the door swung inward, Deborah stepped over the threshold. "We come in the name of Jesus Christ, our Lord and Savior, and mean no harm."

Jim wasn't sure how Bishop Allen would feel about a medium invoking the name of the Lord, but he crossed himself as he stepped inside. The air was stale and scented with ammonia that didn't quite cover the lingering stench of death.

Deborah breezed into the front room, turning on a lamp. "This house has seen a lot of sorrows, but nothing compared to what happened here last week."

Jim stayed beside her.

"The woman is gone, and the boy is safe," she called. "There is nothing for you here."

An oppressive sense of dread swept over Jim. Hopelessness, detachment, as though he'd lost everyone he ever cared about. A lump welled in his throat and moisture pricked his eyes before the moment passed.

Deborah blinked and went for the bedrooms. Jim stayed in the hall, his back to the kitchen in an attempt to ignore the looming memory of how he'd weakened there the night of the murder.

After looking in the other rooms, Deborah met his quizzical gaze. "That's never happened before."

"The heavy feeling?" he asked.

She shook her head. "The switch from that to nothing without any attempted communication. I don't know if the spirit left for good or if it's hiding, but I can't sense it anymore."

"That's good, isn't it?"

"Perhaps." She switched off the light. "We shouldn't stay. This place needs a proper airing."

Cordelia was still in the parlor when they returned to Francesca's house. Deborah went straight for the kitchen, but the artist beckoned Jim.

"The fact that you're completely at ease with a group of ladies proves you're used to female attentions." She raised a page from her sketchbook. "I see how Fran looks at you when she thinks no one is watching. She never looked at my brother like that. Please be kind to her, Officer Abbott."

Jim retrieved the paper. The likeness of him standing beside Francesca, his hand on her shoulder as she sat in the chair with Rochester on her lap, filled the page.

"Thank you, Mrs. Barnes-Wolf. You're very talented."

"Del, please. Have you heard of me?"

He nodded. "You and your husband host artist salons."

"Mathias loves me to be the center of attention so long as I'm showering adoration on him in the process. You and Fran will be invited to my next soiree. A night of drinking and dancing would be good for her."

The memory of Francesca in his dream returned, causing Jim to smile.

"Fran is as beautiful and graceful as ever. Put a little fire in her veins and she's the life of the party." Cordelia whispered in a conspiratorial tone.

The others arrived, and Jim set the sketch on the side table.

Ernest came for a hug. "Goodnight, Officer Abbott."

"Did you drink your tea?"

"With honey, and I liked it."

"I'm glad to hear that." Jim smoothed his hair. "I'll see you tomorrow, Ernest."

After he said goodnight to the ladies, Francesca took Ernest and the kittens to his room.

"Schedule Jo for a house cleansing next door tomorrow evening, Fran," Deborah said when she rejoined them, "and telephone anytime you need me. Goodnight."

Cordelia and Jo said goodbye as well, and Francesca accompanied them to the door.

Alone in the parlor, Jim flipped through the gramophone recordings and started a piano score by J.S. Bach. He slipped off his suit jacket, placing it on the back of the nearest chair.

"Will you dance with me?" Jim asked Francesca when she returned.

"It's not a tune for a waltz or anything modern."

"No, but we can move to it." He placed his hands on either side of her waist. "Put your arms around my shoulders."

She did and he began swaying as he studied her brown eyes. Smiling, Jim led her in a slow box step.

"This is nice," she whispered.

"I'm glad you're enjoying it. Is there anything else I could do for you?"

"Tell me what you found so fascinating about Josephine's pants."

Jim laughed and shifted his hands around Francesca to feel her hips. "I was intrigued with the thought of what *you* might look like in trousers. How your curves would fill out a pair and what this might look like." He smoothed a hand over her buttocks. "I was mesmerized with the thought of seeing your shape outlined more clearly."

"And how is it now that you've felt more of me?" Her broad smile caused him to grin in return.

"Even better than I imagined."

Their lips met with a lingering kiss.

"Jim, I feel so alive with you."

"You feel wonderful, Francesca."

He kissed down her throat and she nipped his earlobe.

"I want you more than anything else in the world," Jim whispered, "but Ernest could walk in here any moment."

"You're still thinking of him even when he's not in the room?"

"I'm fond of the boy—and you." He kissed her temple. "I'll keep reminding you until it's written on your heart. Goodnight, Francesca."

She nodded solemnly but left a hot kiss on his lips when they reached the front door.

***

On Tuesday, Jim was scheduled to work the afternoon shift, but he walked to Francesca's at seven in the morning. He stayed long enough to eat breakfast with her and Ernest. When he returned home, Nathan invited Jim to have dinner with his family at noon. He accepted before going to his apartment for a nap.

Jim slept until Winnie hollered that dinner was ready. After buttoning on his shirt, he hurried down the stairs and entered the back door. Winnie stood at the stove in a checkered apron, transferring corncobs onto a serving dish next to sautéed onions and cauliflower.

"It smells great, Winnie. What can I bring to the table for you?"

"The iced tea and platter of fried chicken, please."

"I'm glad you're here, Jim," Nathan said as he came into the dining room, herding Percy ahead of him.

Percy hugged Jim's legs and then dove under the tablecloth.

"Come on, you." Nathan wrestled his squirming son with practiced ease despite his missing limb and set him in the highchair.

Winnie arrived with the vegetables and bread and everyone was soon seated.

"How was the science club yesterday?" Jim asked Winnie while they dished up food after the blessing.

"More spirited than usual. Hattie reminded everyone about the approaching election and made sure we were all registered to vote. After that business was seen to, she served mint julips to the ladies wanting them and spoke about altered states of mind from peyote the natives in the southwest use during their ceremonies. Melissa Davenport told about something similar in African tribal ceremonies she witnessed during her travels. Mrs. Woodslow drank too much, and Mrs. Melling had to drop her at home afterwards."

"Should you be telling a police officer about alcohol consumption?" Nathan teased.

Jim laughed. "Like federal prohibition means anything in Mobile. Montgomery didn't bother us when the state outlawed it five years ago, and people haven't stopped during the last ten months. Besides, Judge Spunner's house would be off limits."

Winnie's mouth pursed as she shredded a drumstick with her fork for Percy.

"The judge knows everyone in town and Mobile protects their own," Nathan said. "Sean keeps his hands clean from the bootlegging and running, but he likes his indulgences—as does his wife."

Winnie nodded, then looked at Jim. "How is Fran doing? Mama and Papa are going to the funeral tomorrow morning, but Catholic funerals always overwhelm me. I guess you're used to them."

"They're a bit long, but Fran is doing remarkably well considering her circumstances."

When they finished eating, Jim helped Winnie clear the table then joined Nathan on the front porch for a smoke.

"I wasn't going to call you out in front of Winnie," Nathan said as he tossed Jim the lighter, "but what the hell is going on with you and the spinster?"

"What do you mean?" Jim lit up.

"You're smiling like a kid in George's Candy Store when you talk about her."

Jim threw the silver lighter at him, but he caught it before it could strike his chest.

"Is she the latest conquest to replace the memories of that crazy redhead?"

"Shut up, you one-armed bastard."

"So she is!" Nathan laughed.

"She's nothing of the sort. Our connection is pure, so don't try to sully it."

"I won't, Jim," he spoke around the cigarette dangling from his lip. "I just never thought you'd take up with an older woman. You gotta be careful when you let yourself fall in love."

"I'll happily worship at the shrine for one as passionate as she is."

"Now you're waxing poetic. Do I need to loan you some Keats?"

"I think I've got your volume of Byron upstairs already."

Nathan laughed. "You're hopeless, but I wish you well. Finding the right girl is the most important thing in life."

"Officer Abbott!" Ernest ran up the sidewalk.

Jim immediately put out his cigarette and met Ernest at the base of the front steps.

"What is it, Ernest? Is Francesca all right?"

Nathan chuckled from his seat on the porch.

"Well, she looked sad, but—"

"Ernie, you hellion!" a voice with a brassy twang called from the road south. A young blonde minced her way toward them and stopped beside Ernest. Her eyes were wide and blue like Ernest's and her round face as youthful. "Is this Officer Abbott?"

"Yes," Ernest said as he held Jim's hand.

"Are you Narcissa Hart?" Jim asked.

"Guilty as charged."

Nathan came to the edge of the steps, shifting his still smoldering cigarette between his lips as he watched the introduction with an amused smirk.

Narcissa's eyes roamed Nathan from the shortened blue sleeve over the stump of his right arm and then back at Jim. "I'm sorry to interrupt, but Ernie had it in his mind he had to see you, Officer Abbott."

"I'll leave you to business, Jim." Nathan turned on his heels, crushed his cigarette in the tray, and went in the front door.

Jim was certain Nathan had taken a seat just beyond the screen door to listen, but ignored his friend to focus on Ernest. "Did you need me?"

He nodded but didn't say anything, though he cast a sidelong look at his aunt.

"I don't mean to be impertinent, Miss Hart, but how old are you?"

"Nineteen this past April. And you're not the first to ask. I get that all the time."

Jim could understand why. "When did you arrive?"

"A couple of hours ago. I took a taxi ride around the city to see a few of my favorite haunts before going to Willy's house. Some neighbors heard me calling out and pointed me to the woman next door. I told her I had every right to go into my brother's house, but she said she needed to check with the police first. At least she let me take Ernie for a walk."

"I'll bring you to the police station so you can speak to the lead detective." Jim ruffled Ernest's hair. "You can sit on the steps while I change. It'll only take me a minute."

Jim hurried around the corner. Picking up the telephone in his apartment, he asked the operator for Francesca's house and disrobed while he waited.

"Hello?" her voice wavered.

"Fran, I've got him."

"I was worried when she walked off with Ernest, but I didn't think I had the right to stop her."

"I'm bringing them to the station. She's upset you didn't allow her inside the Harts' house, but I completely agree that she needs to speak to Detective Callaghan first. She doesn't look old enough to care for herself, let alone Ernest."

"I already have a call into Finnigan and Spunner to see about getting the custody situation straightened out."

"Call them back and ask someone to meet us at the station as soon as possible. Tell the secretary it's an urgent police matter."

Ten

After calling Mr. Finnigan's office, Francesca placed Rochester and Sunny in the bathtub with a towel to sleep on and closed the bathroom door to help contain any mischief they might get into. She scribbled a note for Becca and hurried toward the trolley on Government Street.

Jim might be upset about her showing up at the station, but she cared for Ernest too much to allow others to decide what was best for him.

When Francesca walked into the stuffy police station, Narcissa sat awkwardly in a corner chair, picking at her fingernails.

Francesca stopped several feet away. "Where's Ernest?"

"With that nugget of an officer. I was told to wait here."

Francesca crossed to the reception desk and asked to see Officer Abbott.

"You'll have to wait, ma'am," the officer on duty replied.

The front doors opened, and the scent of Sean Spunner's French cologne softened the stale air. He looked immaculate in a gray suit, his black shoes shiny enough to see a reflection in.

"Francesca, darling, I'm sorry to keep you waiting." He kissed her cheek, took hold of her elbow, and swept her along with him to the policeman at the front desk.

"Judge Spunner, what can I do for you?"

"Miss Wilton and I have an appointment with Detective Callaghan," Sean smoothly replied.

"Do you know the way, Judge?"

"I do, thank you."

"What about me?" Narcissa whined. "I've been waiting longer."

"I'm sure Officer Fitzwilliam would begrudge your absence if you left," Sean said with a wink. "You do brighten the place."

"How could you?" Francesca whispered once they were down the hall.

"I've learned to play to people's weaknesses, which someone sweet like you wouldn't understand."

"I know devilry when I see it, Sean Spunner."

He stopped and turned to her. "Francesca, I'll do everything in my power on behalf of Finnigan and Spunner to see your wishes fulfilled. Tell me what you want from this situation."

When she set out, her focus was keeping Ernest safe. But under the spell of the judge's amber eyes, she knew what it was she really yearned for.

"I want to adopt Ernest."

He almost frowned. "Ask me to give you the moon, it would be easier, darling. No judge would give a child to an unmarried woman."

"Not even you?"

"I couldn't, Francesca. The system wants orphaned children placed in homes with a solid family unit. If Miss Hart doesn't wish to keep her nephew, he'll be turned over to the boys' home."

"I would give him better care than an over-crowded institution."

"I know you would, darling, but that's not the point."

"I love him, Sean. These past days have strengthened our bond from his previous hours at my house. I've come to think of Ernest as my family. If you won't carry out my wishes, I'll wait for Mr. Finnigan to arrive."

"Uncle Patrick sent me because he doesn't have the stamina for this. I think he knew what you would ask, the sly dog." Sean grinned. "You're enthusiastic, Francesca. Be sure you save some of this energy for your mother's funeral tomorrow."

She huffed but allowed him to take her arm as they continued down the corridor.

Sean paused outside an open door. Jim's back was to them, and Ernest clasped his hand—Jim's uniform hat sitting crocked on his little head. Francesca breathed a sigh of relief at seeing the boy safe.

"Good afternoon, Detective Callaghan," Sean said as they entered the office, "and Officer Abbott and Ernest."

The two turned and the detective stood.

"Miss Fran!" Ernest ran for a hug. "Where are the kittens?"

"Safe at home. Becca will see to them if she gets there before me." Francesca looked at Jim and whispered her thanks.

He nodded and eyed Sean expectantly.

"Could you take Ernest around the station?" Sean asked Jim.

"Come on, Ernest, let me show you the file room."

Ernest clung to Francesca. "Can Miss Fran come too?"

"Not this time," Jim replied, "but you can tell her about it when we get back."

Ernest kissed her hand before letting go. Jim didn't touch her when he passed, but the look he gave felt like a loving embrace.

"I'll be damned," Sean muttered as his gaze shifted between the two.

When the door closed behind them, the detective motioned to the two seats across from his desk. "What brings you here, Judge Spunner?"

"The welfare of the boy. Now that the next of kin is here, it's time to get down to business." Sean sat after Francesca did. "What is that aunt of his, nineteen—maybe twenty? A secretary or something with a studio apartment or sharing a little one bedroom with another young woman?"

"Next of kin is next of kin, especially if there isn't a will," Detective Callaghan said as he propped his feet on his desk. "Anyone would turn the boy over to her, as you well know, judge."

"My clerks have checked with all the law offices from Mobile to New Orleans and Montgomery to Tallahassee. No one has William Hart's file."

"Then we'll need to run a public notice in the newspaper and wait the allotted—"

Sean smirked. "I know how to manage an estate, what I need help with is securing the boy's well-being. What's the department's plan with Narcissa Hart? If it was up to me, I'd send her back to whatever boarding house she lives in and leave Ernest with Miss Wilton."

"Why, because she wants the boy? That's out of the question. Now that a relative is here, Miss Wilton's job is done."

"I want to legally adopt Ernest," Francesca said.

"And what did the aunt say about that?"

"She hasn't been informed."

He looked at Sean. "You need to talk some sense into your client."

Sean bit his lip as he plotted his next move. "Why don't you bring Miss Hart in and see what she expects out of the situation. She might not even be here *for* Ernest."

"But she's here. The boy needs to go with his aunt or to the boys' home."

Sean gave a noncommittal shrug. "Let's see what happens."

Detective Callaghan stood. "Move your chair into the corner and stay quiet, Miss Wilton. I'll be back with Miss Hart in a minute."

As soon as they were alone, Sean gave Francesca a smug grin as he relocated her chair. "Have you and Jim made a physical connection or are you just making eyes at each other?"

"That's none of your business." To distract from her blush, Francesca quietly took her seat.

"Judge Spunner," the detective said when he returned, "this is Miss Narcissa Hart, Ernest's aunt. Miss Hart, Judge Spunner has been brought in on this case as a legal advisor. I hope you don't mind if I ask you questions while he's in the room."

"I never shy away from a handsome man, detective."

Sean leaned against the filing cabinet in her line of sight, enjoying the play.

Once Detective Callaghan took his chair, he started speaking. "The judge's people have reached out to law offices within two hundred miles, but no one has legal papers for your brother."

"Willy would never plan for what would happen when he was gone because he couldn't imagine a world that didn't revolve around him."

"Was he a violent man?"

"I understand the judge," Narcissa pointed over her shoulder at Francesca, "but why is the neighbor here?"

"She's a key witness," Sean said.

"Witness to what? There's no one to put on trial."

"Do you wish her to leave?" Sean inquired.

"I don't care what she does, but I don't like the privilege she's getting."

"Our apologies, Miss Hart. Miss Wilton is an established ally, and we're just getting to know you."

"Was your brother violent?" Detective Callaghan asked again.

"When it suited him. He wouldn't pick fights with strangers, but he pushed people around if he knew he could rule them."

"Like his wife?" he followed through.

"Yes."

"Did you ever witness his brutality?" Sean asked.

"Am I on trial here?"

"Just answer, Miss Hart," the detective sighed with annoyance.

"Yes, but it isn't my business what a man does with his wife when she isn't willing to leave him. Before I left Mobile, I tried to talk Sue into bringing Ernest and coming with me, but she wouldn't part from the bastard. Willy was just like our old man and getting worse each month. I knew where he was headed and didn't want to be around to see it. I guess I should have warned someone, but I didn't think it was possible he'd turn out worse than our father."

Sadness turned to anger, causing Francesca's posture to stiffen. It should be their business if someone was being hurt. If she had telephoned the police when she heard the fights, especially the days when Mrs. Hart sent Ernest to her for safe keeping…. Francesca's chest tightened with regret.

"What do you plan on accomplishing while you're in town?" Sean questioned.

"Accomplish? I came because I was told to. I figured there would be a funeral and since I'm next of kin, I'd oversee my brother's things."

Sean raised his brow. "You don't think the son should inherit?"

"He's just a kid. Wouldn't he need a guardian?"

"Did your brother have a lot of assets?"

She shrugged. "Beyond the mortgaged house, I doubt it. He wasn't much for banks."

"As there is no will, a public notice must be shared, allowing any unknown relatives to step forward. Nothing can be parted from your brother's belongings until that happens."

"There's no one else."

"Not even on the wife's side?" Sean countered.

"My brother earned everything. Sue never worked a day in her life. She was from Conecuh County without a lick to her name except the curves God endowed her with. When my brother picked up Sue Guthrie in Atmore on her way south, all she had was the clothes on her back and a black eye from her daddy."

The detective wrote down the information. "Thank you for her maiden name and county of residence. We'll be sure to post notices there."

"I doubt any of her kin could read."

"I'll send one of my clerks to check things out in person," Sean said with a smile. "Leave no stone unturned."

Narcissa huffed. "What am I supposed to do until the time has passed for these notices? Do I return home and come back when it's over?"

"Ernest won't be able to leave the state until everything is finalized," Sean pointed out.

"Don't you have homes for boys like Ernie?"

"Yes, but with the trauma he went through, we thought it was best he stayed somewhere quiet," Sean said as he motioned to Narcissa. "He's familiar with Miss Wilton and asked to stay with her."

"She's done us all a great service in caring for Ernest these past days," Detective Callaghan said.

"If I keep Ernie while we wait for the notice to go around, do I get use of my brother's house?"

"The estate must stay intact—not a penny spent to pay for anything outside of keeping ownership of the home. Do you have means to buy food and other necessities to provide for yourself and the boy?"

"Wouldn't the estate pay for the boy's keeping?"

"We don't know what all the estate entails yet, so you need to be prepared to financially support Ernest and yourself. Can you do that, Miss Hart?"

"I'm prepared to do what I can for the boy. I owe him that much."

"We're glad to hear that, Miss Hart," Detective Callaghan said. "Judge Spunner will help you with any further questions that might arise."

Though crestfallen, Francesca remained placid. Then she remembered Josephine was supposed to cleanse the Harts' house that evening. She motioned Sean over so she could whisper to him. "I need to leave, but Jim has to stall bringing them home. There's something that needs to be seen to."

Sean nodded and approached the detective. "The check-ins will continue, correct?"

"The department will do that until the boy's living situation is finalized, Judge Spunner."

"I'm glad to hear that, but I'm afraid I need to get my client home," Sean said. "There's much to see to before Mrs. Wilton's funeral tomorrow."

"Of course. And my condolences, ma'am."

"Thank you," Francesca replied on their way out.

Sean left a quick note for Jim at the front desk, then he and Francesca were on their way across town.

Eleven

The first thing Jim noticed when he and Ernest entered the detective's office was the lack of Francesca and Judge Spunner. Jim balled the note Fitzwilliam had given him and tossed it into the waste basket. Only something important would have caused Francesca to leave without telling Ernest goodbye. He focused on doing his part to help.

"You can escort them home, Officer Abbott," Detective Callaghan said. "The Harts' funeral will be Friday morning in Magnolia Cemetery, and Ernest will be staying at his parents' house with his aunt."

"But I want Miss Fran!" Ernest's panic vibrated Jim's clasped hand.

Jim went to his knee before the boy. "Miss Fran will be next door. I'm sure you can visit her often." When tears fell, Jim embraced him and spoke into his ear. "Breathe, Ernest. Breath like Miss Deborah taught you. Miss Fran and I will keep you safe."

Jim felt him relax as he leaned into his chest.

"That's it, Ernest. Keep breathing." Jim lifted him and the boy rested his head on Jim's shoulder, slipping his arms around his neck.

"Stay a minute, Abbott," the detective said.

"I'll meet you out front, Miss Hart." Jim crossed to the desk, a hand on Ernest's back to keep him relaxed.

"I'm glad the boy trusts you. The sergeant will tell you to keep checking on him twice a day. I have a feeling Judge Spunner is waiting for something to go wrong and I don't want that happening on our watch. Do a walkthrough with Miss Hart when you get there. Take note of anything of value so we can be sure it doesn't go missing."

"I will, sir."

"Ernest," Jim said as he carried him down the hall, "how would you like to patrol the south side before going home?"

"Could we see Miss Eilands and the cats too?"

"That's our special place with Miss Fran. Besides, you said your aunt was allergic."

Ernest nodded and tucked back on his shoulder. Jim hoped whatever it was Francesca needed time for would be done before they arrived.

As they approached the Harts' house more than an hour later, Jim noticed the open windows. The cleansing. Francesca didn't want Ernest going there with the stench and unsettled emotions.

"I want to see Sunny," Ernest said.

"Let's see if Miss Fran is home."

Narcissa loitered on the sidewalk while Jim walked Ernest to the house. Francesca met them on her front porch.

"May I see Sunny?"

"You're welcome here whenever you'd like, Ernest, but you have to get permission from your aunt first."

Before he could run down the steps, Narcissa hollered, "Go on, Ernie."

Francesca put a loving hand on the boy's shoulder. "Becca has them in the kitchen. They'll be happy to see you."

After he was through the screen door, her sorrowful brown eyes turned on Jim.

"I don't like it any more than you do, but I'll watch out for him. Detective Callaghan asked me to do a walkthrough with her."

Francesca fished the key from her pocket. "I hope it's safe for him. Jo burned sage and the windows have been open nearly an hour."

Jim nodded and cut across the lawn.

Narcissa held out her hand and he dropped the key in her palm while continuing to the porch. After unlocking the door, she picked up her suitcase that was on the porch and looked around the front room.

"It's in better shape than I expected. Not that there's a lot here. Willy wasn't home much to care for all the comforts. I'm surprised he bought a house. They always rented apartments before."

Jim scanned the room. No gramophone, no shiny trinkets.

Narcissa paused at the table beside the sofa and lifted a lid on a small wooden box, causing a sprinkling of dust to fall. Frowning, she set the lid back crooked. She walked to the main bedroom, looking over the sparse furniture. Jim followed, keeping his gaze away from the kitchen doorway.

Seeing there was nothing of worth, Jim checked Ernest's room. The bed was crisply made and the dresser and rocking chair polished—further proof that Francesca cared for the boy. There were no wall decorations, but the blue curtains were tied back, allowing more air into the space.

"Be sure you telephone a grocer before four o'clock if you want a morning delivery," Jim said.

"Thank you for the tip, officer. Please send Ernest home—without the cat."

Next door, he let himself in the kitchen.

"Good afternoon, Officer Abbott," the cook said while she stirred a pot of gumbo.

"Hello, Miss Becca. It smells wonderful."

"They'll be plenty for you if you stop in later."

"I appreciate it."

Jim continued through to the parlor, where Francesca sat on the floor with Ernest while he joyfully pulled a ribbon around the rug for the kittens.

"You aunt wants you home, Ernest. Sunny will need to stay here with Rochester and Miss Fran. You knew that was a possibility."

Ernest nodded, then buried his face in Sunny's fluffy orange neck.

"You can visit as often as your aunt allows," Francesca said as she hugged him.

He kissed her cheek. "I love you, Miss Fran."

"I love you too."

Jim heard the catch in her voice as Ernest slipped his kitten into her arms.

"I'll walk you over," Jim said. Ernest took his hand, and they went outside. "I'll be watching out for you, Ernest, even if I'm not always here. But I'll see you later tonight."

When he returned, Francesca stared at the kittens that were under a side chair.

"Francesca, if I could take the pain from you, I would." Jim helped her stand.

She embraced him with the tightest hug he'd ever received. Jim silently held her, enjoying the way their bodies fit together.

"Do you want me to come over after I'm done for the day?"

"I want you to, Jim, but I don't think you should." Her soft lips bused his cheek. "My mother's funeral is in the morning. Seeing you will stir things and…and I don't know if I'll be able to sleep tonight as it is."

"If I can stop in the cathedral, I'll pay my respects, but I'm working the early shift."

Francesca nodded as she shifted back. "I understand. I'm going to offer the gumbo next door to be sure Ernest eats a proper meal, but please come for supper tomorrow."

Taking her hands, he kissed her knuckles. "I'll come sooner if you need me."

"I know you would, Jim."

"The Harts' funeral is going to be Friday morning."

"I'm sure that will help Ernest have a bit of closure."

The orange tabby climbed his trousers to his knee as though he were a tree trunk.

"Damn, Sunny! There's flesh under these pants." Jim pried the cat off by the scruff and handed Sunny to Francesca. "You'll need to play with them to expel their energy since Ernest isn't here."

She smiled. "I need the kittens right now as much as I've needed your support."

He left a lingering kiss on her cheek. "Take care, Francesca."

Jim looped around the block and came up the next street. Seeing the kids he'd spoken to the other day, he approached them.

"Keep watching out for Ernest, fellas," Jim said. "His aunt moved in and will be with him."

"Golly, I couldn't sleep where my parents died."

"It'll be rough. Try to cheer him up if you see him."

"We will, officer," Tommy Reardon, the oldest one, promised.

Jim continued his walk toward Broad Street with a feeling of security over his junior neighborhood patrolmen.

Twelve

In the morning, Francesca was ready at eight o'clock, wearing the black dress she had last worn to her father's funeral. It was old-fashioned along with her drab bun, but tomorrow she would go shopping. She wasn't sure when she would be brave enough to venture to a beauty parlor for a haircut.

Bartholomew Graves knocked at the door. His black suit was crisp, his spectacles shiny.

"I appreciate you and Merritt accompanying me today," Francesca told him as he walked her to the limousine Sean's uncle had hired for the day.

"It's our pleasure, Miss Wilton."

At the cathedral, Merritt and Josephine stood beside her on the portico, welcoming the parishioners. Since Mrs. Wilton hadn't attended Mass in over a decade there wasn't a large crowd of mourners, but several of the old families from the neighborhood were there besides the Finnigans and Spunners including Barnes, Wolf, Marley, Stuart, and Melling.

Mass was a fog of incense amid all the standing and kneeling. At Magnolia Cemetery, Merritt and Bartholomew were on either side of Francesca as Father Quinn presided over the grave.

Patrick and Cecelia Finnigan hosted the wake at their house on Palmetto Street. Francesca drank two glasses of wine just because she could—Prohibition or not.

On her way out with her family, Cordelia hugged Francesca. "I'm inviting you and Officer Abbott to my salon Friday night. You're well overdue for a night out."

"I'd like to attend if Jim would escort me."

"I'm sure he'll jump at the chance. I'm dropping an invitation at his house on my way home."

"How do you know—"

"I asked Mrs. Graves where her daughter lives. I know he's in an upper apartment from her. I'm resourceful when needed." She laughed and hurried down the Finnigans' steps.

An hour later, Sean and his wife, Hattie, dropped Francesca at home with a platter of leftovers. Francesca refused Sean's offer to escort her to the front door, but he promised to return with his uncle mid-afternoon to read the will.

With a few solo hours looming, Francesca took the kittens outside, settled on a blanket in the grass with a glass of iced tea, and watched their antics. The squeal of the side gate opening broke the peace. Francesca immediately straightened.

Ernest ran around the corner of the house, hugged her, gave Rochester a few strokes, and captured Sunny. "I miss you all."

"We miss you too. Have you had dinner?"

"I had grits for breakfast after Officer Abbott woke Aunt Narcissa this morning. She's sleeping again."

"Let's take these boys inside and fix some food."

"I came over last hour, but everything was locked," Ernest said as they entered the kitchen.

"That's rare, but today is very different."

"Officer Abbott said my parents' funeral will be Friday morning. Why did it take so long when your mother's only took three days?"

"I know it's been difficult for you, Ernest. They had to wait for your aunt to arrive, but then it took that same amount of time to finalize things with her. If you get the kittens fresh water, I'll fix a plate of leftovers for you."

By the time Ernest was at the table with ham, shrimp, green beans, potatoes, and glass of milk, Rochester and Sunny were curled together on the rug in front of the stove.

"Did you sleep well last night?" Francesca asked him.

Ernest shook his head. "I had bad dreams and woke up Aunt Narcissa. We couldn't sleep because I knew my father was waiting to get me if I did."

Francesca's skin prickled with his words. "Why don't you take a nap here after you finish eating?"

Ernest ate, washed, and gathered the drowsy kittens in his arms before marching to the guest room. When Francesca followed a minute later, he was already snuggled under the blanket, Sunny and Rochester settled beside him. Smiling, she pulled the door closed.

Sean and his uncle arrived at a quarter to three to go over the will.

"I need to confess something," Francesca said as Mr. Finnigan sat in the armchair and Sean settled in on the sofa beside her. "Ernest showed up after I got home. He said Narcissa was sleeping, and he hadn't eaten since early this morning when Jim stopped by. I fed him, and now he's napping in his old room."

"Francesca, you should have brought him home since he didn't have permission."

"I'm not going to send him back if she needs sleep. They were awake most of the night because of his nightmares."

"But his aunt is his guardian right now, darling."

"It's not my responsibility to keep her on track." Francesca crossed her arms. "If she comes looking, I'll say goodbye to him, but I'll not send him home when I know he'll be unchaperoned."

"If you woke her—" Mr. Finnigan started, but Sean held up his hand.

"As Francesca said, Uncle Patrick, it isn't her job to keep a grown woman on task." Sean looked back at her with a knowing smirk. "But you need to put in a dutiful effort, darling. If it happens again, go next door and knock as *softly* as you can so you can honestly say that you tried to return him but your knock went unanswered."

"Thank you!" She hugged the judge.

"I'll go attempt to rouse her," Sean said before going out the door.

Mr. Finnigan shook his head. "When I hear him like this I don't know if I should be proud or embarrassed."

"Proud, Mr. Finnigan. He's helping others."

The judge returned with a satisfied sigh. "No response from Miss Hart."

Mr. Finnigan removed a file from his briefcase. "Now, if you're ready, Miss Wilton, I'll read your mother's will."

Francesca nodded and Sean sweetly took her hand, continuing to hold it while the two paragraphs were read.

As expected, ten percent of the bank account went to the church and the rest of the money, property, and investments Mrs. Wilton had inherited from her husband reverted to Francesca, along with the insurance claim for her life in the amount of five thousand dollars.

"With proper investment, you'll be fine, Francesca," Sean said as he squeezed her hand.

"If you stop by the office Friday, I'll have everything ready to sign," Mr. Finnigan said. "And we hope you'll continue to trust Finnigan and Spunner with your legal needs."

"I wouldn't go anywhere else."

"Do you need any cash to get you through until next week?" Mr. Finnigan asked.

"I had hoped to purchase a few new clothes. After wearing this old dress today I know I'm in sad need of new ones."

"Go to Mademoiselle Bisset's," Sean said. "I shall telephone her and explain the situation. I'm positive she would wait to bill you until next week."

"I appreciate it, Sean. And I'll see you, Mr. Finnigan, on Friday afternoon."

"Call if you need anything before then," he said.

"There's one more thing. I'd like to purchase a headstone for Ernest's mother so he could visit her easier if he wishes. And he needs a suit. I'd like to take him shopping."

"With Miss Hart's permission," Sean chided.

"Yes, Judge Spunner."

"I do like the sound of my title coming from your lips." He grinned. "Take Ernest to Hammel's. I know Mathias Wolf will give you a line of credit without issue."

"Ernie!" a shout came from outside.

Sean hurried out the front door, Francesca on his heels.

"Good afternoon, Miss Hart," he said as they stopped on the lawn between the houses. "Sorry to alarm you, but Ernest has been here for a while. We knocked on your door, but there was no answer. Miss Wilton was kind enough to feed him and put him down for a nap. As soon as he's awake, she'll send him home."

"Oh," she sighed. "Thank you. My sleep schedule is all messed up from working nightshifts, and then Ernie's nightmares last night."

"Have you any experience with children?"

"Just my own childhood, which was a constant wheel of school and chores and shouting, besides the heavier things mixed in to keep us on our toes."

Francesca's middle tightened with pity. Narcissa was young and didn't have the proper role models in her life to teach her about mothering a child.

Sean frowned. "I suggest you let the boy continue to rest for now, Miss Hart, but Ernest should be attending school. See that he gets to Leinkauf Elementary tomorrow morning."

All was quiet after Sean and Mr. Finnigan left. Francesca peeked into the guest room to be sure Ernest was still resting. He was—or at least appeared to be. But he was

welcome to stay if he was secure in bed. Sean had promised
them that much.

Thirteen

"That woman is trying to steal Ernie from me," Narcissa complained as soon as she opened the front door in response to Jim's knock.

"Officer Abbott!" Ernest came for a hug.

Jim placed his hat on Ernest's head and grinned. "Hey, Ernest. Could you give me a minute with your aunt?"

"May I play in the yard, Aunt Narcissa?"

"Stay away from Miss Wilton's house."

"Yes, ma'am." He shuffled out the door.

"Don't try to give me half-stories about what's going on. Judge Spunner already informed me about the situation." Jim stared straight at her shadowed eyes. "Francesca did you and Ernest a service this afternoon. Ernest going to school tomorrow will give you hours to take naps or whatever it is you deem more important than caring for a child."

"I'm used to sleeping most of the day," she practically whined, making her look and sound as young as her nephew. "It's not my fault I work nights at the hotel.

116

And Miss Wilton makes me feel inferior. He's my nephew, but I know he prefers her to me."

"He's used to her, is all. I'm sure once you get better acquainted, he'll be fine with you."

"I hope so."

"I'll see you tomorrow, Miss Hart."

Jim waved to Ernest, who was pacing the invisible line between the two houses and met him under the oak.

"You're leaving already?" Ernest asked.

"I'm afraid so. Sit down with me a minute, Ernest." They settled on the curb. "Going back to school tomorrow will allow your aunt the private time she's used to and ensure you're able to play. Do you have friends you walked with?"

He shook his head.

"How about I walk with you tomorrow morning?" Jim flicked the hat Ernest wore. "It's my day off, so I'll be in regular clothes."

"Are you going fishing again?"

"Would you like some fresh fish?"

He nodded.

"Do you think your aunt knows how to cook it?"

"No, but I'm sure Miss Fran does!"

"I bet you're right." Jim removed his hat, ruffled Ernest's hair, and said goodbye.

At home, Jim found an envelope stuck in his door. It was a letter from Cordelia Barnes-Wolf asking him to bring Francesca to her salon Friday night. He took a long shower, trying to keep his excitement down at the thought of supper with Francesca the next hour and then the party with her on Friday evening.

He dressed in a gray suit with a blue bowtie and suspenders. After shining his shoes and slicking his hair, Jim second guessed his clothing choice.

Downstairs, he let himself in the Patersons' back porch and stopped in the open kitchen doorway.

"Hey, Jim," Winnie said as she looked over from the stove. "You must be going out tonight."

"Is this too much for supper at Francesca's house?"

"Not at all. If she's casually dressed, you can always remove your jacket. I'm sure Fran could use cheering up today."

Nathan came in from the hall wearing an undershirt and trousers. "Sprucing yourself up for the spinster, Abbott?"

"Stop that!" Winnie snapped a dishtowel at her husband. "Fran is a perfectly respectable woman. Leave them alone or sleep on the sofa tonight."

"That's how it's going to be, is it?" His left hand went to his hip, his annoyed stance because he couldn't cross his arms.

"You don't need to tease Jim about liking Miss Wilton."

"Then I'll rib him about that girl from Florida," Nathan said with a smirk.

"Hell no! But thank you for the advice, Winnie." Jim kissed her cheek on his way out just to goad Nathan.

He crossed Government Street in the shadowy twilight. Once on Francesca's back porch, Jim knocked on the kitchen door though it was open to expel the heat from the oven.

"Come in, Officer Abbott," Becca said while transferring dishes. "Miss Fran is waiting for you in the parlor."

"Thank you. Supper smells wonderful." He looked at the empty table along the wall.

"Y'all are dining at the formal table."

He smiled in relief. "Then I am dressed appropriately."

"And you look right nice." She smiled conspiratorially. "I'm sure Miss Fran will appreciate your effort."

Francesca wore a pink dress with a layer of frills across her shoulders and an A-lined skirt that gave her an hourglass shape. It reminded Jim of something one of his girls would have worn before the war.

"You look sweet, Francesca." Jim kissed the back of her hand, then turned it gently to kiss the inside of her wrist.

Her cheeks flushed with pleasure. "It's at least five years old. I plan to go shopping tomorrow because I have nothing to wear to Cordelia's salon. She told me she was going to leave you an invitation—did she?"

"Yes, and I'd be honored to escort you. I'm off the next two days, so there's no need to worry about my schedule beyond checking Ernest."

"I'm going to pack a boxed lunch for him tomorrow with a bit extra should he need something on his way to school."

"I'll be walking him there in the morning."

"That's wonderful, Jim." She paused, watching their linked hands. "Could I cook you breakfast? We could eat after you get Ernest to school."

"Francesca?"

Her brown eyes hesitantly rose. Jim wanted to hold her all night so there wasn't a need to return the next morning. She must have read his unspoken thoughts because her blush deepened.

"I'd enjoy breakfast with you, Fran. Thank you."

"Supper's ready," Becca called.

Jim tucked Francesca's hand around his arm. Two place settings were at the head of the dining table and on the right-hand side of it. He pulled out the armed chair at the head for Francesca.

"The man sits here," she whispered.

"The head of household does. That's you, Francesca. I assume the will was read and this is officially your home."

She nodded and gracefully took the cushioned chair. After pushing it in, Jim took his seat on the side. Becca brought in several serving dishes and a crystal pitcher of iced tea.

"Thank you, Becca," Francesca said after the platter of sautéed yellow squash was set down. "I don't think we'll need anything more."

The cook left with a pleased smile, and Francesca looked at Jim with hesitation.

He took her hand. "No matter that we've shared several meals, it feels like the first time, doesn't it? There's something about the formality of a dining room that tries to make the situation awkward, but it isn't. Everything about being with you is natural."

Francesca glowed at his words and then dished up blackened shrimp, seasoned rice, and vegetables.

Once they were eating, Jim looked around the room. "Where are Rochester and Sunny?"

"They should be in the kitchen with Becca by now, but were in the bathtub when you arrived. That's been my holding pen for them, but it won't last much longer."

"Not with Sunny at least, the little scamp."

She laughed. "What were you like as a boy?"

"Ernest has a layer of caution I never had. If I wanted to climb a tree, I attempted it without bothering to ask how to do it. I learned through broken bones, busted noses, and plenty of paddling about what not to do and who not to do it to." Jim ate a shrimp. "What about you, Francesca?"

"I'm afraid to say I was devious. I played pious to the adults but was a bit wild with my peers. They all liked that because they could say they were with me or that I was attending a party, and it was assumed what was happening was completely proper." Francesca's dark eyes sparked mischief.

"Will I get to see some of that wildness at the salon Friday night?"

"Quite possibly. Del was one of the girls who took advantage of my good standing, so she knows what I'm capable of. I'm concerned that I don't know the new dances though."

"We can practice after supper."

They ate and talked about their school years and interests. Francesca loved dancing, the shoreline, and literature. The conversation further cemented Jim's belief that Francesca Wilton was the perfect woman for him.

"I know you can cakewalk and waltz, but do you foxtrot?" he asked after dinner as they entered the parlor.

"I never had the opportunity to learn."

"Then we'll focus on that tonight. It's the most popular right now, though people still tango."

Before they could begin dancing, Becca called Francesca to the hall. They whispered back and forth while Jim went through the phonographs to find a recording that had the proper beat. Fortunately, Francesca kept up with current music. Jim moved the coffee table, rolled the rug, and started "Smiles" by Joseph C. Smith's Orchestra.

"I've always liked this song," Francesca said as she joined him in the middle of the room.

"A familiar tune helps people learn the dance quicker. The basic steps for you are two slow backwards, then two quick to the side. Practice doing that to the beat."

He watched, enjoying her fluid movements.

"Now, I'm going to nestle to your right side, holding your right arm high, so we look over each other's shoulder." Jim closed the distance, inhaling her fresh scent as he took her right hand, adjusting hers so it rested over his left hand like a hook. "My right hand is going to be under your other arm. Once we get going, I'll signal to you with pressure for turns and spins."

He situated himself, trying in vain not to be aroused by her nearness as his groin was at her right hip when their feet settled in between and to the outside of each other's.

"You smell great, Jim," she whispered. "Is it your aftershave or hair oil?"

"Probably both." Pleased she was open and comfortable with their closeness, he grinned. "We aren't supposed to look at each other once we get going, but ask questions if you need to. The last thing is when we promenade sideways, make sure you face the way we're going while our bodies stay parallel. I'll restart the recording and we'll give it a go."

Francesca incorporated her natural grace into each movement of the foxtrot.

"You're wonderful, Fran. Let's give it another listen, and I'll show you a few advanced turns."

When he returned from restarting the gramophone, she hugged him. "You're a wonderful teacher."

"And you're a superior student." Jim kissed her temple as they settled into position.

Francesca's body was supple, hypnotizing with the smooth glide across the bare floor and the slight rise of her chest with each breath. With the dying strains of the tune, she pressed sensually along his right side while capturing his gaze.

"If you could read my thoughts, Francesca, I fear you'd run from me."

"Tell me what you want to do with me, Jim," she whispered.

"Not tonight, Francesca." The bump of the finished recording continuously spun. "Let me pick another song."

"Please." Her brown eyes were luminous. "Allow me to imagine with you. Becca will be leaving soon, if she hasn't left already."

Jim fingered the curve of her lower lip. "I don't want to go too far and ruin what we have right now."

"I trust you, Jim." Her mouth captured his in a slow kiss that started warm, but switched to scalding in its intensity.

He took her hand, shut down the gramophone, and settled on the sofa so she leaned against his side, his right arm around her. Jim briefly kissed the shell of her ear before closing his eyes so he could pretend he was daydreaming out loud.

"Feeling you beside me, Francesca, stirs me in a way I've never experienced before. When we dance, I feel the pulse of life within me echoing the beating of your heart. The scent of your skin makes me drift into a fantasy of shared touches."

Her hand went to Jim's knee.

"I yearn to run my fingers through the length of your hair and feel your smooth skin as you reveal it to me by slowly removing each piece of clothing. I want to kiss your shoulders, your thighs, and taste every inch of you."

She caught her breath.

His hand trailed to her arm, rubbing it gently. "I'll stop. I'd never force that on you."

"Don't stop, Jim." Her hand on his knee squeezed and she leaned her head on his shoulder. "Tell me more."

"I'd kiss down the column of your throat. After caressing each breast, I'd devour their perfection." His hand at her waist explored up. When she didn't stop him, he palmed a breast, pleased with the way it filled his hand. "A perfect mouthful. I'd shower them with attention before dipping my face lower."

She shifted onto his lap. Nibbling her neck, he explored every inch of her chest through her dress while she whimpered with delight.

"I'd make love to you all night, bringing you pleasure to let you know how much I adore you." His arms crossed around her back. "It's only been a week, but what I feel for you surpasses everything I've ever felt for a woman. Please allow me to continue to be here for you, Francesca."

She nestled into his neck, resting her head on his shoulder. "Thank you for sharing your passion with me, Jim."

"I'm glad you're not scandalized."

Her laughter rumbled his chest. "Scandalized? No. I want to experience all those things with you, but I know tonight isn't the right time." Her lips brushed his jaw. "I want to feel the hot skin of your muscular arms. See you poised above me as—"

Jim stopped her with a hard kiss. "If you keep talking, I might lose control."

"Then dance with me. With a little more practice, we're sure to impress Cordelia's guests Friday night."

"Is there anyone special you want to show off for?" Jim asked as he set "Smiles" back on.

"You." She gave an exaggerated curtsey and grinned.

Jim bowed in reply and they began. They danced twice more. On his walk home, Jim's body hummed as he counted down the hours until he'd see Francesca in the morning.

***

Jim walked down George Street with a couple fishing poles over the shoulder of his white shirt. A basket and satchel crossed his body, navy suspenders held his trousers of the same color, and a wide-brimmed hat shaded his face as he watched Francesca and Ernest on the front steps of her house.

"Mornin'!" he called as he crossed onto Francesca's property.

"You're really going fishing, Officer Abbott?" Ernest asked. When Jim nodded, Ernest turned to Francesca. "He's going to catch fish for you to cook us for supper!"

Jim laughed. "I'm going to *attempt* to catch some fish, but the polite thing to do is ask if the lady wishes to cook them rather than demand it."

"Would you, Miss Fran?" Ernest's eager blue eyes begged as much as his pleading voice, but Francesca looked pensive.

"How about if Officer Abbott can get some fish back here by the time school is over, I make an afternoon treat of it? That way there's no pressure for him to catch a lot of big fish."

"Could you, Officer Abbott?" Ernest asked.

"I'll do my best. Is it all right to leave my gear on your porch so I can walk Ernest to school?"

"Of course, Jim. And you have a good day, Ernest. I'll see you both later."

Ernest handed Sunny and Rochester to her.

Jim set his things on the porch and opened the screen. "It smells great already."

"Fresh biscuits." She pointed to the tin lunchbox in the corner of the porch. "There are a couple buttered ones on top in there for you two to eat on your way."

"You're amazing, Francesca."

She blushed at his words and he grinned as he descended the steps. Jim opened the lunchbox and showed Ernest the surprise.

"Isn't Miss Fran the greatest?" Ernest said as he scooped up one of the biscuits. "Aunt Narcissa didn't have time to fix anything this morning before she sent me out. I waited for you with Miss Fran."

Jim kept hold of the box while they walked. Ernest gobbled half the biscuit before he questioned him. "How are things with your aunt?"

Ernest shrugged and kicked a rock in the road.

"Are you comfortable with her?"

"I don't like being back in the house."

"Why is that?" Jim watched the boy chew pensively.

"I keep having nightmares about my dad. I wake up and I know he's watching me."

"Do you go to your aunt?"

"Yes, but she gets scared too and doesn't know what to say or do like Miss Fran."

Jim patted Ernest's shoulder. "I'm sorry about that, Ernest. Your aunt's had a rough life and has no experience with kids. It's not fun for you to be the experiment though, is it?"

"Nope." Ernest shoved the rest of the biscuit into his mouth, and Jim passed him the second one.

"Call out or go to her when you're scared. She needs to know even if she can't help. Hey, aren't those the kids from your street?" Jim motioned up the block to where a group of boys were battling with sticks as though they were swords. "The Reardon brothers and their friends?"

Ernest nodded as he ate.

Jim increased his pace. "Hey, fellas! Wait up."

The five boys stopped, the oldest narrowing his eyes.

"That you, Officer Abbott?" Tommy Reardon asked.

"Sure is. I'm going fishing today."

"I wish I could go fishing instead of to school," Tommy replied. "Why are you headed this way?"

Jim and Ernest stopped in front of the boys. "Ernest is going back to school, so I'm walking with him."

Tommy thumbed toward his younger brother. "Jack's in his class."

"Oh yeah?" Jim smiled. "How about you fellas and Ernest walk home together this afternoon?"

"Sure, Officer Abbot." Jack rubbed his freckled nose with the black of his sleeve.

Ernest smiled. "I'd like that."

"Come on, then." Jim started walking. "Do y'all still play baseball before the bell?"

"If we've got time," Tommy replied. "But we do at recess."

Ernest was quiet unless the others spoke directly to him. The interest in his gaze and the hopeful smile when he waved goodbye at Leinkauf Elementary told Jim all he needed to know. It would take a while for Ernest to fully immerse himself with friends, but he was on his way.

Fourteen

By the time the bacon was done cooking and Francesca had pulled the scrambled eggs off the heat, Jim slipped in the back door. He eyed the apron around her middle before approaching.

"Are you done cooking?"

When she nodded, his arms went around her, tugging at the laces as he nosed her ear.

"Allow me to undress this layer from you to quench my fantasy for a little while."

Goosebumps bloomed up her arms at his words. Then his fingers skimmed her backside across the tapered green skirt. Jim shifted closer and both hands smoothed over her hips.

"Aren't you naughty today?" she teased.

"The aroma of biscuits does that to me."

"One wasn't enough?"

"I let Ernest eat both." He slipped the apron over her head and tossed it onto the counter. "Allow me to enjoy this connection."

"Connection? You haven't even kissed me yet."

His hands splayed over her curves, pulling her back to him. "I could say the same thing about you."

"Hush your mouth."

His kisses roamed down her neck to her exposed collarbone.

"Jim, we better eat so you have time to fish."

He dutifully took the platter of biscuits, bacon, and eggs to the table. They dished up their food and poured coffee.

"I got the Reardon boys to walk with Ernest to and from school from now on. Jack is in his class."

"That's terrific. Ernest was always alone when I saw him before."

"It turns out the other kids were afraid of his father, so they never invited him to play. I have a feeling William Hart is going to continue to be a problem even though he's dead."

"A haunting of the ghost of his evil deeds."

"But enough of that melancholy topic for now. Would you like to go fishing with me after we eat?"

Francesca dabbed her mouth with the napkin from her lap. "I have to go shopping today."

"How about supper out?"

"I need to attempt to get more rest, especially since the funeral is in the morning and we're going out tomorrow night. I'm having trouble falling asleep since I'm alone."

Jim took one of her hands, green eyes sincere. "Would you like me to stay tonight?"

"That's the most forward offer I've ever had, Jim Abbott."

He grinned. "I meant I could sleep in the parlor, just so you aren't alone in the house."

"I don't need the gossip, but that's sweet of you to sacrifice your reputation for me."

Jim laughed and caressed her hand. "I'd do anything for you, Francesca. And you aren't alone with your sleepless nights. Ernest is having nightmares, thinking his father is coming for him."

"He had a few when he was here, but I had hoped they'd lessen over time. I guess him being at the house where his parents died keeps it fresh in his mind." She sighed. "I wish he were still with me."

"So does he."

After eating, Jim deposited a load of used dishes in the sink. His arms went around Francesca, his lips to her neck. She indulged in the sensation for a moment, then pulled back and fingered his collar.

"I love the way you make me feel, Jim. It's ambrosia to my starved soul, but I need to figure out if what I'm feeling is just a creature of the flesh response or if it's deeper."

"You know damn well it's deeper."

His mouth moved across hers in a possessive way as she felt the strength in his shoulders and the broad expanse of his back through his thin shirt.

"I want you, Jim. I ache for your touch and crave every connection I can get, whether it's a smile across the lawn or your lips on my skin."

"It's the same for me, Francesca." A finger traced her cheek as he gave her the most longing look she'd ever received. "And it's the real thing—I know it to my bones."

Her heart dropped to her stomach with his aching need. "It's all going too fast, and with everything else happening it doesn't make sense."

"Love seldom does from what I've read." Jim's dimpled grin brought lightness to the situation.

"I want to believe," she whispered, "but it might not be enough to merely want it."

"You have to fight for it—cling to it rather than walk away."

Her hands trailed around Jim's back. "I'm clinging to the belief that you're the sweetest and best-looking man I've ever laid eyes on, Jim Abbott."

He held Francesca's gaze. "If I'm going to have any chance of catching anything, I better go. I'll be back this afternoon."

Jim turned for the front door.

"I'm sorry for pushing you to the edge."

Grinning, he quickly kissed her cheek. "I'd happily travel to the edge with you every time we meet for the chance to feel you in my arms."

Before he left, Francesca asked one more question. "What's your favorite color?"

"Whatever you're wearing."

***

After pausing to observe the display of shimmering evening gowns in the window, Francesca walked into Mademoiselle Bisset's shop.

"Miss Wilton!" Mademoiselle Bisset approached in her signature black dress that was updated with modern lines. "It's a pleasure to see you, my dear. When Judge Spunner telephoned yesterday, I was thrilled to hear you would be coming, though I am sorry about the loss of your mother. She was always so proud of you."

They kissed cheeks.

"Thank you, mademoiselle. She's resting with Father now."

"And you, Miss Wilton, are ready to step out at last."

She opened her mouth to protest, but was shushed.

"It is not a crime, my dear. You have lived your life these years as if you mourned her loss before it happened. Do not feel guilty for wanting to live now that she has moved on."

Francesca swallowed the lump in her throat.

"I have the corner dressing room stocked for you as Judge Spunner swore your measurements have not changed an inch. I trust that man's eye for both beauty and character. But there's room for more. Is there a special someone you wish to impress?"

Francesca's face heated.

"What is his preferred palette, my dear?"

"I asked him, but he said it's whatever I'm wearing."

Mademoiselle Bisset laughed, her brunette bob swishing with the movement. "Keep that one close, Miss

Wilton. I shall use tones that complement him, and you of course. What is his coloring?"

"Brown hair, green eyes, and a healthy color as he works most often outdoors."

She paused before the curtained dressing room. "And what does the lucky man do?"

"He's a policeman."

"Is there anything as handsome as a man in uniform?"

"He does look splendid in blue." Francesca inspected the array of dresses hanging in the space, excitement over the chance for a new wardrobe bubbling to the surface. "Could I also have foundation pieces to look at? I'm tired of the mail order things I've been purchasing."

"But of course, my dear. It is an honor to assist you, once again."

Francesca couldn't help but imagine Jim caressing the silk and lace as she ran her fingers over the beautiful undersets.

"Well, Miss Wilton?" Mademoiselle Bisset said.

She traced the lace on the pale pink chemise and smiled. "If it wasn't too indulgent, I'd buy them all."

"My dear, I only showed you the seven that would work the best. That's one for each day of the week. I fear you've been too hard on yourself these years, denying yourself all luxuries. If you wish to skimp, pass on shapewear as your figure doesn't merit it. You would not be spoiled if you walk out of here with a receipt for everything you truly want."

"And then you could lock up for the day."

They laughed, and Francesca looked over the pieces once more. Thinking of her old party clothes and the fact that it had been years since she had a new set of French lingerie, she grinned.

"I *will* take them all."

"Would you be interested in also seeing a silk trouser lounge set?"

"Yes," Francesca said, remembering Jim's fantasy of seeing her in clothing like Josephine's. "And day trousers, if you have some. Then I'll try these lovely dresses."

She enjoyed every moment of trying on the clothes, from the feel of the fabrics to her reflection in the mirror. When Francesca left, it was with the promise her new wardrobe would be delivered by two o'clock.

Hammel's Department Store was her next stop. Francesca asked to speak with Mathias in the accounting department and waited near the perfume counter for him to emerge from the elevator.

"Hell must have frozen over," Mathias Wolf said with his sardonic tone, "for Francesca Wilton is out of her house."

"Hello, Mat." She kissed his cheek and returned his squeezing hand clasp.

He took her by the elbow and promenaded her around the wide aisle. "Del told me you're attending our salon tomorrow night with a handsome *younger* man."

"Yes, but I'm here today to discuss something Judge Spunner told me."

Mathias raised his peaked brow. "And what has that handsome *older* man said?"

"Judge Spunner said you would give me a line of credit so I might purchase a suit for Ernest Hart to wear to his parents' funeral."

"Fran, please know that you don't have to toss around Judge Spunner's name to get a line of credit from me. Don't tell Cordelia, but you were always my favorite out of Jo's friends, though I do remember you telling me once that your father advised against debt."

"The paperwork on my mother's bank account will be finalized tomorrow afternoon, and then I'll pay it in full next week."

Mathias laughed. "I trust you, Fran. When will you be shopping?"

"After he gets out of school today."

"I leave at three, but I'll draw up the papers and have them waiting for you in the children's department."

"Thank you, Mat."

"And I'll see you and your young man tomorrow night."

Francesca walked to a delicatessen to purchase a sandwich and bottled soft drink. She took them to a bench across from the water fountain in Bienville Square. Awed at being in the heart of the city, Francesca settled in the shade of the oaks.

A woman hurried around the fountain. "Francesca Wilton, as I live and breathe! I would never have dreamt of running across you here."

"Hello, Sadie." She greeted her childhood friend who was now living across town. "It's good to see you."

Sadie adjusted her ostentatious red hat and sat beside Francesca. "I'm sorry I couldn't make it to the funeral yesterday, but my nanny had a day off she requested ages ago. Mother and Marie told me the service was lovely."

"It was."

"And that horror that happened in Cordelia's old house last week! Bless your heart. You've had too much to bear, though you look to be managing it all splendidly."

"Thank you, Sadie. I'm at peace."

"Does that have anything to do with the policeman that's assigned to the Hart boy?"

Francesca tried to keep a straight face, but that answered the question.

"Cordelia was right! She always is, but at least she isn't smug about it like Jo. My little sister always spoke highly of Officer Abbott. I thought Marie fancied him, but she appears too busy seeking a high society man these days. Richie and I were invited to Cordelia's salon tomorrow to see if you still have what it takes to rule a party. Don't disappoint me, Fran."

Francesca gave a smile filled with all the self-assuredness she ever possessed. "I just came from Mademoiselle Bisset's and have a beautiful dress for the occasion."

"Then it'll be just like old times." Sadie laughed. "Welcome back to the social scene, Fran. We've missed you."

Fifteen

Jim knew he smelled foul, but he wanted to get the fish to Francesca before Ernest was out of school. After dropping his supplies in the yard, he went to the back door.

"It's me!" Jim hollered into the house from the stoop. "Where do you want the fish?"

"I left a bowl on the porch!"

After loading the fish into the large ceramic bowl and setting his creel outside, Jim washed at the sink. He found Francesca in the parlor, flat on her back on the rug with Rochester sitting on her stomach.

"Do you need rescuing?" he questioned.

She smiled up. "No, my gallant knight, but you appear to need showering."

Jim laughed and Sunny ran out from under the sofa to pounce on his left boot. "I wanted to get the fish here in time, but I'm going home to shower. I'll return soon."

"Could I change my mind about this evening?" She held Rochester to her chest and sat up. "Apparently my friends have an interest in my appearance at Del's party.

There will be a lot of eyes on us, and I want to make sure my dancing is great.”

“I’d love to dance more with you, Fran.” He helped her stand while Sunny scrambled around his feet. “Tell me what time and I’ll be here.”

“Before supper, maybe after as well. I’d like you to eat with me.” Her eyes stayed focused on his face. “I also want to see about taking Ernest to Hammel’s for a suit this afternoon.”

“I’d be happy to accompany you downtown, if it’s all right with Miss Hart.”

“I don’t look forward to speaking with her about that.”

“I’ll return next hour and seek permission in your behalf.”

“I’ll show my appreciation once you’re cleaned up,” she said with a smile.

Francesca’s words fueled Jim’s hasty walk home. The hot shower was what he needed, the afternoon shave a bonus. Dressed in a brown suit and derby, Jim made it back to George Street as Ernest came up the block with the Reardon brothers.

“Did you catch any fish, Officer Abbott?” Ernest asked.

“I did, but let’s check in with your aunt to see about you going to eat with Miss Fran.”

Ernest slung open the front door.

“Miss Hart?” Jim called as he removed his hat.

She meandered out of the bedroom. “I’m up, but this is an earlier check-in than typical.”

"It's regarding Ernest. Miss Wilton has offered to take him shopping for a suit to wear to the funeral. Would you allow it?"

She shrugged. "I suppose."

"Thank you for the permission. Ernest will return in time for supper."

Ernest took Jim's hand. "I washed up, Officer Abbott."

"Then we can go to Miss Fran's now."

Francesca set a platter on the kitchen table. The fish was fried to perfection in bite-sized pieces. Claiming to have already eaten, she took the time to change her clothes while Jim and Ernest ate.

When she returned to the kitchen, Ernest was too busy playing with Sunny to notice. Jim's gaze perused upwards from her ankles to the pleated pencil skirt of her navy dress. The red and gold embroidered detailing trailed the side pockets, hem of her three-quarter length sleeves, and the yoke of her dress, adding a touch of brightness to the ensemble. Paired with the long, tasseled belt, it highlighted her figure with classy distinction. Mouth suddenly dry, Jim licked his lips and met her brown eyes.

"I either look wonderful or something is seriously wrong," she said.

He stood from the table. "You're a vision, Fran." After a glance at Ernest proved his back was to them, Jim kissed her. "I'm glad you changed your mind about tonight."

When the streetcar stopped for them on Government, Jim put in the tokens for himself and Francesca and gave Ernest one to place in the box. The boy eagerly sat on the bench beside Francesca, and Jim watched over them with a growing warmth in his soul.

In the shopping district, the policeman on the corner near the department store stared as Jim escorted Francesca and Ernest towards Hammel's. Jim tipped his hat to the fellow officer and kept close to his companions.

To Ernest's pleasure, they took the elevator to the children's department. As he hurried between the displays of Sunday finery, Francesca spoke to the saleswoman.

"Come over here, Ernest," Francesca said a minute later. "The clerk needs to measure you."

The worker's lean face was stiff even with a smile. Ernest hid behind Jim.

"Come on, Ernest. It will only take a minute," Francesca coaxed.

The boy clung to Jim's suit jacket, refusing to go closer.

Jim caught Francesca's eye and mouthed the words "give us a minute."

He turned to Ernest and offered his hand. "I saw a suit over here that looks terrific. Have you ever had a suit before?"

"No," Ernest whispered as they held hands.

"It's a real treat, Ernest. A rite of passage. Every young man needs a suit, and Miss Fran is kind enough to see that you have that." They stopped before a gray knicker set with a belted jacket. "See those pockets? I bet there are one or two on the inside as well. Just think of all the stuff you could fit in them."

"Marbles? Rocks?"

"Toads, paper boats." Jim grinned. "To get a suit, you need to be measured first. The tape measure goes around your chest and down your legs and arms."

"I don't want that lady touching me."

"It doesn't hurt," Jim reassured him.

"I don't want her too close." Ernest gripped Jim's hand tighter. "She looks like my father."

"What if me or Miss Fran takes the measurements?"

"Could you, Officer Abbot?"

"Do you think they'd let me use their measuring tape?" Jim whispered. "I've never done it before."

"I'll let them know you're a policeman, then they'd know you're capable, and I'll be safe."

"That's a good plan."

When they returned to George Street an hour later, Jim walked Ernest to his front door and handed Narcissa the garment bag with the new suit. "Mission accomplished, Miss Hart."

"Thank you, Officer Abbott. I've got a pot of grits and fried ham on the stove for supper, Ernie." Her gaze moved to where Francesca stood near the street. "And thank you, Miss Wilton."

Francesca waved in reply.

Ernest tucked his shoebox under one arm and hugged Jim. "I'll see you tomorrow, Officer Abbott."

The aroma of roast filled the air when Jim and Francesca went inside her house.

"Allow me to check with Becca about supper," Francesca said as Jim hung his hat on the coat tree in the front hall.

By the time Francesca came to the parlor, his jacket was off, the rug was rolled back, and a dance tune played.

"Supper will be an hour."

"Then dance with me, my glorious Francesca."

She accepted his offered hand and fell immediately into position for the foxtrot. Three tunes later, Jim encouraged her to tango. The beat was different, but the steps were similar, though more connection was allowed. Francesca fell in line beautifully. He couldn't help brushing his leg along her thighs to enjoy her pretty blush.

After their leisurely meal, Jim promised to behave so they could practice a few more times before he went home.

***

Friday morning, Jim drove his neighbor's automobile over to George Street so he could collect the funeral attendees. Magnolia Cemetery was only a handful of streets south, but it would be quicker to get there and back in Leo's automobile. Jim was eager to complete the task. Eight days of uncertainty was more than enough for a child to have to bear the memory of the unnatural deaths of his parents before reliving it graveside.

Ernest—in his new gray suit the same color as Jim's—and Francesca in a modest black dress sat on the front steps of the Hart house. When Jim walked up the path, she stood.

"Narcissa is still dressing. Since you're here, I'll go home and wait for my escort."

"I assumed you'd ride with us," Jim said.

"Judge Spunner insists on accompanying me. I'll see you both there."

When Narcissa excited the door in a black dress and veiled hat, he took Ernest's hand.

"Sit by me for the ride, Ernest. Leo and I washed the automobile and wiped it down early this morning so it won't get your suit dirty."

Narcissa opted to sit in the back by herself.

"Are you settled in the house all right, Miss Hart?" Jim asked as he drove.

"Watching Ernest is more difficult than I expected. I figured once a kid was out of diapers, he'd be on his own. It seems like that's how it was for me and Willy, but Ernie needs more than I can give—especially with his nightmares."

"Adjusting to people takes time," Jim said, flashing a grin at Ernest in hopes of softening his aunt's words.

Ernest frowned but shifted closer to Jim.

The Harts' plot had been secured in a barren side lot. Judge Spunner's car pulled in a few minutes later, followed by the chief of police's automobile.

"Chief O'Shaughnessy," Sean said with a smile while offering a hand to the robust man. "It's good of you to come."

"I'm glad you asked me, judge. It's probably for the best that I see all the players that have been the talk of the station," the chief said with his booming voice. "Detective Callaghan is ready to wash his hands of this case."

Sean laughed. "I keep proclaiming my trust in Officer Abbott's abilities."

"You've been right about him so far," the chief said. "Thanks to you, I've got something lined up for him once this kid-watching gig is done."

"Allow me to introduce you to Francesca Wilton," the judge said.

Jim could tell from her stiff posture that Francesca didn't like that Ernest's predicament was gossip at the police station, but it couldn't be helped after what his father had done.

The chief shook her hand. "Officer Abbott praises your skills with the boy."

"Miss Wilton has a heart of gold," Sean assured him.

"You got yourself a favorite here, huh?" Chief O'Shaughnessy grinned down at Ernest.

"Officer Abbott is the greatest policeman ever!" Ernest said with conviction.

The chief laughed. "That's what the judge keeps telling me by using the term 'promotion.'" Chief O'Shaughnessy glanced at Jim, who held a small bunch of chrysanthemums, and then nodded back at Ernest. "I'm sure he'll go far, boy."

The chief looked beyond Ernest to Narcissa. "And you're Miss Hart?"

"Yes, sir."

"Are you finding Mobile satisfactory?"

"I haven't been out on the town this visit, though I previously enjoyed living here."

The minister stepped forward from his space across the open graves already housing the pine coffins. When he started his brief sermon, Ernest angled back, reaching his hand that didn't hold Jim's for Francesca, who stood behind them. He didn't let go until Jim passed the flowers to him so he could drop them onto his mother's casket.

When they shifted away to allow the cemetery workers to fill in the graves, Jim and Francesca made eye contact over Ernest's fair head. She gave a reserved smile. Feeling his hand vibrating, Jim looked down at Ernest. Tears cascaded his cheeks as he stared at the graves.

"Hey, Ernest." Jim squatted before him. "You don't have to watch this. Do you want to move away?"

He nodded and all three of them walked toward the dirt lane.

"Don't forget to breathe, like Miss Deborah taught you. Would you like to see her again?" Jim asked as he freed his hand to pull a handkerchief from his pocket.

Ernest nodded and wiped his nose with the offered handkerchief.

Chief O' Shaughnessy followed them to the road. "Keep up the good work, Officer Abbott. I'll see you soon."

Sixteen

After the chief of police left, Francesca looked at Ernest. "I'll see you at home in a little while."

Ernest kissed her hand, and Jim offered a dimpled grin.

Francesca waited for Sean, who was paying the minister. "I'd like to walk to my parents' plot. Would you pick me up there in a few minutes?"

"Of course, darling. I'll talk with Jim and Ernest before heading over."

Pleased he didn't offer to escort her or make a fuss over the exit, she quietly walked down the dusty road. She felt the stares burning into her back more so than the October sun on the shoulders of her dark dress, but she didn't turn around.

The concrete bench beside her father's headstone was where Francesca stopped. She stared at the sparse grass and the drying floral arrangements marking her mother's plot.

"Josephine always spoke to her mother after she passed, so I'm going to try it. If you're watching me, you might be shocked at my behavior." Francesca clasped her hands as though in prayer and dropped her voice. "I used to think I loved Tristan, but it's nothing to what I feel for Jim, though it's only been a handful of days. He speaks to my soul, Mother. I can't ignore it forever. I hope you understand it's not a show of ingratitude to you on the timing."

Sean pulled to a stop in the lane. "I don't think you should be in the sun much longer, darling." He came to her side and helped Francesca into his Cadillac. "How is the aunt doing with Ernest?"

"I could laugh, but there's nothing funny about her offering him grits at every meal."

"It's as bad as that?"

"She can barely care for herself, Sean."

"At least he's not suffering with you nearby." Sean patted her hand.

After supper, seeing the emerald party dress in the reflection of her mirror caused a flutter of excitement to rise in Francesca after the solemness of the morning. The cap sleeves showcased her lithe arms, and the shin-length hemline with a short slit exposed more of her legs than she had since she came of age. Her hair was pinned into a loose chignon, but she fantasized about the freedom of chopping the weight so her hair would swing above her shoulders. The thought was delicious, even if the nagging voice of her mother told her for the hundredth time "women should wear their hair long."

Francesca spritzed a dash of perfume on her wrist and rubbed it against the other one. She debated allowing Jim entrance when he arrived, but decided not to. With the physical nature of their budding relationship, Francesca knew she would be rumpled before they left and she wanted to arrive at the party looking fresh. But afterwards….

When the knock sounded on the door at eight, she hurried the kittens into the bathtub before answering. Jim's appreciative stare coupled with his sleek hair and well-fitted pinstriped suit set her heart racing.

"Francesca, you're even more beautiful than usual." He took a hand and kissed the back of it before leaning in to quickly kiss her lips. "It's an honor to escort you to Del's party."

"I don't want to be burdened by a handbag. Would you keep my key for me?"

"Of course." He accepted it and locked the door. "We're in Leo's old Ford tonight, but I figured it was better than worrying about switching streetcars."

He opened the passenger door, and she settled on the bench seat while he cranked the automobile.

At Cordelia's house on North Monterrey, Jim rang the bell. "I want you to enjoy yourself, Francesca. Do whatever will bring you joy."

Startled at his words, she was gazing at Jim rather than the door when it opened.

Mathias Wolf let out a low whistle. "You're ravishing, Fran."

She looked over the dark good looks of the tuxedoed host and smiled. "Thank you, Mat."

He leaned in to kiss her cheek, then studied Jim with an appreciative eye. "And who's the fresh blood you're with?"

"Mat, this is Jim Abbott. Jim, Mathias Wolf, our host—Del's husband and Jo's brother."

"Thank you for having us," Jim said as he offered his hand.

"The guest list is Del's doing, but I appreciate her extending the invitation to you both." Mathias winked, but Francesca knew it was at Jim rather than her. "Come in and get yourself something to drink before the band starts."

They entered beneath the fourteen-foot ceilings.

"Fran and Jim—my favorite officer." Cordelia's red and black silk gown shimmered under the chandeliers. She held her cigarette to the side and kissed both on the cheek. "I'm sure Mat was impressed with y'all. There's champagne and reds, if you still prefer those, Fran."

"Yes, though I haven't had much of an opportunity to indulge."

"Be liberal with her refills, Jim. She has a lot of missed time to make up for. And if you want something harder, we have that too. Take the time to experience Shelly's art in the parlor. I rotate through my artist friends and she's the featured guest tonight. I expect to see you on the dance floor after that," Cordelia said before her attention was pulled away.

Francesca clung to Jim's arm as they moved through the rich furnishings and flamboyant guests on the way to the art display. Shelly worked in oils and her preferred subject was nudes. The artist herself stood before a self-portrait in a thin evening gown that didn't look to have any undergarments beneath the thin lining, though Francesca refused to stare.

"Cordelia is something else, isn't she?" Jim asked. "I prefer her sketches to this bold display, but I think it's great she shares her love of art by featuring her friends."

"Del has always been eccentric, but she's gotten more outlandish since she married. Her and Mat are an odd couple. Be careful around him."

"All right," Jim said with a quizzical grin. "What can I get you to drink?"

"Always a glass of red, please."

The Harringtons were filling their own glasses when they reached the refreshments. Josephine was in a gorgeous navy pantsuit with a pink blouse and sash. Cyrus's azure eyes and square jawline were always mesmerizing to Francesca. His tailored suit, navy to match his wife, had a pink bowtie that made his complexion glow.

"I'm glad you made it, Fran," Josephine said with a smile and a challenging look at Jim. "Officer Abbott, allow me to introduce my husband, Cyrus Harrington."

They shook hands and exchanged a few words before the Harringtons moved along.

Jim poured Francesca a generous amount and handed her the crystal goblet. They each took a sip and migrated to the side of the room, watching the other guests. Francesca steeled herself when Sadie approached.

"I'd accuse you of being a cradle snatcher, Fran, but you're youthful enough to get away with it." She offered her hand to Jim. "I'm Sadie Beauchamp, one of the old Washington Square regulars. You know my younger sister, Marie Marley. I think we've crossed paths at one of her piano recitals."

Jim swallowed hard and shook her hand. "Yes, and it's nice to see you, Mrs. Beauchamp."

"Treat Francesca right or there will be a line of women ready to beat you with their handbags."

Jim gave a forced laugh. "I'll be on my best behavior."

"I'm sorry about that," Francesca said when Sadie retreated. "She's always been dramatic."

From the hall, the strains of a foxtrot started. Jim downed the remaining contents of his glass, and Francesca did the same. After discarding them on a collection tray, he led her into the next room.

No one was dancing yet, but that didn't stop Jim from positioning them in the middle of the floor. They began their choreographed display amid the disinterested crowd. By the time the first verse was over, they'd captured the attention of everyone nearby. Jim's movements were crisp, his manner almost cocky. Francesca expected him to be grinning, but what she saw of his face out of the corner of her eye was the satisfied façade of a man who knew he was desired.

When he ended with a flourishing dip, they were surrounded by applause.

The band paused a few beats, then started on a tune fit for a tango. Several other couples came out to dance. Jim tugged Francesca closer with a wicked glint in his green eyes. His knee brushed the inside of her thigh as he took position, but his gaze fell back to its center focus over her shoulder.

"You don't play fair," she whispered.

"Tease me back, Francesca. I can take it."

They danced into the night, stopping every few songs for a new glass of wine. Jim dripped sensuality as they kissed, touched, and writhed together. Feeling like the past decade was a bad dream, Francesca was alert to each shift of their bodies as they connected to the music and each other.

Close to midnight, Francesca caught Jim's gaze. "Would you take me home?"

"Certainly, Fran." He slung an arm around her hip for their walk through the house.

Josephine stopped them to tell Francesca goodbye and whispered something to Jim that made him blush.

Cordelia was lounging with the guest artist. Mathias, perched on the arm of the sofa next to her, watched their approach with his dark eyes as he smoked a cigarette.

"Thank you for the invitation, Del," Francesca said. "I thoroughly enjoyed the evening."

"Do you mean to deprive us of the best dancing that's ever been done within these walls?"

"Jim has the morning shift."

"Pity." Cordelia said with a pout.

Mathias put a hand on her knee. "Maybe they'll return another time."

Cordelia nodded and waved Francesca away. "Go on, you two. I'll be in touch."

The cool night air made Francesca realize how warm she'd gotten dancing. And how much she'd drunk. She leaned on Jim all the way to the car. At the automobile, she slid to the center of the seat so she could sit beside him on the drive home.

After opening her car door at her house, Jim offered the key.

"No, please see to it. And free the kittens. I need to get headache powder."

"I guess I refilled the glasses a few too many times." He held her arm up the path.

"I'm out of practice."

As soon as they were inside, he clicked a lamp on.

"Don't turn on too many."

He hung up his suit jacket and went towards the bathroom. Hearing their approach, Sunny started meowing. Jim gathered the cats, and their purrs overtook any distress.

Packet of medicine in hand, Francesca followed Jim to the kitchen. She mixed the powder into a glass of cool water, drank it fast, and sat at the table to slip off her shoes.

Sunny and Rochester circled Jim's feet, rubbing their heads against his ankles.

"I imagine I looked a bit like that at the party, rubbing against you while we danced." She met him in the middle of the kitchen.

Jim took hold of her hips and pressed their bodies together with a playful rhythm. Francesca captured his mouth, a slow kiss building into a ravenous exploration.

Jim flinched back. "Damn, Sunny!"

Francesca removed Sunny from Jim's suit leg. "Let's go to the parlor. They need to play for a while before I'll be able to get to sleep."

She lay on the rug on her stomach next to Jim's cross-legged figure. His hand immediately went to Francesca's back in a gentle massage, but Sunny thought it was a game and attacked his moving flesh.

"He's something else, isn't he?" Jim remarked.

"He's bright and playful rather than studious like Rochester."

"And which type do you prefer?" Jim questioned.

She slowly turned onto her back, displacing Sunny, and smiled at Jim. "Someone who knows how to have a good time but can discuss Hawthorne and the Brontës."

"Yeah?" He raised his eyebrows.

"And the type of man who knows how to kiss and touch and dance because making love involves everything physical as well as emotional and intellectual."

"That's asking a lot." He leaned closer, holding eye contact as his hand trailed the emerald fabric over her hip.

"But not impossible. There's a man named Jim Abbott who appears to check all those boxes."

"He's a fortunate guy." His touch roamed down the outside of her thigh to her knee and he dipped his face to leave a gentle kiss on her lips.

Francesca wrapped her arms around his shoulders. She managed to undo his bowtie and the top few buttons of his shirt so she could nibble his neck. Jim gently pulled up her dress. His hand caressed her stockinged knee, then trailed higher to tease the bare skin of her thigh. First one leg, then the other. She shifted, restless with want, need.

"Jim," she whispered.

"Yes, Francesca." He grinned while fingering the edge of her stockings.

"I feel so good when I'm with you."

"And you feel incredible to me." He sweetly kissed her brow.

"What did Jo whisper to you?"

He nosed her ear, kissing her neck while his hand grew heavy on her skin. "That I need to pleasure you until you cry out the last of your restraints."

Love and lust collided within her, and she widened her legs. "Touch me, Jim."

He didn't hesitate, but his motions were controlled. He bit his lower lip when his fingers brushed over the lace edge of her undies.

Sunny pounced, making her yelp.

"Damn. Are you okay, Francesca?"

"That's not the cry of passion we were expecting," she said with a laugh.

Then a scream pierced the night.

Jim was up in a flash.

"That was Ernest," she managed to say before he rushed from the house without his shoes.

Francesca went to the front porch, praying for Ernest's safety.

Seventeen

Jim pounded on the front door of the Harts' house so hard it popped open. Ernest's screams continued as he rushed for the bedroom. The single bare overhead bulb was on, casting a harsh glare in the space. Narcissa in her nightgown stood in the middle of the room, staring at Ernest on his quaking bed.

Jim shouldered past her and scooped the boy into his arms, which caused the bed to stop moving. "Ernest, it's me. I'm here. You're okay."

His breath hitched with sobs, and he squirmed.

"It's me, Jim Abbott. You know me, Ernest." Jim rubbed his back. "Don't forget to breathe."

The boy took a few halting breaths and turned his face to Jim.

"Officer Abbott!" His arms were around his neck, squeezing.

Narcissa stepped closer. "Offi—"

"Not now," he snapped.

She slumped into the chair.

Once Ernest was calm, Jim dug for the truth. "What happened to frighten you?"

He shifted so his head was near Jim's ear. "My father came."

The whispered words chilled him.

"I didn't want him to touch me." Ernest paused, dropping his voice even lower. "Then Aunt Narcissa screamed too, and he came closer."

"Did you see him?" Jim asked even though he didn't want to know.

"I could feel him. Watching."

"You're all right now, Ernest."

"Can I go home with you?"

"I'm afraid not."

"What about to Miss Fran's so I can see Sunny?" His blue eyes were large and rimmed with tears.

"No, but I have an idea. Wait here so I can speak with your aunt."

Ernest tensed. Jim didn't have a hat to bestow, so he unbuckled his wristwatch.

"Take this for me. I'll come back for it." Jim folded Ernest's hand around the leather band before moving him to the bed.

Jim crossed the room, snatching Narcissa's arm on his way to the hall. "Ernest's welfare includes his peace of mind, Miss Hart. Why didn't you try to help him?"

Narcissa's eyes as wide as Ernest's. "Because I was scared. I felt Willy too, and then Ernest's bed was shaking. My knees were knocking so bad I couldn't move."

Surprised, Jim paused and thought how best to help them all. "I think Ernest should keep his kitten at night. It will be no strain on you with feeding and cleaning, and if Sunny stays in his bedroom, you shouldn't be bothered with allergies. He can collect Sunny before he goes to bed and bring the kitten straight to Fran when he wakes in the morning. Will you agree to that?"

"If it will help Ernest."

Jim nodded and left, a wave of nausea sweeping over him as he passed the kitchen doorway. Half blind with emotions, he barely made it to Francesca's front steps.

"Bring me Sunny," he said, releasing too late that he shouldn't have commanded her.

When she came back with the kitten, Jim touched her shoulder. "Forgive my harshness, Francesca. I'll be back soon."

"Tell Ernest I love him."

When Jim returned to the Harts' house, Narcissa was still in the hall, looking dazed, but Ernest perked up.

"Sunny!"

Smiling, Jim handed the cat to him in exchange for his watch. "Sunny has permission to sleep over every night. You can collect him when you're ready for bed and return him to Miss Fran when you wake. She sends her love."

Ernest nuzzled the purring kitten. "Thank you, Officer Abbot. I'll be safe with Sunny."

Jim buckled on his watch. "I'll see you in the morning, Ernest."

On Jim's way out, he whispered, "Is there anything I can do for you, Miss Hart?"

"No, but thanks for helping Ernest."

Jim returned to Francesca next door.

"Is he all right?" Francesca asked as Jim followed her inside.

"He claims his father was coming for him. He's been having more nightmares since he left here. I'll speak with Deborah Farley in the morning. I need to return Leo's car, but I'll be back soon."

After slipping on his jacket and shoes, Jim kissed her once more.

At the apartment house, he left Leo's key inside the door to the front stairwell before going to his room. He quickly dressed in uniform so he wouldn't need to return before reporting to the station.

Jim walked back to George Street, pausing under the oak between the Wilton and Hart houses. The only sounds were crickets, an owl hooting, and the occasional croak of a late-season frog. He sat on the edge of Francesca's porch, stretching his legs down the steps.

The screen door opened behind him and a cup of steaming coffee was handed over his shoulder.

"Bless you, Francesca."

She lowered to the top step beside him, putting herself snug between him and the slatted banister. Rochester settled on her lap. It felt cozy and private under the blanket of stars.

"I've kept the doors open but haven't heard anything," her voice was like velvet in the night—soft and luxurious.

"How's this little one?" Jim took a sip of coffee and rubbed Rochester's chin.

"Lonely, but I think having some time away from Sunny will be beneficial for him."

"The coffee tastes great. Thank you."

"I figured you wouldn't want to sleep."

She had braided her hair so it hung in a thick plait down her back. Jim stroked it all the way to the tip. Francesca leaned into him, resting her right arm on his thigh so her hand cupped his knee.

"You don't need to sit out here with me, Fran. There's no reason both of us need to be sleep deprived."

She tilted her head up and kissed his jaw. "I'd like to keep you company for a while and cook breakfast for you in the morning."

"And sleep sometime in between."

Francesca nodded and stroked Rochester. Jim watched her while he drank, enjoying her companionship. He set the remaining coffee behind him and the next moment his arms were around her as he nosed her ear.

"It feels completely natural to be with you like this, Francesca. I hope you realize how special you are to me."

Her brown eyes looked black in the pale moonlight when she nodded. "There's a pot of coffee on the stove if you need more before dawn. Wake me at six if you don't see me by then."

She lightly kissed him, then cradled Rochester to her chest and stood.

Jim leaned against the banister, sipping the rest of his coffee. A mixture of pleasure and worry stirred his soul. Concern for Ernest and the unsettledness of his house churned with his love for Francesca and the elation over their growing connection. Protection and passion—an emotional storm that helped him stay alert.

Around three o'clock, Jim slipped inside to heat more coffee. Francesca's room was open and he couldn't resist looking in. She was on her back, and the lacy neckline on her pale nightgown slowly rose and fell. Rochester, curled on the pillow, slept beside her braid. It was an angelic scene he hoped to join one day. The thought carried him through the next few hours.

As the sky lightened, the sound of the Harts' door opening caught Jim's attention. Ernest, in his faded pajamas that were a few inches too short, tiptoed down his front steps carrying Sunny.

"Morning, Officer Abbott. You're on duty early."

"I sure am. Did Sunny do all right with you?" Ernest nodded and Jim stood. "It's about time to wake up Miss Fran. Want to help?"

Ernest smiled in an impish way. "Could we put Sunny on her bed?"

"That would probably do the trick."

Ernest followed Jim inside. Francesca was still in repose, Rochester on her shoulder. Jim motioned Ernest to enter. He gently set Sunny at the foot of the bed. The kitten immediately meowed, waking Rochester, who stood on his spindly legs and stretched before padding toward the end of the bed.

"Where are you going, Rochester?" Francesca kept her eyes closed but reached for him.

Her movement caused Sunny to pounce. She jerked when the paws captured her hand, sitting upright in a flash.

"Sun—Ernest!" Her surprise switched to joy. "Good morning."

He went to her side for a hug. "Sunny helped keep me safe," he declared.

"I'm glad to hear that. Would you watch Rochester while I dress and cook breakfast?"

"Yes!" He took a kitten in each arm. "I'll bring them to the back yard."

Francesca watched him leave, then focused on Jim leaning nonchalantly in the doorway. The blue and white gown barely covered her knees when she stood. Jim's eyes traveled up those shapely limbs to the thin cotton as she crossed the room. She was soon in his embrace, and he kissed her neck.

"Thank you for waking me."

"A chance to see you like this is much more to my benefit than yours. I only wish your hair was loose so I could see all its splendor." When he released her, he stared a moment longer to burn her image in his mind before going for the back door.

When Jim and Ernest came in from the yard, Francesca was at the stove.

"Jim, would you slip next door and invite Miss Hart to join us for breakfast?"

"Of course."

"I can stay here?" Ernest asked with an eager tone.

"For now," Francesca said with a smile.

"I'll be back in a minute." Jim ruffled Ernest's hair and grinned at Francesca. Her cheeks went rosy before she turned back to her preparations. She still went shy occasionally, but bold or blushing, Francesca Wilton stirred him body, heart, and soul.

A damp chill that went beyond temperature permeated the Harts' house when he reached the front door. The evil was seeping back, but hopefully Deborah would be able to help.

"Miss Hart?" he called through the screen.

Narcissa came down the hall, still wearing her nightgown. "What are you doing in here so early, Officer Abbott?"

"After Ernest's fright, I sat outside in case he became upset again. Francesca is making breakfast for all of us—including you."

"I appreciate it. I'll get dressed and come over."

Jim returned to the kitchen next door. "She'll be here in a bit. Do you think it's too early to telephone Deborah Farley?"

"Yes. It's Saturday for one thing, but with four children, you never know who might be sleeping. It would be less of a disturbance to go over in person. If you go to the back door, you'd probably catch her in the kitchen, so you won't even have to knock."

Jim nodded and poured himself a fresh cup of coffee. "I'll do that. Thanks."

Narcissa arrived in a blue pleated dress that brightened her complexion. Jim found himself watching her while they ate pancakes in the formal dining room. Narcissa had a soft expression that crossed her countenance whenever she looked at her nephew. That near-loving gaze turned sad when Ernest paid all his attention to their hostess.

"Could I stay here and play with the kittens this morning, Aunt Narcissa?" Ernest asked when he had finished eating.

She sighed. "I suppose, but I expect you back by noon, Ernie."

He jumped out of his chair and scooped the kittens off the hardwood floor on his way out.

Smiling, Francesca met Narcissa's gaze. "Thank you, Miss Hart."

She shrugged and stood to leave. "And thank you for breakfast."

"Could you stay a moment?" Francesca asked. "I'd like to ask you more about what happened with Ernest last night—and the other nights he's been upset."

"It's only nightmares and imaginings."

"So you don't feel or see anything when he does?" Jim asked.

Narcissa hesitated. "It's not like I see a real person, but the suggestion of Willy is there."

"An outline? A ghostly shape?" Francesca questioned.

"I might just be catching Ernie's hysteria," Narcissa said uncertainly. "Do you believe this ghost thing?"

"You don't?" Francesca countered. "Haven't you noticed things about Ernest that are out of the ordinary?"

With the tilt of her head, Jim saw a bit of innocence that hid behind Narcissa's tough exterior. Not innocence from life's experiences, but naivety about kindness, charity, and spiritual matters.

"He's on edge a lot of the time and gets physical," she said with a dismissive shrug. "He pounds the furniture and walls."

Jim raised a brow. "But how does he do that without using his fists?"

"I don't know!" Narcissa snapped. "I don't understand any of this."

"None of us do exactly," Francesca said, "but I have friends that can help us. Hopefully one will be able to come over this evening."

"I'm going to take Ernie out to supper. A night on the town might cheer him up. It typically does me. Thank you, again, for breakfast."

When they were alone, Jim hugged Francesca. "You know she's jealous of your relationship. She feels like yesterday's catch when Ernest is paying all his attention to you and the kittens."

"I don't mean to downplay their connection."

"I know you don't, but it's obvious he's closer to you. Narcissa is struggling with that on top of everything else. You even bought his clothes this week, not to mention all the meals he's taken here."

"Those were necessities, Jim."

"I know, but tread carefully with her."

Francesca nodded. "Will you come for supper after your shift?"

"I'd love to. I'll talk to Deborah and invite her to come over tonight."

***

On his return to George Street that evening, Jim met Narcissa and Ernest heading out of the neighborhood. The boy was in his new suit and his aunt in a lacy red dress, her lips painted to match.

"Hello, Ernest."

"Hi, Officer Abbott! We're going downtown for supper."

"I heard. Y'all have fun."

166

At Francesca's house, Jim entered the kitchen door. "It smells wonderful, Becca."

"It'll be a quarter of an hour yet," the cook said from the stove.

"I'll keep Francesca occupied until then."

Becca gave him a knowing look and grinned.

Francesca was in an armchair, Rochester on her lap, while Sunny batted a marble around the parlor floor. Jim went straight to the gramophone and put on a tango. He dropped his suit jacket and fedora on a chair and the gray kitten was placed on the sofa. When Francesca was in his arms, she answered his unasked question with the proper stance. Even barefoot, Francesca went through the steps perfectly.

Once they were in the rhythm, Jim spoke. "Becca says we have fifteen minutes. I thought we could spend at least a few of them this way."

"You're a wonderful dance partner, Jim."

"I hope to be more than that to you, Francesca." He left a kiss below her ear.

They ate and then settled in the parlor. Francesca answered the knock when it came and returned a moment later with Deborah Farley. The petite woman sat beside Jim and took his hands into hers.

"I'm glad to see you, Jim." She closed her eyes, keeping hold of his hands. She smiled slightly as she continued her connection. "I know you're staying grounded and helping those around you."

A moment later, Deborah went to Francesca in the side chair. Holding her hands, she concentrated on Francesca's face as she spoke in her clear, deliberate way.

"Your mother knows you served her valiantly and that you'll do well moving forward, Fran. She's proud of the woman you are and your open heart, and she wanted me to tell you."

Tears silently cascaded Francesca's face as Deborah continued to minister to her.

"Your mother is glad you welcomed Ernest into your life, and she's pleased you've found an honorable man. Don't hide, Fran. Love and lean on those around you. You must know how blessed you are to have Jim with you. He's the most grounding person I've ever met. Don't tell Alvin, but Jim surpasses him with calming effects, and we're practically strangers. I can only imagine what extras he gives you with his presence."

Francesca opened her mouth, but Deborah politely shushed her.

"There's no shame in needing someone. Our souls are made to be knitted together. There's no weakness in craving companionship."

Francesca's slim shoulders shook as she freed her hands to cover her face.

Deborah motioned for Jim to take her place. He immediately lifted Francesca into his arms and carried her to the sofa so he could cradle her in his lap. Her sobbing melted into soft tears that continued while Deborah sat nearby in silence.

When Jim kissed Francesca's temple and pressed a handkerchief into her hand, she wiped her nose.

"I think I needed that cry." Her voice was raw.

"I want nothing more than to help you, Francesca. I don't need to have known you years or even months to realize you're the most important piece of my life. I'll do whatever you'll allow me to as means of helping because I love you."

Her arms went around his middle, and he nearly flew to the sky at her favorable response to his declaration. Jim didn't need to hear her say it—not yet—but he did need the validation that she accepted his words. He hadn't meant to declare his feelings with an audience, but he wasn't embarrassed, and Deborah wasn't the type to spread gossip about what she witnessed during her vocation.

"As lovely as this tender scene is," Deborah said, "I'm needed next door."

"Ernest and his aunt are out for supper right now," Jim said.

"That's even better. I can get a sense of the place while it's quiet. Will you come with me, Jim?"

He nodded and stood.

"I'll wait on the porch for you after I wash my face," Francesca said.

"You're beautiful, Fran, red nose and all." Jim left a kiss on her salty lips.

At the Harts' house, Jim knocked on the door to be sure they hadn't returned. When no one answered, he opened the unlocked door.

"Allow me to enter the rooms first," Deborah said as Jim crossed himself.

Not wanting to disturb Deborah, he watched silently as she passed through the parlor. When she switched on the kitchen light, the sight that had met him after the murder filled his mind. His stomach quivered as the tile floor came into full view for the first time since then. Jim's knees weakened on his way to Deborah, causing him to reach for the nearest counter.

"Jim, you're as white as flour!"

That was the last thing he heard before the deafening echo of artillery struck his unit as they climbed out of the trenches.

Blood and flesh rained down on him. Jim ran, shot, and crouched when he could as he blindly followed the plan. The shouting. The screams.

Moist pieces stuck to his cheek. He had to scrape his best friend's brain matter from his ear and wore the stains on his uniform for days.

"Jim. Jim, come back to me." A gentle hand on his trembling arm.

He was curled in on himself, rocking like a lunatic on the tile floor of the Harts' kitchen.

"Oh, God!" Jim jerked away from Deborah and scrambled on his knees to the hall.

Body giving out, he leaned his head on the wall.

"Show me what plagues him," Deborah whispered as her hand caressed his cheek. Her breath caught. Moments later, her hands were in both of his, head on his shoulder. "If only you could bring comfort to yourself as you do to others. God brought you through that, Jim. You have a purpose. It just might be for the boy who lives here and the woman next door."

His eyes opened in fright and gripped her hands. "Don't tell Francesca how I weakened."

"You aren't weak, Jim. You have shellshock. You need to talk to someone about this. There are too many potential issues in your line of work."

"Don't I know it." He closed his eyes again. "I'll never make detective if I can't tolerate murder scenes."

"That's what did it?"

Jim explained how the sights in the kitchen his first evening brought him to the edge and that the room was now linked with it. Deborah listened, never interrupting with questions as he released the pain. "I feel empty now."

Deborah smiled. "Talking can be therapeutic. I suggest you speak to Jo. She's a bit of a…well, she knows how to harness more of the brain's capabilities than people typically utilize."

"She's a witch," Jim said with a grin. "At least, that's what I've always heard, but people say the same thing about Miss Eilands, and she's harmless."

"I wouldn't go so far as to call Jo Harrington harmless, but she might be able to teach you how to control the memories."

"I appreciate it, Deborah." Jim slowly stood, bringing her to her feet once he was upright. "What needs to be done here?"

"The presence veiled itself again. If it's Mr. Hart, he's the most resourceful new spirit I've come across. That doesn't bode well."

"Can you do anything to protect Ernest?"

"I could seal his bedroom against unseen visitors."

"Can't you do the whole house?"

"It would be too difficult to be sure there's nothing lurking somewhere, but with his room, I could be certain."

Deborah immediately commanded that nothing follow them inside Ernest's bedroom. Jim stood in the middle of the space, watching the deliberate way she scoured the room as though with a third eye. She felt the walls, touched the corners, and even searched the little closet. Her quiet voice once again took on a tone of superiority as she sealed the room with words that sounded like a blessing. Perhaps she was a priestess of sorts with her otherworldly powers.

When they returned next door, Francesca still waited on the porch.

"It's all right, Fran," Deborah said, sweeping her inside. "But I need you to promise you'll speak to Ernest about staying in his room at night. He'll be safest there."

Francesca nodded.

"Telephone or stop in if you need me." Deborah kissed her cheek in parting.

When Francesca returned from seeing Deborah out, she fell into Jim's arms. "I was so scared. You were in there for an hour."

"Was it that long?" He checked his watch over her shoulder, marveling at the length of his stupor. "I'm sorry you were concerned, Francesca."

Her arms stayed around him. "You're pale, not yourself. What happened?"

"It's nothing." He managed to smile.

"Don't lie to me, Jim."

"It's nothing that concerns Ernest."

"But it concerns you, and that concerns me." Her brown eyes swam with unshed tears as she held his gaze. "How can we love each other properly if we can't share everything?"

He knew that even if in telling Francesca she lost respect for him, he needed to know that he did everything honorable on his side. They settled side-by-side on the sofa holding hands.

"I had an episode." Jim paused. When she stayed silent, he proceeded. "It was as bad as the ones I'd had in the weeks immediately following the attack. I felt it coming on when I was at the Harts' that first night. All the blood and Mrs. Hart's clothing was the same shade as our uniforms, but was able to walk away. Tonight it struck suddenly. I must have been out of my senses for half an hour, but Deborah stayed with me."

"The war?" When Jim nodded, she added another question. "Shellshock?"

He nodded again. Her hand squeezed his.

"I wore the remnants of my best friend for days, unable to do anything but drink enough water to keep from dehydration. Once I was hospitalized, I realized I wasn't as bad off as some of the others, but the tremors persisted for weeks. Afterward, they stationed me near a quiet village because I wasn't severe enough to be sent home, but they knew I'd be dangerous in a firefight. That's where I met Anna and her family. They gave me a sense of security I desperately needed. She had recently lost her fiancé at the Somme. You understand, don't you, Francesca?"

"Yes, Jim."

"I love my job, but some days it's perilous to keep the bloody scenes at bay. Deborah suggested I speak with Jo for help."

"She would be a great resource, whether for calming teas or thought control." Francesca held eye contact. "Thank you for telling me. And I'm glad you weren't alone when it happened."

"Deborah was wonderful."

A knock broke their conversation.

Francesca answered it. "Hello Ernest. Miss Hart."

"We had supper at the top of the Cow Horn Hotel, and I drank three colas!" Ernest's pleased voice carried through the house.

"Cawthon Hotel, Ernie, and we're here for the cat," Narcissa said.

"Could I bring Sunny over in a minute? I need to be sure the kittens finished their supper."

"Take him straight to Ernie's room," his aunt said. "You don't need to knock."

Becca was gone, but Sunny and Rochester were happily playing with a ball of newspaper in the kitchen. Their saucers were empty and their bellies bulging.

Jim caught the kittens and handed Sunny to Francesca along with leaving a kiss on her cheek. "I'll be waiting with a dance tune."

Eighteen

A sense of relief washed over Francesca when she entered Ernest's room, reminding her of Deborah's plea.

"Sunny!" Ernest sat up in his bed, reaching for his cat.

"Did you enjoy your supper?"

"It was much better than what Aunt Narcissa cooks, but not as good as you and Miss Becca."

"Miss Deborah stopped by while you were gone. I was hoping you could talk to her, but you stayed out later than I expected."

"Aunt Narcissa let me look out the windows at the city lights. We were higher than the oak trees in Bienville Square!"

"That was nice of her. I bet you enjoyed that." Francesca looked around. "Miss Deborah wants you to stay in your room all night, no matter what. She thinks you'll be safer in here. It feels comfortable, doesn't it?"

"That's because you and Sunny are here."

"Sunny is staying, but I need to go home." She leaned over to hug him.

"Goodnight, Miss Fran. I love you."

"I love you too, Ernest. Remember to stay in your room. Call to your aunt if you need something."

He nodded and snuggled under the blanket with Sunny. Francesca clicked off the overhead light and pulled his door closed on her way out. She stopped in the doorway to the other bedroom.

"I hope you had a nice evening out," Francesca said to Narcissa.

Narcissa nodded, but looked remorseful.

"What's wrong?" Francesca didn't want to enter the bedroom without an invitation, but Narcissa looked like she could use a hug so she inched closer.

"Supper took most of my money, but I wanted to do something nice for Ernie."

"Oh." Francesca paused, searching for the words that would least likely offend her. She placed her hand on her arm. "I'd be happy to order groceries for you for this coming week, and if you need a job, Judge Spunner knows everyone in town. He'd know where to send you for a reputable position. What is it you wish to do?"

"Cleaning hotel rooms is all I know. I hope I can keep my job when I get back to Tallahassee."

"If you get a position in Mobile, couldn't you stay here? I'd be happy to watch Ernest if your hours are outside his school ones."

Narcissa smiled. "Thank you, Miss Wilton."

"Call me Fran." She opened her arms, and Narcissa hugged her as though Francesca was the only security in her life.

"Thank you, Fran." Narcissa said when she stepped away.

"My friend, Deborah, stopped by while you were out. She's put a layer of protection around Ernest's room. It will be the safest place for you both, so if he's scared or you get nervous during the night, stay in there, all right?"

"How did she do that?"

Francesca lifted a shoulder. "I'm not sure exactly, but she's trustworthy. Remember to keep to his room if there's trouble."

Narcissa nodded and they said goodnight.

Francesca walked home and stopped to pet Rochester on the parlor chair he perched on while Jim flipped through the music recordings.

"I'll be a minute," Francesca said.

Jim turned. "Is everything all right?"

She smiled. "Better than ever."

In the bedroom, Francesca removed her clothes and loosened her hair. She brushed her brown locks until they shone, seeing the beauty in the contrast between their luster and her pale skin. After tying on her blue dressing gown, she walked slowly to the parlor.

Jim met her in the middle of the room.

"I'm here to fulfill your unspoken request, James Abbott."

"James?" He took her elbow, fingering the silk.

"It is your true Christian name, isn't it?" Francesca lifted a brow, hoping to keep his attention on her face.

"Yes, but I only use it during oaths."

"Then swear to me you'll remain a gentleman."

Playing along, Jim raised his right hand. "I, James Baxter Abbott, promise to be gentlemanly to Francesca Wilton. Only if she begs me for favors will I—"

"Jim!" A shocked laugh escaped.

His mouth captured hers. When his hands began to roam, Francesca guided one to her sash while they continued to kiss. Jim worked the knot open. The moment his hand touched the bare flesh of her stomach, they both gasped.

"You're my undoing, Francesca." His breathy words feathered hot on her ear.

"You don't have to touch me. I thought you'd be pleased with looking." Francesca straightened in his arms which caused the robe to gape open in the front. "I wanted to show you my hair down wearing nothing else because I'm going to get it bobbed this coming week."

He groaned and rested his head on her shoulder as he hugged her. She put her arms around him in return but held still, unsure how far she was willing to push him when he'd already had a trying night with his flashback. Francesca relaxed in his warm hug, the scent of him, the weight of his head on her shoulder. It was perfect.

"I love you, Jim."

His head rose so he could look at her. His green eyes held her captive until he leaned in for a slow, deep kiss. When the kiss broke with his huge smile, she moved out of his arms so she could remove her covering. The silk slid off her body, causing her skin to prickle and her body to crave Jim's touch.

He closed his eyes. The dark, straight line of his eyebrows showed how much he concentrated. "I don't know if I'm strong enough to resist."

"Then I'll step away, but look upon me all you wish, James Baxter Abbott."

He regarded Francesca with awe as she slowly turned. The tip of her hair skimmed her buttocks with each movement, keeping her alert to her nakedness. Jim grinned and she glowed with the power he bestowed on her with his want. To break the spell, Francesca dipped into a curtsey, picking up the robe from the floor as she straightened.

Jim took the dressing gown and held it open so she could slip her arms inside. He lifted her hair free from the covering, letting it fall around her as he released it. After kissing her collarbone, he tied the sash closed.

The tenderness left his face and his voice turned rough. Pulling her against him, she felt his need. "I used every ounce of my control watching you. As much as I hate to admit it, I'm at my limit, Fran. I have to go home."

"Would you join me for breakfast?"

He gathered his jacket and hat from the chair. "Yes, but I'm sure I'll see you in my dreams before that. I look forward to touching every inch of you, Francesca."

"And I await that experience too."

"Thank you for the vision of my future."

The surge she had felt over Jim's open admiration whooshed from her the instant he walked out the front door. Never had she felt so alone. Empty. After baring her soul and body to Jim she was bereft in grief over his absence, though she loved him even more for leaving.

Rochester's pitiful meow changed her focus. Francesca picked up the kitten and carried Rochester to her bed. The purr wasn't as loud as Sunny's, but it brought a smile to her face and a feeling of companionship to her soul. When Rochester fell asleep, she stayed where she was, allowing the kitten to rest. Her mind replayed the sight of Jim's intimate gaze as he watched her, the feel of his hands on her bare skin, the strength of his arms as he held her.

The parlor clock struck eleven. She had spent a glorious hour fantasizing about Jim and what he would do to her when they finally set their passions free. After moving Rochester to her pillow, she braided her hair, washed, and pulled on a floral nightgown. In bed, the kitten curled on her shoulder, and she drifted to sleep.

***

Francesca jerked awake in the dark.

Only the pale curtains moving in the night breeze stirred in the shadowed room. Rochester was still sharing her pillow. There were no odd sounds, so after a few minutes of watchfulness, Francesca closed her eyes and tried to get back to sleep.

A scream.

Out of bed in a flash, she hurried down the hall. Francesca hastened across the lawn and threw opened the Harts' front door without pause.

The hall light was on and knocking sounds came from the shadows. She ran straight to Ernest's bedroom. The odor of urine filled the space, and Ernest stood in the middle of his room, crying. Only when she stopped before him did she feel the trembling of the house that caused the rocking chair to move.

Francesca crouched and took him by the shoulders. "What's wrong, Ernest?"

"She didn't come!"

"Try to breathe like Miss Deborah taught you."

"I called for help, but she didn't come!" He choked on his tears. "I needed to go to the bathroom and called for Aunt Narcissa because you told me to stay in my room. I called and called, but she never came. I opened the door and saw my father waiting for me."

Francesca hugged him. "It's okay. I'm here now."

"I wet myself and screamed."

His trembling voice brought tears to her own eyes. "It's all right, Ernest."

The walls rattled so much the bedroom door slammed shut, causing Sunny to fly off the bed. The knocking turned to pounding in the distance, then a shout of Ernest's name. Sunny pawed at her bare legs.

"Look, here's Sunny. Hold him a moment while I go check on your aunt."

"No, Miss Fran, don't leave me!"

"Ten seconds, Ernest. That's all. Count aloud, with a breath in between each number." She handed him the cat. "One…"

Across the hall, Francesca opened the door of Narcissa's bedroom. The young woman stood inside, shaking as much as Ernest had.

"I couldn't open the door," she spoke through panting breaths.

Francesca grabbed her arm and rushed back to Ernest as he said "ten."

"Ernie, I'm sorry. I tried to get to you but my door stuck." Narcissa put a hand on his shoulder. "I tried, I really did."

"He didn't want you to help me," Ernest replied with a sniff as he hugged Sunny. "I'm sorry I wet the floor."

"That's all right, Ernie. Miss Fran can stay with you and I'll clean the floor right quick."

As Narcissa cleaned the puddle, Francesca kept hold of Ernest's hand as she gathered clean underwear and a playsuit for him.

"Y'all are coming home with me." She passed the bundled clothes to Narcissa.

"I don't want to go out there, Miss Fran."

"Stay with me, Ernest. Narcissa will be right behind us."

The house was vibrating before they reached the hall. Behind them, the bulb in the ceiling of Ernest's room exploded.

Pausing, she looked down at him. "You must try to breathe."

He nodded and bit his trembling lip.

"I know you're scared, but you must control your emotions, Ernest. Remember Deborah said you had to harness them?" She looked back at Narcissa to be sure she was keeping up with them.

Francesca thought she saw the figure of a man near the kitchen doorway, but when she turned her head fully, nothing was there except a chill autumn breeze that seemed to flow through the open doors. Ernest yipped like a kicked puppy and squeezed her hand so hard she lost feeling in her fingers, refusing to move.

"Come on, Ernest."

"My father is in the kitchen."

Goosebumps bloomed up her arms. "Then let's get out of here. Quickly."

He continued to stare at the dark entry into the scene of the crime.

"Let's go to my house. You'll be safe there."

"He'll keep coming for me," Ernest whined.

The floor buckled with the vibrations coming from him. In the kitchen, there was a pop and a hiss.

Sunny's fur stood on end. The cat jumped from Ernest's arms toward the front door as the kitchen lights flicked on and then shattered.

"Ernest!" She yanked him toward the exit with both arms at the same moment fire lit the kitchen.

The heat was on their backs, but she managed to carry him to the lawn while turning back to see Narcissa, who had dropped Ernest's clothes to run with them.

Neighbors were already gathering.

"Someone telephone the fire department!" Francesca shouted.

Mr. Reardon and a few other neighbors brought buckets. They hurriedly filled them at the spigot and soaked the back of the Harts' house.

Francesca carried Ernest inside, stopping in her dining room. "I need Judge Spunner's house," she told the telephone operator the location and it rang through while she continued to hold Ernest.

"Spunner," Sean's sleepy voice answered.

"It's Francesca. I need you right away. And if you hear sirens, they're going next door."

"Dear God! I'll be right there."

Once they were in the bathroom, Francesca started warm water running. It covered the sound of the sirens and shouting outside. She soaked his soiled pajamas in the sink while Ernest washed in a shallow bath. He dried himself and pulled on one of her plain button-up shirts.

Standing in white, Ernest looked like a cherubic angel. His big blue eyes were moistened with unshed tears. Only then did Francesca realize what she'd witnessed. Either Ernest had caught his house on fire or Mr. Hart's ghost had tried to kill them.

"I want Sunny, Miss Fran."

"Let me go check outside. I'm not sure where Narcissa is, either." She tucked him in a blanket on the sofa and kissed his forehead.

The youngest Reardon boy had Sunny in his arms as he watched the firemen from across the street.

Francesca put an arm around Narcissa, who was standing on the front walk, too shocked to move. "Come inside, Narcissa."

"Fran!" Bartholomew Graves hurried over. His nightshirt was tucked into a pair of wrinkled trousers. "When I rounded the corner, it looked like it was coming from your house."

"I'm fine, and we got Ernest out in time."

"Praise the Lord."

Sean joined them, looking just as disheveled as Bartholomew. "The block was too crowded, so I parked by Merri's house. Are you all right?"

"Fine, and Ernest will be once I bring him his kitten."

He looked Francesca over, then Narcissa beside her. "Darling, we need to get you both inside. Where's the cat?"

She looked down at their nightgowns and blushed in the dark. "With Jack Reardon."

Sean strode toward the crowd.

"Thank you for checking on me, Bartholomew. Be sure to tell Merritt we're fine." She took Narcissa's hand and led her inside.

"Where's Sunny?" Ernest called from the parlor.

"Judge Spunner is getting him. We need a minute to change, but we'll be right back."

In her bedroom, she gave Narcissa her robe and told her to sit with Ernest. Then Francesca tossed her nightgown into the sink with Ernest's pajamas and put on a simple house dress.

By the time Francesca returned to the parlor, Ernest was curled beside Jim on the sofa and Narcissa sat in the corner chair.

"I had hoped you'd come," Francesca said, "but I didn't want to disturb the household."

"Fortunately the sergeant on duty isn't concerned about waking people. I ran straight over when I heard."

"I come bringing gifts!" Sean swept through the front door. "The wayward kitten has been found."

"Sunny!"

The kitten meowed in reply.

"I want to stay with Officer Abbott." Ernest yawned.

Francesca pulled a needlepoint pillow to the side of the sofa and patted it. "Put your head there, and you can rest your feet by Rochester."

Francesca tucked a blanket around Ernest, kissing his forehead.

"Goodnight, Miss Fran. I love you."

"I love you too, Ernest." When she passed in front of Jim, she paused to kiss his cheek. "Thank you."

He took her hand and mouthed "I love you" before letting go.

When Francesca turned, Sean was grinning with that chipped-tooth smile that made him look as young as Jim.

"Could we go check on the house?" she asked the judge, who nodded.

"Do you want to come with us, Narcissa?"

She shook her head, eyes still unfocused from her fright.

Outside, a few neighbors lingered, as well as the fire team. Sean easily found the chief and questioned him about the Harts' house.

"It's the darnedest thing, Judge Spunner. It was quite a blaze, but it stayed in the kitchen," the fire chief explained.

Hearing the effects of Ernest's powers—for she was certain it was him and not his father who had caused it-- made goosebumps rise on Francesca's arms.

"The residents will be able to go inside in the morning to see what's salvageable. I suggest having a contractor look at the structure to see if it's safe, but from what I can tell, all the damage is in the kitchen."

Sean thanked him and they returned. Francesca immediately motioned Jim and Narcissa over. Jim carefully stood so as not to disturb the slumbering little ones.

"We need Deborah, maybe even Jo," she said as soon as Jim joined her in the kitchen along with Sean and Narcissa.

"What happened?" Jim asked, a hand resting reassuringly on her forearm.

She told of the house quaking, the state of agitation Ernest was in when she found him, and how Narcissa had been trapped in her room. When Francesca described Ernest's belief that his father was in the kitchen and the sounds that followed, both men stared.

"Is there any possibility he was part of the murder scene?" Francesca asked, needing to know her faith in the boy was pure. "Did he kill his father because he had killed his mother?"

"No, he was hiding under his bed," Jim assured her. "You saw him, Fran. He didn't have a spot of blood on him and no one in that kitchen could have escaped without blood splatter. But tonight he wanted to destroy his father. It's more symbolic than anything. Don't you think, Judge?"

"Yes, but what the hell are y'all doing in Washington Square these days? Only a powerful telekinetic could accomplish what that boy did. Is it something in the water here?"

Jim chuckled, as though Sean was trying to lighten the mood, but Francesca saw the judge's deadly earnestness.

Narcissa paled. "Ernie is a what?"

"Ernest is your nephew," Francesca assured her. "He's a boy—a special boy who went through many traumatic experiences that have set off a wave of emotions that come out as energy that moves things without him touching them."

Narcissa shook her head, refusing to accept the obvious.

"Why didn't you tell me all this before?" Sean asked Francesca.

"Would you have believed me?"

"I've seen a lot of things in this neighborhood involving Deborah and Jo over the years. Ernest is just another example of extraordinariness."

"Then I'm sorry for withholding information from you."

"Would you like medical intervention? Dr. Woodslow is my closest friend and he—"

"Deborah already informed Jo about his further agitation and nightmares." Francesca met his hooded gaze. "Between the two of them, I'm sure we can get him under control."

"He might be better off in an asylum. At least there he could be restrained."

"Restraints would do nothing if what y'all say is true," Narcissa said. "And if he did try to take out Willy, then he's braver than me or Sue ever were. I don't understand it all, or even want to believe this ghost business, but I know Ernie isn't crazy."

"Of course he isn't," Francesca said. "But as your neighbor and friend, I'll give you all the support I can to help with him. Please don't take him to Florida. I can only help you both here."

"My job is in Tallahassee. I have just enough money left to make it back there."

"Help her find a job, Sean, so she can stay. I've already offered to watch Ernest when he's out of school if she's working."

"Francesca, be reasonable. You saw the look of horror on her face. She's not up for this and you know it."

"She can grow," Jim said. "Give her that chance. I'll continue to be here for Ernest and them all. The best way you can help right now, judge, is to assist Narcissa in securing a job."

Sean shook his head in resignation. "I'll see what can be done."

"Thank you." Francesca kissed the judge's cheek. "I appreciate you coming when I telephoned."

"I'll talk to you tomorrow, darling." He nodded to the others and quietly left.

"The judge is right," Narcissa whispered. "I'm not up for this."

"Maybe not alone, but we're with you," Jim said.

Narcissa turned away and closed herself in the bathroom.

"I should check on her," Francesca said, avoiding Jim's gaze.

He took her hand and kissed the back of it before she could leave. "I'm here whenever you need me, Francesca."

She smiled despite the heaviness of the situation. "Thank you."

"Would you like me to stay?" Jim asked as they held each other.

"No, but thank you. Ernest seems to be settled, and I'll make a cup of Jo's lavender tea to help Narcissa relax."

Jim took a step back. "I'm on duty at noon."

"We'll be fine, so don't rush over. And thank you for what you said to Sean. Narcissa needed to hear that as much as he did."

"I hope you get some sleep, Fran. I'll see you tomorrow."

Nineteen

Jim lit up as soon as he was in the yard and walked slowly down the street, worrying his cigarette under the indigo sky.

When he passed the front of the house on Hallett Street, the steady tapping of Nathan's typewriter came through the screen door. He had a little desk in the front corner near Winnie's grand piano, in the spot furthest from the bedrooms for moments like these when he needed to write. He was probably covering the Harts' fire.

Jim trudged up the back stairs, pulled his clothing off down to his underdrawers, and collapsed on the open bed. His mind immediately went to where it had been when he got in bed several hours ago. Francesca—naked. Her beautiful lines and pleasing smile. He would marry her tomorrow if it were possible, but he knew no matter how willing she was to share physical experiences with him, he'd never ask her to rush formalities.

Jim tossed and turned, too restless to read. Sleep finally found him when the world woke.

He rose at half past ten, showered, dressed in uniform, and downed a cup of coffee. The Patersons were already gone for their Sabbath service and family visits, but

Leo hollered goodbye from his balcony when Jim walked down the driveway. Unsure whether Francesca would have company or not, he knocked on the front door.

She answered wearing a tailored black and gold dress. "You don't need to knock, Jim. Come in."

"I figured with Narcissa and Ernest staying here, it'd be for the best." He removed his hat as he entered. "How are they?"

"He's well, but Narcissa is still in bed. I gave her use of my mother's old room. I was waiting for you to arrive to go next door. I need to collect Ernest's things but didn't want to go inside without someone to help me spot trouble."

He knew she spoke of both physical issues with the house as well as the unseen. "I'll take you, Fran. Where's Ernest?"

"Playing with the kittens on the back porch. He's still wearing one of my shirts."

"I'll say hello and let him know we'll be back in a few minutes. Why don't you check with Narcissa and ask her to come as well?"

"All right." Francesca paused, then threw her arms around him. "I love you, Jim."

He relished the floral scent that always clung to her and the feel of their bodies touching while they hugged. "I love you too, Francesca."

He went through the kitchen to the back porch. "Hey, Ernest."

"Officer Abbott, look!" He held up Sunny. "He's bigger than ever, isn't he?"

"You've been doing great with him this week." Jim placed his hat on Ernest. "I'm going to take Miss Fran to your house to get your clothes."

Ernest flinched back. "Do I have to go too?"

Sensing his dread, Jim smiled. "Could you stay and watch the kittens for us?"

The boy nodded, causing Jim's hat to practically fall off. "But be careful."

"I will, Ernest."

Francesca waited by the front door.

"Narcissa says she'll listen out for Ernest, but wants me to collect her luggage. Sean got her a job interview lined up for tomorrow at the Cawthon. I told her she and Ernest are welcome to stay with me as long as necessary." Francesca paused on the front porch and fingered the buttons on his uniform jacket. "It will cut into our privacy, but their situation is urgent."

"Agreed. And the waiting will make everything between us that much more delicious."

Francesca blushed, then hooked her arm around his for the walk next door.

The few pieces of Ernest's clothing that ended up being discarded were trampled in the hall, but otherwise the only sign of disorder in the main part of the house was the lingering odor of smoke.

"I don't want him to ever have to return here," Francesca said on the way to Ernest's bedroom.

She bundled Ernest's meager clothing plus his two pairs of shoes, brushes, and the few toys he had into a blanket.

Jim took the load from her so she could pack Narcissa's things in the other room.

"She really doesn't have much," Francesca remarked when she carried the suitcase to the hall.

"I don't think she planned on staying."

They crossed the yard and ascended the front steps.

"Please bring Ernest's things to the back porch for cleaning."

"Then I need to check my call box, but I'll stop in later."

"Have supper with us."

"I'll be too late tonight, but appreciate the invitation. Don't worry about me. Winnie typically puts a plate of food in my icebox on Sundays. She always looks out for the well-being of my stomach."

"I'm glad you have such nice neighbors." Francesca dropped her voice. "Deborah is coming over at two to visit with Ernest. It would be great if you were here as well."

"I'll do my best."

***

Washington Square Park—typically filled with people on Sunday afternoons, slowly emptied as the threat of rain drew closer. Just before two, Jim met Deborah Farley as he walked down Palmetto Street.

He tipped his hat. "Good afternoon, Deborah,"

194

"Hello, Jim." She switched her folded umbrella from one hand to the other, tapping it on the road as she held his gaze. "I hope you're headed to Francesca's."

He nodded and fell into step with her as they turned onto George Street. "Ernest is happy to be back at Fran's, but he's shaken up over what happened—and so is his aunt."

"Do you think she'll be open to my assistance?"

"I have no idea. Francesca has developed a bit of a camaraderie with her. Maybe she'll be able to talk her into it if needed."

"We can hope," Deborah whispered as Jim knocked on the frame of the screen door.

Francesca unlatched it. "It looks like you arrived in time to stay dry." She took Deborah's umbrella and Jim's hat.

"How is he?" Deborah asked.

"He's settled back into his old space, but I'm worried about Narcissa. She's hardly spoken since the fire." Francesca's brown eyes looked at Deborah. "I told her a friend was coming to help, but that didn't interest her."

"Allow me to speak with Ernest first." Deborah settled on the sofa.

Jim followed Francesca, taking hold of her hand in the hall.

She smiled. "I'm glad you could make it."

"We can thank quiet Sunday afternoons for that." He leaned in for a kiss before returning to the parlor.

"Your aura is glowing pink, Jim," Deborah said as he sat beside her.

"Is that good?"

"It means you're happy and in love."

He grinned. "You know I am."

"Hold to the brightness—for all our sakes. I'll rely on your strong spirit during this session." She studied him a moment. "Jo told me you're meeting with her tomorrow evening."

Before Jim could respond, Ernest jumped between Jim and Deborah on the sofa, bare legs kicking excitedly. "Hello, Officer Abbott! Miss Deborah, are you going to teach me more about my power?"

"Yes, Ernest, but not quite yet." She took his hands. "You've been scared recently but are having a good day, right?"

He nodded as Francesca walked in.

"You're healing." Deborah smiled and closed her eyes. "Your mother is glad you're at Miss Fran's house."

"So am I!" Ernest nearly bounced on the sofa with energy.

"There's another…" Deborah turned pale.

Jim laid a hand on her shoulder. A current of energy tingled up his arm with the contact.

"What, Miss Deborah?" Ernest asked when she quieted.

"It's coming," she whispered.

A flash of lightning brightened the room immediately followed by a clap of thunder that snapped as though it struck a nearby tree. Francesca jumped and Ernest cowered on Jim's lap.

"This isn't helping him," Francesca said as she crossed the room. "Come to me, Ernest."

"I want Officer Abbott." The boy's arms encircled Jim's waist.

"It's in the house," Deborah warned, causing Francesa to step back.

Between his contact with the medium and Ernest, Jim's skin prickled as though lightning had struck him. But he felt it. Whether it was the suggestion of a ghost or the real thing, Jim knew an unseen presence was drawing closer.

Deborah stood, Jim's hand falling away from her. "I command you not to touch anyone!"

The empty side chair slid across the floor, leaving scrapes in the polished wood before it tipped toward the kittens. Sunny and Rochester screeched and scurried out.

"You shall not—" Deborah's face jerked as though it had been slapped.

Jim's hands went to Ernest's arms to loosen the hold to free himself.

"He needs you more. Protect him," Deborah's said with as much authority as when she spoke to the dead.

Jim's first thought was the Colt in his holster beneath his jacket, but he knew the revolver would do nothing against their current aggressor. He needed something to combat the unseen evil as hatred heated the charged air.

Love.

Jim gazed at Francesca, pale and shaking, but posture still erect. He would do anything for her, and that meant protecting Ernest.

Imagining his love radiating with the rosy glow Deborah had mentioned, Jim drew Ernest to his chest in a hug as he swayed to quiet the sniffling child. He concentrated on the glow of love, brighter than any darkness.

Ernest snuggled to his neck as his breathing calmed. "You're warm, Officer Abbott, like Miss Jo's tea."

"Pretend you're in the kitchen with Fran enjoying tea and cookies."

Around them, books and sheet music were knocked about like a Gulf wind was ripping through the room though the windows were closed. Jim continued to speak to Ernest about the comforts of Francesca's cozy kitchen while Deborah chanted things he couldn't understand and refused to allow Ernest to hear.

Francesca fled from the room. A short time later she brought Narcissa in, forcing her to link hands with her and Deborah amid the tumultuous atmosphere.

"Hot tea with honey and fresh lemon cookies to go with it," Jim continued to prattle as the women's triangle of power caused further uproar.

Narcissa squirmed between Deborah and Francesca as though wanting to escape, but they gripped her wrists tightly as Deborah's voice rose higher.

"So be it, in the name of our Lord and Savior!" Deborah shouted above the wind.

All went still, like the quiet after a clock tower's twelfth stroke at midnight.

Then the clatter of rain struck the roof like artillery. Jim flinched at the sound of the heavy drops, and Narcissa fainted. Deborah and Francesca on either side lowered her gently to the ground. Jim stood with Ernest clutched to his chest and transferred him to Francesca's arms. He lifted the young woman from the floor and carried her from the room.

Jim laid Narcissa on the bed in Mrs. Wilton's old room, wondering if she knew she slept where a woman had died a week ago. Surely that would do no favors for her nerves.

"Miss Hart." Jim watched for a response, noticing that the curve of her nose and chin were exactly like Ernest's. He perched on the edge of the bed and waited. "Narcissa, you're safe. You can wake up now."

He didn't want to leave her alone, nor did he wish to stay gone from the others.

As though she read his mind, Deborah came into the room.

"How did you know to do that?" Deborah asked wonderingly.

"Do what?"

"Expand your aura to protect Ernest."

"I did?" Jim shrugged. "It just felt right. How are Ernest and Francesca?"

"Ernest is fine, thanks to you. Francesca could use a hug. I'll stay with Narcissa so you can see to them."

"And what was that séance-looking thing you did?"

Deborah smiled. "Actually it was a bit of a reverse séance. It should protect the house for a while."

"I thought you couldn't seal a whole house."

"Not properly, but it might be worth trying sometime. Maybe with your strength combined with mine it would work."

"I'm not strong in that way."

"Yes, you are, Jim."

He returned to the living room, going straight to Francesca, who had Ernest on her lap. Without thought, he sat beside them and kissed her.

Ernest immediately put a hand on Jim's sleeve. "Do you love Miss Fran, Officer Abbott?"

"I do, Ernest. Very much. I'm glad you're both safe." Jim ruffled the boy's mop of hair. "How do you feel?"

"Still warm, but I'm hungry. Do you have any cookies, Miss Fran?"

"Go check the tin on the counter," she said with a smile.

Ernest slipped off her lap and hurried out. Jim's arm went around Francesca's middle as he pulled her close.

She hugged him in return and rested her cheek on his shoulder. "You're like fire, Jim. Are you sick?"

"I've never felt better."

"Narcissa wants to see you, Fran," Deborah said from the doorway. When Francesca lifted her head, she continued. "Did Jim tell you about his ability?"

"It was nothing," Jim said as he stood. "I didn't even know what I was doing."

Francesca clasped his hand. "What happened?"

"Ernest isn't the only one in this house with budding abilities," Deborah declared. "Jim used his aura to protect him."

Trying to downplay it, Jim shook his head.

"Don't forget I can see them. Most people have a slight glow about them based on their thoughts, mood, or intentions. Your rosy glow expanded until it surrounded you and Ernest several feet. No dark soul could have penetrated it if they tried." Deborah stepped closer. "It's still heightened. When you walked out with Narcissa, it expanded again like you could sense she was weak and needed protection. Now the color is pinker than ever and clear as a bell around you, especially where your hand is linked with Fran's."

Jim and Francesca both looked at their hands as though they wanted to witness it for themselves.

"I told you that you were hot when you hugged me. You still are, but it isn't uncomfortable. It's rather cozy."

"So you'll keep me around on winter nights?" he teased.

Francesca lifted her shoulder playfully. "Among other times, but now I need to go to Narcissa."

Twenty

When Francesca walked into her mother's old room, the sight of Narcissa lying on the bed sent a chill down her spine.

"I know Ernie can move things without touching them," Narcissa said as she slowly sat up. "Was all that hubbub Ernie or Willy?"

Struck by the possibilities, the sound of the rain and thunder temporarily overshadowed Francesca's thoughts. "I think it was ghostly in nature. Jim was holding Ernest and didn't mention anything strange going on with him during the commotion."

Narcissa shivered. "I can't stay here."

"But you must." Francesca sat beside her on the bed. "You and Ernest can say with me as long as you like, plus you have a job interview tomorrow."

"If I return to Florida, I can claim my old job. No one is keen for the nightshift."

"What about Ernest?"

"He'd be better off with you, Fran. Everyone knows that."

"But the law—"

"I'm sure that fancy judge of yours could work something out, especially if I put in writing Ernie living with you is my wish. Not to mention Sue trusted you with him. His mother's voice should count for something, even if it's from the grave. She put her life on the line enough times to protect him." Narcissa stared at her hands in her lap. "Not everyone has a cozy home like you." Narcissa lifted her chin. "I'm doing the best I can, but my best isn't enough to keep up properly with a growing boy that's doing unexplainable things."

"Deborah can help him. That's why she's here."

"I can't stand that spiritism stuff. I used to think it was crock, but I guess there's something going on. Not that I want to see it happening ever again. And I sure don't want to be involved in a conjuring circle or whatever that magic was you made me do with that woman."

"We needed at least three people and Deborah told me not to take Jim away from Ernest."

"You're lucky to have a guy like that. I may be young, but I'm not stupid. I see the way you look at each other." Narcissa's eyes were pleading. "Officer Abbott would be a wonderful father for Ernie. Don't try to hide real love—Ernie needs to see how good people can be."

"And you can be here too, Narcissa."

She shook her head.

"At least see about the job at the Cawthon in the morning. I'd be happy to go downtown with you after Ernest gets off to school. There's something I'd like help with as well."

"What's that?"

"I want to get a bob, but I don't know where to go. Your hair is always pretty, so I thought you could help me find the best beauty parlor."

Narcissa gave a little smile. "I know a place downtown from when I used to live here."

"We could leave at eight-thirty. Is that good for you?"

She nodded.

"And now," Francesca said as she stood, "I need to go back to check with Deborah. Will you come with me?"

"I don't have it in me to witness any more horrors. I'm staying here."

"Would you take some coffee?"

"Yes, thank you."

While Francesca waited for the water to boil, Jim's arms slipped around her middle from behind. "Everything go all right with Narcissa?"

"As well as can be expected. I'm making coffee for her. Would you like some?"

"I need to get back on patrol."

"In this rain?"

"An officer of the law has a responsibility to the community, rain or shine, Francesca." He turned her to face him. "My uniform is water repellent—not that I'd want to stand out in a downpour. I'll stop under a magnolia tree if the lightning lets up or take shelter on a porch if needed. I've done it plenty of times."

"But not with me willing to shelter you."

"True, but there are plenty of friendly folks in the area. I've passed lots of time on porches or inside shops during summer thunderstorms."

Francesca smoothed her hands over his chest, the wool jacket creating friction against her palms. "I'm sure your company is highly sought after, Officer Abbott."

"Whether it is or isn't is not my concern. I have the attention of the only woman I'll ever need."

His fingers brushed her throat as he trailed his touch upwards to cup her cheeks as he lowered his mouth agonizingly slow.

"I'm forever yours, Francesca." The whispered words heated her lips before his kiss did.

She clung to him as the kiss deepened, hoping to store all the love and strength he could impart.

***

Monday morning, Francesca let Ernest sleep as long as possible to make up for the hour she'd spent awake with him at one in the morning because of a nightmare. She had pots of oatmeal and coffee ready when Jim arrived.

"I needed something Ernest could quickly eat," she said as an apology.

"There's nothing wrong with a respectable bowl of oatmeal," Jim replied as he helped himself to a cup of coffee. "But why isn't Ernest out here yet?"

"Nightmares last night. I let him sleep half an hour longer than usual."

"Are you sure it was only nightmares, not a visitation?"

"Yes, positive. I didn't see, hear, or feel anything, and Narcissa wasn't disturbed. Ernest was crying, but he didn't make the house shake." Francesca took Jim's hand that didn't hold the coffee and kissed his knuckles. "He seems all right now."

"Good." Jim lifted their linked hands and kissed hers in return.

"Supper tonight?"

He shook his head. "Sorry, but I have an engagement."

Francesca raised her brow. "Police business?"

"No, it's with an unconventional woman who wishes to see me at eight o'clock outside of town."

She paused, then questioned. "With Jo?"

"Yes, about my shellshock." He leaned in for a kiss.

Ernest barreled into them, hugging their legs as they embraced. "Morning, Officer Abbott. Are you going to eat breakfast with me?"

"Sure thing, Ernest. But we gotta make it quick. You've got school, and I gotta get to the station."

Narcissa didn't get out of bed until Ernest and Jim were gone. When she finally came into the kitchen, Francesca had the breakfast dishes done and was wiping down the table.

"That's a nice outfit," Francesca said about Narcissa's beige skirt and white blouse. "I've got a brown coat that would look lovely with it if you'd like to borrow it."

"I'm a bit thicker than you," Narcissa said. "I doubt it would fit."

"It isn't too chilly out, so leaving it unbuttoned wouldn't draw attention and it would give you a polished look, which bodes well for a job interview."

"And just how many job interviews have you completed successfully?" Narcissa quipped.

"None, but I've read about them in women's magazines."

Narcissa laughed, Francesca joining her.

"There's coffee and oatmeal."

"Just coffee, thanks. I can never eat before a meeting."

Half an hour later, they were on an east-bound streetcar. They looped around to the north side of Government. Francesca looked up St. Emanuel Street when they passed it, hoping for a glimpse of Jim leaving the station, but the men in blue out front weren't him.

"Here." Narcissa stood two stops later.

Francesca allowed her to take the lead, falling into step beside Narcissa. They walked north, crossing Dauphin Street, getting dangerously close to a neighborhood Francesca was never allowed to mention.

As though she felt Francesca's unease, she explained. "It's on this block—not any further. And yes, the red-light district girls tend to frequent it, but that's because the owner knows how to best flatter her customers with haircuts."

Francesca paused outside the door. "How did you find out about it?"

"I lived with Willy and Sue for a summer in their little apartment a few blocks from here when I was sixteen. Ernie had croupe and Willy couldn't stand to listen to him cough all the time. He stayed gone, spending nights with the lady who did manicures here back then. He'd sometimes leave money with her for Sue to buy groceries, but she couldn't bring herself to go face-to-face with Willy's mistress, so she sent me to pick it up." Narcissa patted her arm. "Don't worry, Fran. If you don't like it here, once Cleo gives you the right cut, you can go anywhere to keep it up. But Cleo is a fine person, I promise you that."

Narcissa swung the door open and stepped onto the polished tile floor. Francesca was nearly knocked over by the chemical smell in the warm air, but hesitantly followed her.

"Welcome!" a lady standing over a woman at a sink called. "I'll be right with you."

"There's no rush," Francesca replied.

The busty woman in a green apron dried her hands on her way over. "Is that you, Narcissa?"

"It sure is, Cleo."

"Why I'll be flabbergasted! You were such a pokey thing but you've filled out all over! Who's doing your hair? It looks good enough to have been done here."

"A lady near the capitol building in Tallahassee. I've got a position in a fancy hotel, and the manager likes the staff to look like we're off the fashion pages."

"Well you're perfect, Narcissa. And that coat is divine."

Narcissa smiled. "I'm borrowing it from my friend. Fran here wants to get her hair bobbed."

Cleo eyed Francesca's thick bun and nodded. "You're finally ready to enter a new phase of life, aren't you?"

"Yes, ma'am," Francesca said with a smile.

"I bet there's a man involved too."

"A handsome police officer," Narcissa said with a giggle.

Cleo whistled. "We've got some fine ones in Mobile, don't we? I just love the darlings who patrol my neighborhood—even the old one. Let me finish setting this curl treatment and then I'll get to you, Fran."

Narcissa led Francesca to the sitting area and pointed to the magazines. "You can pick out styles you like in those, but if Cleo knows it won't do for you, she'll steer you to cuts that will work. Are you okay if I leave to go to the hotel?"

"Of course. Would you like to meet in Bienville Square afterwards, then we could go to a luncheon counter, my treat, before going home?"

Narcissa nodded. "Thank you, Fran. I'll see you in a little while."

Once alone, Francesca listened to Cleo's steady chatter with her client as she poured foul-smelling curling chemicals on the woman's hair. Then the lady was set in rollers and placed under a hooded hairdryer—something Francesca had only seen in magazines.

"Now," Cleo said as she approached, "what do you have in mind, Miss Fran?"

She held up a recent edition of McCall's magazine and pointed to a brunette with a chin-length bob.

"You aren't afraid to be daring, are you?"

"No," Francesca said with a smile.

"I like to hear that because it will look fabulous on you. Do you plan on selling your hair? I could cut it for free plus give you…" Cleo unwound Francesca's hair and whistled. "The wig boys will love this virgin coil. I bet they'll give me at least thirty, so with the haircut fee and collecting the service, I could give you twenty-five."

"That sounds more than generous, thank you." Francesca's mind raced with ideas for the money—everything from her luncheon with Narcissa to a new lingerie set to model for Jim.

Less than an hour later, Francesca walked to Dauphin Street lighter than ever. While she paused before the window displays at Hammel's, Mathias exited the doors.

"Dear Lord," he drawled as he took her hand, "Del and Jo are going to have an absolute fit when they see you, Fran!"

"Is it that good?"

"You know it is, you minx." He kissed her cheek and flashed his wolfish smile. "What does your policeman have to say about it?"

"He hasn't seen it yet." Francesca smoothed her hands over the bob. "I hope he likes it."

"Are you meeting him for lunch? I'm on my break and would be happy to join you."

She narrowed her eyes. "I'm sure you would, but no, I'm meeting a neighbor in the square. She's at a job interview right now."

"Pity." Mathias held both her hands. "When you do see him, if he doesn't eat you up, send him my way because he'd be a hopeless prospect for you."

"Don't you wish. Tell Cordelia I'll see her soon," Francesca said before continuing to Bienville Square.

Francesca found Narcissa sitting on one of the benches facing the tiered fountain.

"You look wonderful, Fran!" Narcissa went to her feet and hugged her. "Do you love it?"

"Yes, and thank you for the recommendation. How did your interview go?"

"They were happy to know I've worked nights before because that's what they need. The manger took me right over to the head of housekeeping to introduce me."

"You know I'd be happy to watch Ernest at night or any other time."

Narcissa nodded. "They want me to start training on Thursday."

"That's wonderful! In celebration, we're going to the Trellis Room."

"But I couldn't go in there! The Battle House lobby will put me to shame."

"Nonsense. The coat dresses you up. Besides, I sold my hair and have more money than expected. I'd like to stop at Hammel's afterward and get Ernest a new pair of pajamas, if that's all right with you."

"Whatever you'd like, Fran," Narcissa said with a hushed tone.

By the time they were back home, Narcissa claimed a headache and went to the bedroom to rest.

Humming to herself, Francesca folded Ernest's new red pajamas into the drawer in the guest room. She'd chosen the color in hopes he would be there at Christmas, but a lot could change in two months. So much had already shifted in two weeks.

Francesca fixed a cup of tea before Becca arrived to prepare supper. Narcissa was still in the bedroom, so Francesca settled on the front porch with the kittens to await Ernest's arrival.

The sound of Ernest and the Reardon boys laughing reached her ears before they came into view. Never knowing them to be so loud, Francesca smiled at the sight of Jim in their midst when they turned onto George Street.

They reached the edge of the property line, and she let the kittens down the stairs. Ernest scooped up his cat and ran with Sunny over to the Reardons' house.

Jim continued toward the porch. "Your haircut becomes you, Francesca. I hope you're pleased with it."

She blushed and smiled. "I am, thanks."

He caught Rochester on the grass. "Shall I bring him in for you?"

"Yes, thank you."

She held the screen open with her hip until Jim joined her. He was right behind her as she slipped into the parlor from the front hall. After setting down the kitten, he took her in his strong arms as he nuzzled her skin.

"Your new hairstyle fans your scent and gives easy access to your delectable neck."

His hot mouth on her throat stirred her to her core, but she laughed over the memory of Mathias's words. Jim's kisses rose until he was at her smile.

"What has you so pleased?" he questioned.

"You, for devouring me."

Jim's grin was devilish as his hands spanned her middle and around her backside. "I haven't even begun to devour you, Francesca. Just you wait." He nipped her with a kiss before going for the door.

She followed him back outside. "I hope Jo is able to help you tonight."

"Thanks, Fran." He captured her hand as they stood on the porch watching Ernest cross the street with Sunny. Jim descended the steps and picked his hat off the boy's fair head. "You be good for Miss Fran and your aunt this evening. I'll see you in the morning."

"Bye, Officer Abbott." Ernest hugged him with one arm. "We can telephone if we need you, right?"

"Of course, Ernest. Miss Fran knows where I'll be."

Ernest paused to hug Francesca before going inside, then she met Jim's gaze.

"I meant it, Fran. You can telephone me at Jo's house or home later if something happens. I'll be here quick as a blink."

His words chased the chilling thoughts of the nightmarish possibilities that awaited them should the ghost of Willy Hart return.

Twenty-one

Jim parked Leo's Ford in the circular lane in front of the brick mansion in Spring Hill. The two-acre property was lined with trees that stood as sentinels in the dark. Under the flickering gaslights on the porch, he took in the lush flowerbeds bordering the entry as he climbed the few steps.

Knowing there were children in the house, Jim knocked rather than ring the bell.

After the better part of a minute, Cyrus Harrington opened the door. Jacketless with his white shirt opened at the neck, he commanded an air of respectful leisure as his angular face fell into an easy grin. "Hello, Officer Abbott."

"Jim, please, Mr. Harrington." He shook the offered hand and crossed through the wide doorway.

Cyrus looked him over under the crystal chandelier as though taking stock, making Jim glad he'd dressed in a suit for the appointment.

"And call me Cyrus because if all goes according to Jo's plans, you'll be here often. She asked me to wait with you until the children are settled." Cyrus motioned to the sofa. "Make yourself comfortable, Jim. Would you care for a refreshment?"

"I'm fine, thank you."

Jim sat in the corner of the plush blue sofa. Cyrus took the other end of it, crossing his legs as he turned toward his guest. "Do you understand what you're getting into with this meeting?"

"No, but that's what I'm here to learn. Deborah recommended I bring my troubles to your wife, and Fran seconded the opinion."

Cyrus smiled as he rubbed his chin. "Deborah is keen, and Fran would know. She's Jo's oldest friend. You two have quite a connection, as everyone at Del's party would agree."

"Don't get him too excited, Cyrus." Jo said as she entered the room. Her silk trousers flowed about her legs with each step. When she paused before Jim, she smiled. "Cyrus will fix a cup of a special tea for you and deliver it to us in the library. The purple label, Cy. You know the one."

Cyrus nodded to his wife and silently left the room.

"Come with me, Jim."

"Yes, ma'am." He stood.

"Though I might be a teacher to you, please keep things informal. I'm either Jo or nothing—do you understand?"

Jim nodded.

Down the hall to the rear of the house, she flicked the switch in a paneled room of mahogany and green velvet. A giant mirror over the mantel reflected the electric chandelier. "Remove your jacket and shoes, then sit on the chaise."

She waved him toward the tufted lounge chair that was large enough for two adults to recline on.

Jim reluctantly shed his jacket and nudged his shoes under the edge of the furniture.

After lighting several candles on the side table, Jo clicked off the overhead switch and sighed. "There's nothing more soothing than candlelight."

Tense with the intimacy of the situation, Jim shifted away from Jo when she sat beside him. She laughed and placed a hand on his knee.

"Trust is the most important factor in our working relationship." She leaned closer. "Even if Fran didn't have her heart set on you, I'd never disrespect my family. Cyrus and our children are everything to me."

Jim laughed nervously and cleared his throat. "Why do I feel like I'm making a deal with the devil?"

"My reputation rears its ugly head," she said with a grin. "I was chided as being Witchy Wolf of Washington Square though I never did anyone harm, not counting Edgar Melvin. He deserved to be run out of town after his raving claim that I got into his head and pushed him around Dauphin Street. But that was nothing compared to what that monster did to my brother."

"Not that old story. It always riles you to speak of it," Cyrus said as he arrived with a silver tray. "Here, my love, I fixed you a glass of water and put a few cookies on here in case Jim should need nourishment afterward."

"Thank you, Cy." They shared an amorous kiss, then Cyrus closed the door on his way out.

Jo brought Jim a dainty teacup wafting steam scented with florals and spice. "Drink this as quick as you can and then lie down."

Afraid to not comply, Jim drank without questioning what it might contain.

Jo placed the teacup back on the tray and sat beside him on the edge of the chaise as he reclined. "Now close your eyes and listen to me, Jim. I haven't attempted to try this with someone since half a lifetime ago, but Deborah assures me your spirit is strong and I felt the power in you myself the day we met."

Her warm hand took his closest one and held it.

"I know you're accepting of things out of the ordinary after witnessing what you have with Ernest, so keep an open mind."

She spoke the ominous words evenly, but Jim wanted to peek at her to see what she was focused on.

"No, Jim. You must follow *all* instructions. Keep your eyes closed." Before he could ask how she knew, she continued. "I can hear a bit of your thoughts, but only if I concentrate completely. What I'm going to teach you I mastered as a child. Listen to the silence, then tell me what you see in your mind."

Jim concentrated on the shadows behind his eyelids and the connection of their hands. As though brightening with the rising sun, a picture began to take shape. Him—on the chaise—with Jo sitting beside him. The vignette began to telescope out until he was looking down on the scene from the height of the ceiling. Then the focus switched to the gilded mirror over the fireplace. That drew closer until it was within touching distance. Jo's hand squeezed his and there was a flicker of an apparition in the reflection. Jim jerked and sat up.

"Well?" Jo asked. "What did you see?"

He shivered. "Your ghost. It was looking down on us and then looked in the mirror."

"Very good, though I prefer the term spirit or astral form as I'm not dead. We'll leave the ghosts to Deborah." Jo laughed.

"But what happened and how did you do that while sitting beside me?"

"It's called astral projection. It's when your spirit leaves your body before death. When someone utilizes it, they can go anywhere, see anything in their spirit form. I used to have to lay down and be still for several minutes before leaving my body, but now I can do it whenever I want."

"What does that have to do with me?"

"I am going to teach you how to use your mind as a means of relaxation. It strengthens the spirit and controls emotions which will help you deal with the war memories." Her hands went to his shoulders. "Lie back down, Jim."

"I'm not a witch."

"Warlock, and no, neither am I, though some people might say I am because of my abilities." Jo lay beside Jim, her shoulder snug against his. Holding his hand, she nestled it between their hips. "Just relax, Jim. Listen to my words."

She spoke of the heaviness of his body, making him aware of each section with her hypnotic voice. When he felt lethargic, she switched to speaking of the lightness of his soul. Tethers holding his spirit to his body were described, then the imagery of how he could untie them. All this transpired while they lay side-by-side, but the furniture was no longer felt. Just the comforting heat of Jo's warm body and her soothing words.

Now, Jim, she whispered, though he didn't hear it with his ears. *You have my hand. Cleave to it with your spirit and rise with me.*

With the gentle tug, he released the tethers and floated up. Jo's shimmering figure was less intense than her physical person but every bit as daunting with her powerful gaze.

Stay focused on me, Jim. We'll circle the room and then return.

A quiver in Jim's middle fluttered to his throat at the sensation of flying. When they passed in front of the mirror, Jo hovered beside him as he looked around the room in wonder. A minute later, she tugged at his hand and led them back to the chaise.

"Stay there a minute," Jo commanded. "If you try to get up too quickly, you'll be on the floor. Concentrate on the connection between your body and spirit. Sit up only after you feel completely attached. Return Thursday night and we'll work on visual imagery."

"And all this magic will help me?"

"If it's magic then you're as witchy as me." Her teasing voice kept its soothing tone. "It all strengthens your inner self, teaching you control. I showed you something physical you couldn't deny to prove to you what your mind is capable of and gain a new perspective. Trust me, Jim, it will all make sense as time goes on."

He rubbed his eyes and sat up.

"How do you feel?" she asked.

"Like my universe just expanded."

"You're more than up for the challenge," Jo said with a grin.

***

Thursday morning, Narcissa was at the breakfast table for the first time when Jim entered the back door. After a general greeting to both women, he paused by the stove to kiss Francesca's cheek and enjoy the way her shortened hair framed her beautiful face.

She touched the shoulder of his white shirt and smiled. "Help yourself to coffee."

He did and brought it to the little table. "Good morning, Miss Hart. Are you ready for training at the Cawthon?"

"As ready as I'll ever be." She drank from her cup. "I just wish they could train me during my regular hours, but the housekeeping management doesn't stick around for nights."

Jim nodded. "And how's Ernest?"

She glanced at Francesca, whose back was to them. "He's still crying in the night, but he goes to Fran."

Ernest ran in. "Morning, Officer Abbott. You goin' fishing today?"

"I am." Jim hugged him when the boy threw his arms around him.

Ernest slipped into the chair pulled close to Jim's and looked at Narcissa. "Good morning, Aunt Narcissa."

"Morning, Ernie."

Francesca opened the oven, releasing the aroma of fresh cornbread into the air. "It's ready."

Jim crossed the kitchen to help carry the cornbread pan and platter of fried ham to the table.

Seeing Narcissa's sullenness after the blessing, Jim sought to draw her into conversation. "What are you most looking forward to with your new job?"

"The paycheck."

"That's always a good thing."

"Independence is important to me. I don't like living on charity no matter how kind the giver is."

At the end of the meal, Francesca hugged Ernest. "Don't forget your lunch. And I have a meal to go for you as well, Narcissa."

After the bustle of gathered lunches, goodbyes, and the closing door, Jim took Francesca in his arms. It had been days since he'd held her so he didn't waste time with subtleties. She met his searching tongue and pressed closer as eagerly as he did. When Francesca's hands roamed lower, Jim's breath hitched.

"I'd apologize and say I didn't mean to go that far, but I won't lie." Francesca's grin was playful, but her eyes were hesitant.

Jim stepped back, appraising her honest blush. "I'm gonna have to jump in the bay to cool off from this, but it was worth it."

"Supper tonight?" she asked.

"I promised Winnie my fish today. Then I've got my second session with Jo."

"When will you check in with Ernest?"

"Some time in between."

"I'll be here." Francesca stepped forward for a hug and kiss. "Think of me when you're trying to cool off in the water."

"It'll turn the bay into a hot spring." Jim laughed, then gathered his supplies and headed for the trolley lines.

When he made it back to Hallett Street six hours later, Winnie was giving a piano lesson to one of her students. Jim entered her kitchen through the porch, gathered what he needed, and started cleaning fish in the back yard on a simple table Leo had rigged up with scrap wood.

He was filleting the final fish when Winnie stepped out.

"Hey, Jim. I thought I heard a critter in my kitchen while Tabitha was practicing. Did you have a good day at the bay?"

"Yes, and there's enough for everyone. I'll do the frying."

"And I'll do the vegetables and cornbread."

Percy toddled onto the porch and pawed at the screen. "Jim! Jim!"

"Hey, big guy." He smiled. "Do you have more students today, Winnie?"

"One more in half an hour."

"Let me clean up, then I'll take Percy for a walk."

"He'd love that. Thank you."

Twenty minutes later, Jim was freshly showered. He rolled his sleeves, forewent a hat, and collected Percy from the first-floor apartment. With the boy on his shoulders, Jim instinctively headed south. He took Percy to say hello to his grandmother and then let him sit on the deer statue in Washington Square Park before heading back.

Winnie was on the porch with Sydney when he returned. The upstairs neighbors—Leo and Sydney Williams—both worked and kept a vigorous social calendar, but at least once a week all of them managed to share a meal.

"Mama!" Percy shrilled.

Jim sat him on the porch, and he ran to his mother with open arms. Then Jim nodded at Sydney. "Hey, lady."

"Hey, Jim. I hear you're frying fish this evening. Leo and I are up for a bite before we go to the cinema."

"Glad you can join us. When is Leo expected?"

"Any minute. He ran to Greer's to look for some okra. Winnie's got a craving."

"Green beans will do, if that's the only option," Winnie said as she rocked Percy in her arms. "How was he?"

"That one's good as gold." Jim sat on the railing and looked between his neighbors' wives. "We went to Washington Square Park."

"You can't help walking a beat, even on your day off," Winnie teased. "Next time you go fishing, invite Miss Wilton to join us. Ernest would be welcomed too."

"Who's Miss Wilton?" Sydney asked.

"She lives around the corner from my parents," Winnie said, "next door to the Hart murder-suicide. Ernest was their son."

"How awful." Sydney shuddered. "Hurry up with the food, folks. I always get hungry when I hear sad news."

Jim laughed. "We might as well wait until Leo comes back so we know what we have to work with."

"Can't blame a girl for trying." She looked Jim over. "So this Miss Wilton is your new interest?"

"Something like that." Jim hopped off the railing. "I'll prep for the frying. I can't stay late."

He went to Winnie's kitchen and pulled out the necessary bowls, pans, and other pieces. A minute later, the lady of the house joined him.

"Where are you going tonight, Jim?"

"I have an appointment with Jo Harrington."

"What do you want with Witchy Wolf of Washington Square?" Winnie asked. "I was scared to death of her when I was little. Sean once made my brother dress up as a court page and deliver Mardi Gras invitations to her house."

"She was recommended to help with a few things that trouble me from time to time." Jim looked at Winnie's kind face, not knowing if her husband had told the confidences he'd shared with him during Nathan's darkest days. Trusting her, he lowered his voice. "I have a bit of shellshock. Not like Nathan had because of his injury, but enough to paralyze me from time to time. So is going to teach me how to control my responses."

Winnie took his hand. "I wish you the best with healing. Let me know if we can ever assist you. We owe you from helping save Nathan's life."

"Thanks, Winnie."

Twenty-two

Francesca attempted to be cheerful over supper, but Narcissa was exhausted and Ernest had experienced his first disagreement with Tommy Reardon. There wasn't much to smile about around the table when neither wanted to talk.

Afterward, Narcissa retreated for a hot bath and Ernest took the kittens to his room. Through the open windows, the sound of the old Ford Jim often borrowed from his neighbor rumbled to a stop. Francesca met him on the darkness of the porch, taking comfort in his arms.

"What's wrong, Fran?" Jim whispered as she laid her head on his suit jacket.

"Ernest is out of sorts, Narcissa is tired, and you're going to Jo's house tonight."

"I'm here now. What can I do?"

"Kiss me, and then see if Ernest will talk with you."

Francesca felt exhilarated as she soaked in his warm affection. When he pulled away, she smiled. "I wish I could change my mind and request you come to my bedroom instead. I'd love for you to hold me all night."

Rather than laugh, Jim's fingers brushed her cheek as he stepped closer. "I yearn for our togetherness as well, Francesca."

"There's nothing so lonely as a house full of grumpy people."

Jim's dimple winked before he leaned in for another kiss. "Allow me to see what I can do for our favorite boy."

"Ernest," Francesca called as they entered the front door. "You have company!"

Francesca settled in the corner chair and pretended to read a magazine. When Ernest ran in, he claimed the sofa with Jim.

"Hey, Officer Abbott. Did you catch fish today?"

"Plenty, and my neighbors enjoyed them with me. They want you and Miss Fran to come over next time. How was school?"

"Well…" Ernest stroked Sunny's head and kicked his heels on the sofa skirting. "It stunk. Tommy said I wasn't good enough to be on his ball team during recess when I've been playing with him for days. And nobody put in a word for me—not even Jack—so I must be pretty rotten."

"I doubt that," Jim said reassuringly. "You just don't have as much practice as the others. Did I ever tell you I was on the police department's ball team this past season?"

"No. What position?" The excitement in Ernest's voice pitched it higher.

"Second base. How about I bring you a ball and we start playing catch every day?"

"Would you, Officer Abbott?"

"I'd be happy to."

Francesca lowered the magazine to watch Jim ruffle Ernest's hair. The grins between them lifted her spirits as much as Jim's loving embrace had.

"I gotta get to an appointment, but I'll be here in the morning."

"For breakfast?" Ernest asked.

Jim caught Francesca's gaze and she nodded.

"Yes, Ernest. And if you want me to walk to school with you, I will."

"Thanks, Officer Abbott." Ernest hugged him.

Francesca walked to the door with Jim, their fingers intertwined.

"I can never repay you for all you continue to do for him," she whispered.

"Seeing him smile is more than enough."

Jim kissed her goodbye and she closed the door for the night.

Once Narcissa was in her room and Ernest bathed and in bed, Francesca sat in the guestroom and read him a chapter from *The Princess and the Goblin* while he drank his tea blend from Josephine.

When she leaned over him to kiss him goodnight, Ernest looked up at her with his luminous blue eyes.

"Do you have any books with spaceships or time machines?"

"No, I'm afraid not. But we could check at the lending library."

"Or with Officer Abbott. He's got a lot of books, remember?"

"Yes, he does. I'm sure he could recommend a great one for us to read. Goodnight."

"Goodnight, Miss Fran." He took her hand. "I can call for you if I need to, right?"

"Always, Ernest."

Francesca brought the empty teacup to the kitchen, then knocked softly on the closed door of her mother's old room.

"Come in," Narcissa called.

She sat up in bed when Francesca entered.

"Is the job terrible?"

"No, not really. It's different than the hotel in Tallahassee, but the other maids are nice. I'm just not used to being on my feet all day—or being awake for that matter. I'm tired, but I think I'm too exhausted to sleep."

"Could I fix you some lavender tea?"

Narcissa made a face. "I never want that noxious stuff again. I hope what you're giving Ernie tastes better."

"I add honey to his."

"You're a living saint, Fran."

"I'm not as pious as you think I am."

"You're the type to care for an ailing mother and take in an orphaned neighbor. I don't have the patience for either."

"That doesn't make me perfect—it makes me different, that's all." Francesca stopped at the side of the bed. "There's lots of good things you do that I never have."

"Like what?"

"Work a fulltime job and support yourself."

"Barely, and that's living with a roommate."

"It's still more than I've ever done, especially on my own. You're brave, Narcissa, and that's no small thing." She held her gaze several seconds. "I hope you get some rest. Officer Abbott will be here again for breakfast."

When Francesca started for the door, Narcissa spoke. "Is Officer Abbott the reason you aren't such a good girl?"

Francesca turned back to her. "I'd tuck him in my room until breakfast if I could."

"It's your house. Don't let me stop you."

The image of Jim on her bed filled Francesca's mind and she smiled. "Someday."

Thinking about what Jim might be learning from Josephine kept Francesca from fully enjoying the L.M. Montgomery novel. She set *Rainbow Valley* on the side table and clicked off her lamp. The hall light, which she left on because of Ernest's troubled nights, lighted a path to the foot of her bed. Josephine was sure to have told Jim about her telepathy and astral skills, but the tiny moments of privacy Francesca and Jim had shared the past few days were taken up with loving rather than talking—something she needed to adjust the ratio of.

She pulled the quilt to her chin and sighed with longing for Jim's companionship. Wanting nothing more than to curl up next to him and whisper about his day gave her a hunger she'd never felt before. A craving of her soul to feel his arms around her while he discussed something funny that happened at the station, the fish that got away, or what might have disturbed him created a gnawing feeling of emptiness that she knew would never be filled until they were one.

Sleep came to Francesca slowly but part of her mind remained active. Was it the one focused on Jim or the section alert to trouble as Ernest continued to wake in the nights distressed?

When the cry came, Francesca was on her feet instantly.

Through her opened bedroom door and over to Ernest's took mere seconds for her to cross, but Francesca was too late.

Amid the trembling walls, Ernest sobbed on the floor of his room, cowering as though being struck on his back.

"Ernest!" She ran forward but was shoved aside before she could reach him.

Righting herself, Francesca approached slowly. A cold resistance met her two feet from the boy. She felt the heaviness in the air and her skin prickled as she tried to pass through it.

"Ernest! Look up, Ernest, I'm right here!"

His tear-streaked face rose. "Help me, Miss Fran!"

"I'm trying," she promised as she pushed against the unseen barrier.

Struggling as though trudging through chilled swamp muck, Francesca gritted her teeth and pushed her body to new strides only to gain an inch.

"Move, you bastard!" she cursed under her breath. "You no longer have a claim on Ernest. You gave that up when you murdered his mother."

The cold set her teeth chattering, and then a blow struck her cheek with force enough to send her to the floor.

Ernest screeched in fright and the bedroom door swung shut as the house trembled all the way to its foundation. The kittens hid under the edge of the bed, fur standing on end, tails puffed and straight out.

Holding back her tears and terror, Francesca stood and opened the door.

"Narcissa, I need you!"

Narcissa's white face was petrified as she met Francesca's gaze across the hall.

"You need to telephone the Farleys on Rapier Street. Tell Deborah it's urgent." When Narcissa made no move that she understood, Francesca repeated herself and added another plea. "Now, Narcissa. It's worse than ever."

She finally nodded. Holding the quivering walls for balance, Narcissa crept toward the telephone.

Returning her focus to Ernest, Francesca vowed to reach him no matter the cost. Skirting the bedroom, she approached him from the opposite side. The cold barrier was there, but not as thick. She didn't speak in case the thing was listening, but she prayed Ernest would see her and calm down before it struck again.

Shivering with cold, Francesca's muscles nearly seized with effort before she fell through the invisible wall. On her knees beside Ernest, she gathered him to her chest.

"I'm not letting go of you, Ernest. Whatever happens from now on, I'll be beside you." She kissed his forehead and rocked him. "Breathe, Ernest. Miss Deborah is on her way. Remember what she taught you."

It felt like hours that they held each other within the demonic cage, crying silent tears as Ernest calmed in Francesca's arms.

Deborah's small but mighty figure entered, clad in a mauve robe. She clicked on the light switch by the bedroom door and advanced, arms swinging as though chopping through kudzu vines with a machete.

She declared her presence, then started her demands. "You *will* remove your malevolent spirit from this room, William Hart. You will not touch another living creature."

The cold around them deepened as though a wave collapsed, smothering all hope.

"Hear me, William Hart!" Deborah was only four feet from Francesca but they felt miles apart with the oppression separating them. "You are to leave this home now!"

Warmth flooded them and then Deborah was beside Francesca, talking directly to Ernest though she didn't try to remove him from her embrace.

"You were brave, Ernest. You did well controlling your fears. I'm proud of you."

It took him a few minutes to speak, but when he did, Francesca's heart soared.

"Miss Fran helped me. She reminded me to breathe and held me." He kissed her cheek. "I love you. And you too, Miss Deborah."

He hugged Deborah, smiling despite the recent scare.

When Francesca felt stable enough to stand, she went to check on Narcissa.

"I just want to be alone tonight, please."

"All right, Narcissa. I'm going to telephone Jim and ask him to come over. I hope you get some rest."

The operator put her through to Jim's house and she said three words when he answered.

"We need you."

"I'll be right there."

The line clicked and Francesca let out a sigh of relief. Seeing Deborah quietly talking with Ernest in his room, she collected her dressing gown from her bedroom, and waited for Jim.

As soon as he was in the front door, Jim gave her a quick hug and then a questioning gaze.

"Deborah's here."

"Hart's ghost?"

Francesca nodded and Jim stepped under the hall light. His clothing was disheveled, as though he'd picked it off the floor in the dark, not bothering to tuck in his shirttails.

Deborah and Ernest were settled at the kitchen table. Jim stopped in the doorway and Ernest jumped for him.

"Officer Abbott!" He hugged Jim around the middle. "Now all my favorite people are here. We're going to have tea and cookies—a midnight party."

Jim ruffled his hair and mustered a smile.

"Tea?" Francesca asked him.

"Coffee, please," Jim replied. It would be another sleepless night, but Jim didn't complain. Instead, his hand captured hers, his thumb caressing her wrist. "There's no place I'd rather be, Fran."

As they ate and drank, Jim's silent strength buoyed Francesca and gave Ernest a solid figure to focus on amid his inner turmoil. The boy finished eating and shifted into Jim's lap.

Deborah returned to the kitchen. "I've sealed Ernest's bedroom, like I did next door. Do you wish me to do the same for yours and Narcissa's?"

Francesca stood. "Yes, I'd appreciate it."

"It's all minor things compared to the scope of what this spirit is capable of. I have an idea I need to discuss with Jo. It will take some planning if she agrees to it, so I'll keep doing what I can in the meantime."

"I appreciate everything, Deborah." She touched the shoulder of her winter dressing gown. "And I'm sorry to have gotten you out of bed."

Deborah smiled. "It's not the first time I've roamed the streets of Washington Square in my nightclothes. I keep this cover handy throughout the year to retain a smidgeon of modesty in my call to serve. It used to irk Alvin to see me run from the house in the middle of the night, but he has finally accepted that time does matter in affairs of the spirit world."

Deborah went to Francesca's room, and Ernest was falling asleep in Jim's lap.

"You can carry him to his bed if you want," she whispered. "I'll get you a fresh cup of coffee."

Ten minutes later, Deborah was gone, Ernest slept in his bed with Sunny by his side, and Narcissa was still silent in her room. Francesca and Jim sat at the kitchen table with steaming cups.

"Would you be able to sleep if I stayed to watch over things?" Jim asked.

"In a little while." Francesca stroked Rochester, who was curled in her lap. "I need to get my mind off everything that happened. Tell me about your meeting with Jo. Is she able to help you?"

"She taught me how to close off the section of my brain that triggers the war memories when I see something potentially damaging. I close my eyes, slow my breathing, and visualize putting my war memories into a box and closing the lid."

"What happens to the box?"

He set his cup down and captured her hand. "I can't neglect it. The longer I wait to deal with it, the harder it will be to control. But when I'm home or somewhere safe, I visualize myself opening the box to confront those images. Jo guided me through the mental imagery so I know how to do it. I'm sure it will be difficult when I have to do it in a moment of stress, but I worked through it with Jo's guidance."

She squeezed his hand. "Jo and Deborah proclaim your strong spirit and I've felt it as well though I don't understand it on the level they do."

"Neither do I." Jim smiled. "Everything in my life changed when I walked into this house."

Twenty-three

Just before sunrise, Jim rose stiffly from the front steps and stretched. He briskly walked home where he showered and dressed in uniform before returning to Francesca's house.

Jim entered the kitchen door, and paused a moment to appreciate Francesca's silhouette at the counter. Even in his sleep-deprived state she stirred him physically and emotionally with just a glance.

"Good morning, Jim." She smiled.

He dropped his hat on the table before capturing her around the waist. His hands roamed before they found the perfect curves to grip.

Francesca hugged him with complete surrender. "I love you. Promise you'll always be here to support me and make me smile."

Jim lifted her off her feet and grinned up at her glowing face. "I promise, but you do the same for me, Francesca."

Her brown eyes held him as though spellbound by her love. "I can't help thinking I'll wake up one day and realize it was all a dream."

"There have been some nightmarish events around us, but never because you and I found each other." He kissed her and then slowly released his hold. "What do you need me to do this morning?"

"Telephone Judge Spunner," Narcissa said from the doorway. "Oh, and good morning. I'm sorry for interrupting."

"What's the matter, Narcissa?" Francesca asked.

"I've thought about it all night, Fran. I can't stay here."

"But what about Ernest and your job!" She took the blonde's hand.

"Ernest is better off with you. Everyone knows that, even Ernest. I can go back to my job in Tallahassee, no questions asked as they know I had to leave temporarily because there was a death in my family."

"But—"

"No, Fran. I can't. It's all too much for me with the haunting and Ernest's...whatever that is." She turned to Jim. "Please telephone the judge. I want to get this taken care of as soon as possible so I can catch the next train."

"Jim, don't," Francesca whispered, eyes rimmed with tears.

Jim went for the doorway though it pained him to ignore Francesca.

When he returned to the kitchen, Narcissa stood with her arms crossed, staring at Francesca while she stirred a pot of grits.

"Judge Spunner will stop by on his way downtown. I told him you both needed his advice, but gave no details. I'm leaving that to you, Narcissa."

"Thank you. I'll wake up Ernie. School doesn't stop because we had a ghostly visitor last night. I'll tell him goodbye before he leaves." She sniffed and wiped her nose with a handkerchief. "I'm not upset. It's because of the cats."

She walked out, and Francesca's dark eyes fell on Jim.

"Just as you proclaimed my capabilities in taking control of my shellshock, I know you're more than suited to discuss Ernest's well-being with Narcissa and the judge. You have, after all, marched down to the police station about it before."

"I know you're right, but I just wish she'd give life here more of a chance." Francesca turned back to breakfast preparations.

The four of them were soon squeezed around the kitchen table with cheese grits, coffee, and milk for Ernest.

Narcissa spent most of the meal watching her nephew. As soon as he scooped his last spoonful into his mouth, Narcissa spoke.

"Ernie, I need to talk to you." She waited until he put down his spoon. "You're happy with Miss Fran, aren't you?"

"Yes, I love her and Sunny."

"You and me, Ernie, we had things rough with our original families. But I have an opportunity to keep building a new life in Florida just like you have an opportunity here." She took his hand, and Jim scooted his chair back to give them a bit more space. "I want the best for you and that means you should stay with Miss Fran. Would you like that?"

His blue eyes clouded over as he listened. "Would you visit?"

"Yes, as often as I could, but it might only be every few months."

"And I'd be here with Miss Fran, not at the boys' home?"

"Yes, I'm going to see to that after you get to school. I wrote a letter to the courts and will be speaking to Judge Spunner. We're all watching out for you the best way we know how."

"Okay, then."

"I might be gone when you get back from school, so I wanted to be sure you know how much I love you, even if I haven't been around much these past couple years. Miss Fran and Officer Abbott will take good care of you, Ernie."

They hugged, and then Ernest looked at Jim.

"Will you walk me to school, Officer Abbott?"

"I'd be happy to."

"Could you play ball on the playground if we get there early enough?"

"I don't think the principal would take too kindly to an adult taking over the schoolyard, even a policeman."

As soon as they were walking, Jim started whistling "Smiles." By the time they passed the Marley house on the corner of Roper and Palmetto, Jim noticed Ernest was trying to copy his lip movements. He spent the rest of the walk teaching Ernest how to whistle.

When he got back to George Street, Judge Spunner was in the parlor, Francesca sitting beside him on the sofa and Narcissa across from them.

"Well?" Jim asked.

The judge raised his head from the page he was reading. "The letter is helpful, but it will still take smoothing things over for the courts to award Francesca custody."

Jim reached for the paper and Judge Spunner handed it to him.

To Whom it May Concern,

Before her death, Sue Guthrie Hart trusted Francesca Wilton with her son, Ernest, on multiple occasions. Miss Wilton acted as a loving neighbor and guardian to Ernie during his months living on George Street, especially amid the fighting between his parents that was a constant source of agitation to him.

After my extended visit, I have seen countless examples and hours of Miss Wilton's loving care. Just as his mother trusted Miss Wilton, I too trust her with Ernie's life.

It is my wish that Ernie continues to live with Francesca Wilton as I am not able to properly care for him. Though I would like to continue contact with my nephew, I will not hamper any guardianship requests from Miss Wilton regarding him. If she seeks it and the court sees fit to allow her to adopt Ernie, it would be with my blessing.

Sincerely,

Narcissa Hart

It closed with her contact information in Tallahassee.

"It looks solid to me," Jim remarked.

"And he can't go to the boys' home," Francesca said.

"I know, and I'm not saying it's hopeless, Francesca," the judge replied. "I'm saying we've got to ease people into accepting what's best for Ernest. I can pull a few strings, get Ernest's case before a friend, and I'm sure temporary custody would be granted to you."

"Temporary? Sean, I love Ernest."

"I know, darling, but adoption is out of the question until you marry. We have to ease the old boys into a modern way of thinking. Ninety-day custody will get us through the holidays and then they can see how well Ernest is doing—and maybe you and Jim as well." The judge winked.

"So it'll all be okay?" Narcissa asked.

"I can guarantee temporary custody within the month. And if you're willing to come back for any court dates, I don't see why this won't work." The judge stood.

"Yes, of course." Narcissa shook his hand. "Thank you, Judge Spunner."

"I'm happy to be of assistance." He looked at Jim. "And Chief O'Shaughnessy will be glad you're free of this daily grind."

"Official check-ins or not, nothing is gonna stop me from seeing Francesca and Ernest."

"We're all counting on that." The judge clapped him on the shoulder and bowed to Francesca. "I'll be in touch."

***

The dismissal bell sounded a block away while Jim waited at the corner of Michigan Avenue and Selma Street. Minutes later, students from Leinkauf Elementary began crossing the road toward him. He smiled and nodded amid their greetings.

"Officer Abbott!" Ernest's hair flopped on his forehead as he rushed over.

"Hey, Ernest." He bestowed his hat on the boy and grinned. "How was your day?"

He shrugged as the kids passed around them. "All right, I guess."

"Look what I found." Jim pulled a baseball out of his pocket.

Ernest dropped his lunchbox to take it. "Gee, thanks, Officer Abbott! Can we play catch when we get home?"

He grinned over the fact that Ernest considered Francesca's house home—and included him in it. "For a few minutes, then I'll need to patrol more. But look what else I have."

Jim reached under his coat tails and pulled out a new child-sized mitt he'd tucked into his belt.

Mouth gaping as large as his wide-eyes, Ernest stuck the ball under his armpit, reverently took the leather mitt from Jim, and slid his left hand inside. "It's the best thing in the world, Officer Abbott! Only two boys at school have one. I bet I could get on a team if I share it."

Jim's hand went to Ernest's shoulder. "Don't rely on bribes—it's no way to live. You're going to get on a team because you're going to be a great player."

"Yes, sir."

Ernest gathered his lunchbox and they set off for George Street.

"Miss Fran!" Ernest called as he ran up the steps. "Look! Look what Officer Abbott got me!"

A minute later, Francesca came outside with Ernest and took a seat on the front steps to watch, her face radiant with joy.

"Come on over here, Ernest," Jim said. "What you need to keep in mind is to follow the ball with your eyes and get underneath it with the mitt. You'll have to use your other hand to cover the mitt to keep the ball inside because if it drops—"

"Everyone groans and yells at you."

"Something like that." Jim grinned. "Just pretend you're an alligator snapping its jaws to eat the ball."

"Have you seen an alligator?"

"Lots of times." Jim snatched the ball from Ernest. "They live along the rivers all around town."

"Would you take me to see one, Officer Abbott?"

"They're getting sleepy this time of year, but we could try if Miss Fran says it's okay. For now, show me how you snap."

He placed the ball in Ernest's mitt, who covered it with his other hand.

"Good. We'll start close, then we'll step apart every time you catch it. All right?"

Ernest nodded.

The first toss from a foot away rolled out of his mitt. That happened half the time over the next ten throws, but Ernest was giving it his all. After he caught it three times in a row from over ten feet away, Jim clapped.

"That's it for now, Ernest, but you know I'll be back."

"I hope we'll see you for supper, Jim," Francesca called.

He nodded, enjoying the look of appreciation Francesca gave him.

On his way to Washington Square Park, Jim went to the front gate of Winnie's parents' house. The dog started barking, and Merritt Graves stepped out the back porch.

"Good afternoon, Mrs. Graves," he called as he rounded the corner of the house.

"Hello, Officer Abbott."

"Is Drew here?" he asked about her teenage son.

"What's Andrew done this time?"

Jim laughed. "Nothing that I know of. I was hoping he'd stop by Miss Wilton's house and give Ernest a few pointers about baseball sometime over the next few days. I got the boy a ball and mitt, and he's eager to learn."

"He's working at the store this afternoon until closing, but he should be able to stop by this weekend."

"Thank you, Mrs. Graves. Let me know if you ever need anything."

"I appreciate it, Officer Abbott."

The next few days were filled with patrolling and playing ball with Ernest every available daylight hour, plus two appointments with Jo.

After supper Monday evening, when Ernest was sent to bathe, Jim and Francesca settled in the parlor where he dug in for the real update on the household. "How have things been at night since Narcissa left?"

"Quiet, but not what I'd call good." Francesca leaned against his shoulder. "Ernest isn't screaming, but he wakes up scared half the nights. Nightmares, though from what he tells me they aren't as vivid as before."

"Jo told me at our last session that she's studying things Deborah asked her to, but she's not ready yet."

"Ready for what?" Francesca asked.

"She didn't say, but I think it's something to stop Mr. Hart's ghost once and for all."

Twenty-four

In the twilight on Halloween, Francesca sat on the front porch and watched Ernest join the Reardon boys. His black bat wings, which Merritt had helped her make, flapped behind him as he caught up with his friends. Pleased that Ernest's improvement in baseball had strengthened the boys' friendship that week, she happily finished off a caramel apple and went inside to wash.

When Francesca returned, Jim walked up the street. The porch light glinted off the buttons on his uniform when he came up the walkway.

"You were always one to arrive in the gloaming, Officer Abbott."

"Are you going to start quoting lines from *Jane Eyre* to me?"

Francesca laughed.

"Chief O'Shaughnessy thought it would be a good idea to watch the Harts' house tonight in case some older kids try daring each other to enter."

"If you need refreshments or use of the bathroom, you know my house is always open to you. I'll leave it unlocked since you'll be out here all night."

"I appreciate that. I'll update you after Ernest gets home." Jim motioned up the street. "I saw him down the road when I was on my way in."

"Would you like to come in for some coffee?"

"I sure would." Jim held the screen door open and she felt his eyes on her from head to toe as she entered the house. "Is there anything you need help with while I'm here?"

"Yes." Francesca turned to him straight on. "I'm in need of a hug—and kiss."

Jim didn't waste time with gentleness. When his tongue swept in her welcoming mouth, he groaned and pulled back slightly.

"You're so sweet, Francesca."

"It's probably the candied apple. Would you like one? I have a few leftovers."

"I want more of this."

His lips were demanding, and she welcomed his insistence. Only when his touch roamed across her backside did she try to separate from him.

"Jim, you're on duty."

"I'm doing what you asked of me."

"And doing it beautifully." Francesca kissed him once more and turned for the stove, careful of Sunny and Rochester sleeping on the rug in front of it. "I'll get the coffee going. The apples are on the table."

"Will you be going to the polls Tuesday? I'm working security."

"I didn't get registered in time," she said with real disappointment.

"You're going to miss out on the first women's voting day in Alabama? Hattie Spunner refuses to allow the judge to escort her. She's bringing a carload of friends with her, including Winnie. I've had to promise the judge they wouldn't be molested when they go. There have been threats about men doing that. Judge Spunner is worked up about it, but Hattie isn't a timid woman."

"No one with Sean could ever be accused of timidity," Francesca said, thinking of Josephine's brief liaison with him before they were both married. "I won't miss the next election, that's for sure."

Jim picked up one of the apples by the skewer and bit into it. "Mm, this is great!"

"I bought fresh caramel from George's and melted it. Then used the plumpest apples I could find."

"No scrimping." He took another bite.

"I like the best of everything." She met his green eyes. "That's one of the reasons I love you."

He set his apple down and embraced her. They kissed until Sunny scaled Jim's trouser leg.

"Dammit, Sunny!"

"You're the only one he does that to." Francesca laughed and collected the kitten.

Jim took Sunny so she could return to the stove. His purring was loud across the room while Jim ate.

"I'm off a week from this Saturday," Jim said between bites. "I plan to go fishing and Winnie wants to host a fish fry that evening. Would you and Ernest want to come for supper?"

"We'd enjoy that, thank you."

"What about going to the bay with me? I could borrow Leo's automobile so we could easily get down there and back. I like to go before dawn, so it might make for a long day."

"I'm sure Ernest and I could handle that."

"Great. I'll let you know what time to expect me closer to then."

Jim tossed his skewer in the rubbish can. When the coffee was ready, they left the kittens inside and carried their cups to the front porch. They sat close on the steps and watched the neighborhood children run amuck amid the ruckus of howling, hooting, and other spooky noises. Francesca leaned her head on Jim's shoulder and soaked in the peace he always brought.

"How was your day?" she asked.

"I was one of the first on the scene of a horrific automobile accident this afternoon. A girl was badly injured, her mother was screaming, and the dad was trapped behind the steering wheel. There was blood everywhere."

Francesca rested a hand on Jim's knee.

"I closed my eyes and slowed my breathing. After that, I was able to refocus and offer help until the ambulance arrived."

"That's great, Jim. I'm sure Jo will be pleased to hear about that as well."

"It's about time I put all those tutoring hours to the test."

Ernest ran up the road, tears streaking his cheeks and his friends behind him. Jim was on the lawn before Francesca could stand.

"What's this about?" Jim asked.

Ernest ran passed him, throwing his arms around Francesca and buried his face in her middle.

Jack Reardon stepped forward. "Some fellas called him Ghost Boy and said his house was haunted. Tommy took off after them to pound 'em, but I hope he doesn't catch up. Dad will tan his hide if he gets into another fight this week."

Jim patted Ernest's shoulder as he continued to cower. "You've got some good friends ready to defend you, Ernest. That's a good thing."

He looked up.

"Words don't hurt unless you give them the power to," Francesca whispered. "Remember to hold your power, Ernest."

He looked at her with what Francesca could only call reverence.

"Like Miss Deborah taught me?"

Francesca nodded. "Now go wash your face and get back out there to have more fun. Halloween only comes once a year."

An hour later, Ernest and the Reardon brothers returned, separating to their houses.

"How was it?" Francesca asked as she stood from the front steps.

"The best night ever! We had cookies and slices of cake and pies at five different houses and games at three others." He hugged her and then looked at Jim, still sitting on the steps. "Are you staying, Officer Abbott?"

Jim nodded. "I'll be on patrol all night."

"Could I stay out here with him, Miss Fran?"

"For a little while. Let me take your wings inside so you don't get them stuck between the slats."

Francesca put away Ernest's wings and cleaned the kitchen. When she returned outside, Ernest was asleep, cradled in Jim's arms.

Smiling, she kissed the top of Ernest's head, then Jim's cheek. "Would you carry him to his room?"

She held the screen open. Ernest shifted restlessly when Jim brought him over the threshold. An oppressive force tingled across Francesca's skin. She berated herself when she remembered she hadn't informed Deborah of Ernest's increasing nightmares.

Francesca allowed Jim to tuck Ernest into bed so she could telephone Deborah.

"The spirits have already whispered your troubles to me," Deborah said. "I telephoned Jo a few minutes ago. We'll be over within the hour."

Jim joined her as she hung up the earpiece.

"Deborah?" he asked.

Francesca nodded. "And she's bringing Josephine."

"Good. Something is off—I can feel it." He hugged her. "I'm glad you didn't wait until things got out of control before seeking help. I'll wait on the porch for them."

"I love you, Jim."

"I want to show you how much I love you every day for the rest of my life, Francesca."

"I want that too." She shifted her hand lower on his back. "I want to share everything with you."

"We will, Francesca. We will."

Francesca busily straightened the parlor, pacing outside Ernest's door often. She joined the others in the front hall when they entered the house.

"Jim, your aura is red with thoughts of sex," Deborah declared as she slipped off her coat. "It's a good thing loving thoughts can go a long way in protecting a person from the ill effects of an evil spirit."

"Then Jim might prove to be invincible." Josephine smirked as she flipped a gauzy jade scarf back over the shoulder of her sleek pantsuit.

"It's no laughing matter," Deborah declared. "Is Ernest asleep?"

"Yes," Francesca said.

"We need to make a circle in the center of the house. Where do you think is closest to the middle, Francesca?"

"The hall outside Ernest's door."

"We'll gather there," Deborah explained in a low voice, "and link hands. Jo will need to sit closest to a wall because she'll be astral projecting, and her body will need the support."

"But if you can see him, doesn't that mean he can see you?" Jim asked.

"Yes, but he can see us in the flesh as well."

"But he might have more communication with you in spirit form," Francesca said. "Are you sure you're up for it?"

"I know the risks and am willing to take them to free you and Ernest from this otherworldly danger. No matter my faults, you should know I'm a loyal friend."

"But what of Cyrus and your children?"

"Cyrus understands my need to help and has complete faith in my abilities, as well as Deborah's. Won't you trust us as well?"

Francesca's brown eyes filled with tears. "I don't want anyone else hurt—or worse."

"You should know a little pain never stopped me. How many fights did you witness me participate in during childhood? How many scraped knees and blackened eyes? You and Ernest are more worthy of needing my protection than my own youthful ego."

Francesca and Josephine linked arms and led the way down the hall.

"What should we each focus on?" Jim asked Deborah when they stopped outside Ernest's door.

"Jo has her responsibilities, but you and Fran can focus on love and happiness. That won't be too difficult, will it?" Deborah gave a reassuring smile. "I'd like you on my right, Jim. You can hold Fran's hand on the other side."

That left Josephine in front of Ernest's closed door as they settled cross-legged on the floor. She held Francesca's gaze with her hazel eyes. "Stay alert, Fran."

She nodded and glanced at the medium. Deborah's eyes were closed as she focused on her breathing.

Jim raised their linked hands and kissed the back of Francesca's. "I'd do anything to protect you and Ernest," he whispered as the temperature of the house dropped.

Without warning, Deborah raised her voice. "You are not welcomed here, William Hart!"

Josephine slouched against the door. Francesca looked around in an attempt to see her astral form.

"The boy is protected. You need to move to the next life." Deborah jerked as though someone had knocked her on the side of the head.

Francesca squeezed Jim's hand to reassure herself he was there.

"You shall leave all inhabitants in this home alone." Deborah flinched sideways just before a dent was punched into the wall beside where she sat.

Though she couldn't see or hear her, Francesca knew Josephine had warned Deborah and was smiling over the slight victory. Then there was a rush of cool air, and Josephine's leg jerked.

Deborah rattled off commands regarding Mr. Hart leaving Josephine's body alone. As though he changed his focus, the medium began squirming, seeming to be strangled by an unseen hand.

Josephine must have succeeded in gaining control of William Hart because Deborah gasped and swayed with release. After a moment, Deborah began to declare the spirit powerless in her presence. Before she could finish the statement, she was struck back. Jim's linked arm jolted with the force, and her lip bled.

Deborah opened her mouth, red staining her lips and chin on her otherwise colorless face. "You have no power over me, William Hart!"

In case the blood triggered Jim, Francesca prayed for him to remain calm. While she was keeping vigil in her thoughts, Ernest's bedroom door opened. Josephine's body fell back—pulling her hand free from Francesca's.

Ernest saw the blood on Deborah's face. Fear turned to anger, his eyes an icy blue. "Don't hurt my friend!"

With the circle already broken, Francesca rose, wishing to be a barrier between Ernest and his father as the house began to shake.

Deborah avowed another command. "He belongs to another now. He's protected by love!"

"My love!" Francesca echoed.

"Miss Fran!" Ernest clung to her. Rather than cower before his father as he had done in the past, he raised his chin as though making eye contact with his father's ghost. "Stop hurting my friends."

A blast of angry wind tunneled down the hall, blowing everyone's hair and rustling Deborah's dress. The medium's words continued while Francesca embraced Ernest. Looking over his head, she saw Josephine's jade scarf slowly being pulled from her shoulders.

"Jo?" she whispered. There was no reply, not even a halting of the scarf's movement. "Deborah, where's Jo?"

"Her aura is there, and it's not moving." She pointed to the floor outside their grouping. "He must have somehow stunned her."

The scarf, now free of Josephine, drifted directly toward Francesca on an invisible current. One moment it was in the air, the next it was coiled around her throat.

"No chance in hell, you fiend!" Jim worked to get his fingers between the scarf and Francesca's neck.

The house bucked with waves of emotion rolling off Ernest. It was his outstretched hand that knocked the evil spirit away, allowing Jim to fully free Francesca. She clung to him, gasping for breath, as he leaned against the wall and held her.

Ernest's arms went around them both. "I love you, Miss Fran. You and Officer Abbott are my favorites."

And then he appeared in his ghostly form. Tall, lean, and sporting the biggest scowl this side of the Mississippi. William Hart's frigid glare looked down with malice on the trio.

"Welcome to your death," he drawled, hovering toward them.

"Don't engage him," Deborah warned. "Y'all are too inexperienced!"

Francesca straightened, knowing she needed to help Ernest.

William's ghost gave a sardonic laugh as it moved closer. "Touching, ain't it? She's like my Sue—another dumb broad thinking her love can save a boy."

Jim clumsily lurched forward.

"No, Jim." Francesca held tight to his hand. "We're stronger together. Remember what you did before with your aura."

"That was a fluke."

"Please try again. Focus on Ernest. He needs you."

Jim steadied his footing and Deborah issued more commands to control the ghost, who, though not as visible as he was moments before, still created a menacing presence as he reached toward Francesca.

Ernest stood before her with deliberate effort amid the shrieks that surrounded them. His stare brought his father to his knees. Slowly, William Hart's ghost crumpled into submission as his vile face twisted in a mockery of physical pain.

"Deborah," Francesca said, "Ernest has him subdued. Banish him!"

"Hold steady, Jim," Deborah replied. "He might lash out again before it's over."

Deborah felt Jim's palm grow warmer though he didn't hold her any tighter. She clung to Ernest with her other arm, watching the apparition whither away though Deborah and Ernest kept their focus on the spot where it was. Seconds later, it felt like midday in July. The hotter it got, the more Jim appeared to wilt.

"Ernest, keep holding me," Francesca said.

She maneuvered to hold Jim upright with both arms. By the time Deborah's final words were said, Ernest and Jim were both on the bare wood floor.

Jim had suffered a swoon and was unresponsive with his head in Francesca's lap. Ernest sat with Deborah while Josephine burned a sage bundle between them.

When he opened his eyes, Josephine poked Francesca's knee.

"See, he's fine, Fran. He used a lot of spiritual energy and will be weak several hours. I'm sure you'd be happy to keep him here tonight and administer to him." Jo grinned and looked at Ernest. "You were amazing. Deborah has taught you a lot, but I could teach you more.

"Not yet, please," Francesca said. "We need to recuperate from this before moving forward."

"Deborah banished him, didn't she?" Jim's voice was weak and deeper than normal.

"Yes, he's gone, but you did your share of the work," Deborah said. "Your aura joined with Francesca's and Ernest's, then expanded further to protect all three of you, plus Jo and me. The colors swirling within it were amazing to witness. But you need rest."

"I'll keep you here as Jo suggested so you can finish your watch duties. That is, if you dare risk your reputation."

Jim smiled up at her. "You own me, Francesca Wilton."

Twenty-five

A week later, Jim walked into the station Monday morning and was given the message to report to Chief O'Shaughnessy's office immediately.

"Better you than me," Officer Fitzwilliam whispered from the desk.

Jim's knock on the chief's door was answered with a booming "come in!"

"Abbott." Chief O'Shaughnessy motioned to the extra chair with a nod. "Judge Spunner tells me the business with the Hart boy is as good as done."

"Yes, Miss Wilton is officially getting temporary custody of Ernest."

"Good for her. She seems to really care for the boy. I'm pulling you from them starting today. You've got bigger things to worry about than the orphan. We need more officers on wheels. I hear your goal is detective, but getting you into more action will be beneficial for that. We've got two additional Harley-Davidsons on the way and you're going to be one of the officers on a new bike. You know how to ride, don't you?"

"Yes, I've ridden several times."

"Good. Cooper's going to train you. Your wheels should be here by Friday, but he can show you some maneuvers before then. Be sure to stop by Dreaper and Burns to get fitted for riding pants, boots, and gloves on your way out. And you'll need an exterior holster. Pick one up as soon as you can and get used to wearing your sidearm over your coat." He handed Jim a paper with orders for the needed supplies. "It'll be a raise, of course."

"Yes, Chief O'Shaughnessy. And thank you."

"That's all."

Jim stood, and hesitated. "Who's going to be taking my place in Washington Square?"

"We're moving Officer Keegan over from the north side of Government. Fitzwilliam is going back on the streets and will take Keegan's old grounds."

"Glad to hear that, chief. Thank you again for this opportunity."

Jim soon strolled up St. Emanuel Street to the men's store on Dauphin that handled the police uniforms. He handed over the paper with the order and planned his other stops while they measured him. By the time he caught a westbound trolley, he was wearing a new holster and two pairs of leather gloves and a pair of goggles were stored in his interior pockets. He would pick up his new uniform pants and boots later in the week.

When he met Ernest walking home from school, the first thing Ernest did was stare at the revolver on Jim's hip.

"Golly, Officer Abbott, you've got a gun like a real cowboy!"

Jim dropped his hat on Ernest's head. "I've always had the gun, Ernest."

"Really? Where?"

"Under my coat. I've got to start wearing it like this because—well, I'll wait to tell you and Miss Fran together."

"Aw, I can keep a secret!"

"Not from me and Miss Fran, young man."

"No, sir. But for the walk home?"

"Nope."

"Do you think Drew Graves will come play with me again today?" Ernest asked as they walked up Palmetto Street.

"He's working this afternoon, but it sounded like he would check in with you later this week."

"Then we better practice, Officer Abbott."

"You're ready for some high pops, but that oak tree's canopy out front is too big. We'll have to move down the street for that."

When they got to Francesca's, Ernest ran ahead. The screen door banged shut behind him. Jim carefully let himself in. He pulled a pair of gloves from a pocket, slipped them on, and held the goggles behind his back.

Ernest carried the kittens into the parlor, Francesca following him.

"I told Miss Fran you had an important announcement," Ernest declared as he sat on the sofa beside her. Francesca's eyes were on Jim's crossbody holster, her brow quizzical.

"It's mixed news," Jim said in warning, "but I hope you'll be as excited as I am about the changes. By the end of the week, you'll have a new patrolman in the neighborhood, my friend, Officer Keegan."

"You won't come check on us anymore?" Ernest whined.

"Not on official police business, but Chief O'Shaughnessy told me today was my last day for that since Miss Fran is getting permission to be your guardian. I hope she'll let me keep visiting."

Ernest clung to her. "Will you, Miss Fran?"

"Of course, Ernest. Jim is very special to me, as he is to you."

Jim grinned. "And I love you both."

"Where are you gonna be if you aren't in Washington Square?" Ernest asked.

Jim pulled the goggles over his head and held his hands like he was steering handlebars. "You're looking at the newest motorcycle officer with the Mobile Police Department."

Ernest squealed and jumped to his feet. "Wait until Tommy and Jack hear about this! It's much better than any other job in the world!"

"I wouldn't go that far, but it's a step up for me at the station."

Ernest picked up Sunny and ran out the door. Jim's chuckle stopped as soon as he saw Francesca's seriousness. He removed the goggles and re-pocketed them and the gloves. Lowering to the sofa beside her, he took her hands in his.

"It's a steppingstone, Fran. Chief O'Shaughnessy knows I want to be a detective, and this will give me broader experience before moving me up. I even get a raise."

She fingered the cross strap on the holster. "You look ready for a shootout."

Jim smiled. "Ernest said I looked like a cowboy, but it's always been there, Fran. Wearing it this way just makes it easier if I have to use it while on the motorcycle."

"Have you ever had to draw it?" she whispered.

"No, not even when I was a guard at the bank. It's been since the war that I was in a firefight." He leaned in to kiss her, then rested his forehead on hers. "I appreciate that you care, Francesca. Now that the possible dangers are on full display, it's more concerning to you."

Her nose brushed his cheek as she nodded. "I don't want to lose you, Jim."

"It'll take more than a change in departments for that to happen." He hugged her. "I'll tell Keegan to look after y'all when he's on duty, but you can bet I'll drive by as often as I can. My one worry is that Miss Eilands will accuse me of scaring her cats the first time I drive to her house."

Francesca smiled. "I'm sure she will. You're still welcome to take breakfast and supper with us when you can."

"And dessert?" Jim nipped her neck.

She laughed and shied away.

"I'd love to stay and taste more, but I've got to get back on patrol."

"I'll see you this evening."

"I wouldn't miss supper with you and Ernest for anything, Fran."

***

On the second Saturday in November, Francesca had coffee and sausage ready and pancakes cooking at four in the morning. Jim came in the back door while Ernest was still dressing.

"Morning, Francesca." Jim gave her a quick hug.

"Could you take over this last batch so I can check Ernest?"

"Certainly."

She pulled the apron off and smiled when Jim saw what she wore beneath—a simple shirt tucked into a pair of belted trousers. Eyes wide, he watched her leave the room.

When she returned with Ernest and the kittens, breakfast was on the table.

After eating, the ride to the bay was dark and quiet. Ernest laid on the backseat beside the fishing poles so he could catch a bit more sleep. Francesca sat snug beside Jim, his right hand tucked between the thighs of her trousers.

The sky was a dusky purple when he parked a hair north of Dog River along the bay. Francesca set out the blankets and picnic supplies while Ernest helped Jim with the fishing gear. The sunrise over the bay mesmerized her with the golden display Jim and Ernest were silhouetted against.

After the sun crested the eastern shore, she spent the morning lounging on the blanket or walking the coast. Ernest flourished under Jim's instructions, making her ache because he had missed such opportunities with his father. At least there was a second chance with Jim. He was wonderful with children—Ernest, Percy, and the boys on the street. Jim was kind but firm and deserved every show of respect the youngsters gave him.

"Are we close to having enough fish to feed everyone?" she asked as Jim ate a sandwich.

"Nearly." He pushed his wide-brimmed hat up his forehead. "I'd like a bit more so we can leave some with Miss Eilands."

"We get to see the cat lady?" Ernest asked.

"Yes," Jim answered. "But that doesn't mean you get another kitten."

Francesca laughed. "Sunny and Rochester are more than a handful."

Ernest ate the rest of his apple before wandering to the shore to check the fishing poles that were stuck in the sand.

"You're doing marvelously with him, Fran," Jim remarked.

"You've been a great help. And now that the nightmares about his father are gone, he stays asleep all night." She took Jim's hand, hot from the sun. "Ernest has looked forward to today, and I'm having a terrific time as well."

Jim glanced at Ernest wading in the water before stealing a kiss. "I'm loving this extra time with you."

"There's a fish on your pole, Officer Abbott!" Ernest hollered. "It's gonna drag it in the water!"

"Grab it, Ernest!" Jim shouted as he ran towards him.

At half past two, Jim pulled to a stop outside Miss Eilands's property. The automobile was immediately flocked by a dozen cats, meowing for food and attention.

Laughing, Jim passed the basket for Miss Eilands to Ernest. "Think you can make it through that gauntlet?"

"If you get the gate."

Jim left the automobile door open for Ernest to scramble out with his load. Francesca followed their lead into the odiferous yard teeming with felines.

"You have company!" Jim hollered.

"As if I couldn't tell with that racket," Miss Eilands shouted back. "You're the only one who can bring my cats to this level of frenzy, Jimmy, but at least you didn't bring that motorcycle this time."

While doing his best to keep the basket out of reach of the persistent cats, Ernest giggled over Jim being chastised.

"I see you brought your friends. I hope they aren't planning on returning those kittens I entrusted to them."

"No, ma'am! I love Sunny," Ernest said as he thrust the basket at her. "Officer Abbott taught me how to fish and we brought you some."

"Well how about that! Jimmy is quite a man, isn't he?" She teased as she accepted the offering.

"He's my favorite," Ernest declared, "and I think Miss Fran's too."

"Oh, I'm sure he is if she knows heads from tails." Her blue eyes flashed in Francesca's direction, causing her sun-kissed cheeks to blush. "The link between the two of you is stronger than it was last month. Don't let it go to waste, girl."

Jim wiped the grin off his face long enough to speak. "We need to get moving, but holler if you need anything, Miss Eilands."

Jim dropped Francesca at home so she could freshen up, but insisted on bringing Ernest back with him so he could teach him how to clean the fish. After caring for the kittens and taking a leisurely shower, Francesca dressed in a blue striped cotton frock and pulled her bobbed hair back with tortoiseshell combs. The hint of sun she'd gotten agreed with her. Coupled with Jim's sweet attentions throughout the day, she felt beautiful as she walked to Hallett Street with a knapsack holding a change of clothes for Ernest.

Jaunty dance music played on a phonograph set on the front porch of the apartment house. A huge man in overalls and a white undershirt sat on the steps, shucking corn into a bucket with Percy.

"Good afternoon," Francesca said.

The man raised his head, brown hair falling into eyes of the same color before he pushed it back with his forearm. "Hey there."

"Hey, hey!" Percy said as he waved a corncob, full radiance on display with his bright smile.

"Hi, Percy. It's good to see you again." She met the man's stare. "I'm Fran Wilton—Jim's guest."

"Oh, sorry, ma'am." He dropped his corn into the bucket and stood. After wiping his hands on his overalls, he offered one. "I'm Leo, from the other upstairs unit. Jim borrowed my car today—among other times. I guess you already know Percy."

"I know his grandparents well. It's good to meet you, Leo."

"I don't know where Jim got to, but he's probably out back. He was teaching your boy to clean fish."

Nathan exited the front door behind Leo. Seeing his cropped right sleeve sent a pang of regret to Francesca's heart at the thought of Jim's invisible wounds.

"Hello, Miss Wilton."

"Please call me Fran, Nathan."

He smiled, making him shine as much as his son. "Would you like something to drink, Fran?"

"Not yet, thank you."

"The ladies are inside, and Jim and Ernest are out back. Could I take your bag?"

"It's a change of clothes for Ernest. I'll go around and leave it on Jim's steps. Thank you for hosting us."

In the back yard, Jim watched over Ernest as the boy worked with a knife, filleting fish at a makeshift counter beneath the live oak tree. The wooden ledge was built for the standing height of a man, so Ernest was on a stepstool. Francesca set the bag on the stairs.

"That's it, Ernest. Slow, firm strokes." Looking up, Jim caught her eye and grinned. "Look who's all cleaned up while we're a smelly mess."

"Watch what I can do, Miss Fran!" Ernest took another deboned fish and carefully sliced it into fillets.

"That's great, Ernest. Jim's been teaching you a lot today."

"Hello, Fran," Winnie said as she stepped out the back screened door, followed by a wiry blonde. "I'm glad you could join us. This is Sydney Williams. She lives upstairs with her husband, Leo, in the front apartment."

"It's good to meet you, Sydney. I met Leo on my way in."

They shook hands.

Sydney looked over Francesca. "Your dress is beautiful."

"I love the floral print on yours," Francesca remarked. "Purple is always festive."

"Pretty and sweet." Sydney sighed. "Jim, you better hang onto this one."

"I plan to." He smiled, but stayed by Ernest as he finished the final fish.

Ernest proudly carried the platter to Winnie.

"You did great, Ernest," Winnie said. "Thank you for helping with supper."

"I brought you a change of clothes," Francesca told him. "It's on the back stairs."

Jim turned on the spigot and rinsed his hands. "Come wash off, Ernest. Then I'll take you upstairs to get cleaned up properly."

"Then clean up yourself," Winnie told him. "We'll keep Fran company."

When Jim and Ernest climbed the stairs, Sydney watched them with a shake of her head before turning to Francesca. "Our Jim has it bad. He's had a few girls over before, but he's never looked at them the way he does you."

Winnie nodded in agreement. "Not even Marie Marley."

"We'll miss him, but I won't prevent a woman from enjoying what Jim can bring to a relationship." Sydney grinned wickedly. "Besides that fine backside, he's got a heart of gold."

"He's loved you from the beginning, Fran," Winnie added.

Francesca helped Winnie and Sydney with the food and chatted with everyone over the meal.

When the men came back inside following their after-supper smoke, Sydney put a finger to her lips. "The boys are being put to bed."

"Do I need to bring Fran and Ernest home?" Jim asked.

"Don't take Fran away," Sydney said. "She's the most fun we've had around here in a long time."

Winnie came out of the front bedroom and went straight to Jim. "Ernest is on the daybed. He was asleep almost as soon as his head touched the pillow. Now you and Fran can have some time together before you take them home. Shall we play a game or dance?"

Francesca began swaying her hips.

"Oh," Sydney said, "get these folks a tango, quick!"

Leo hunted up a recording and Jim moved the coffee table to the hallway. All six of them danced, changing partners several times. Nathan was stiff with Francesca at first, but she treated him the same as Winnie did—leaning close to his right side to compensate for his missing limb.

When they rotated through to some ballads, Nathan and Winnie took the sofa so she could rest her swollen feet. Leo and Sydney were dancing sensuously in a way only a married couple could do without a scandal brewing. But it was nothing to the moves Jim and Francesca had done at Cordelia's party.

"Would you like to get some air?" Jim asked.

Francesca nodded and he held the screen door open. The November night had cooled considerably, causing her to shiver. Jim put an arm around Francesca and pulled her close as they sat together on the wicker loveseat.

"Did you bring a coat?"

"No, and don't leave to fetch one. I'll be fine if you keep beside me."

He kissed her cheek. "I had a wonderful day."

"So did I. I loved every moment, and your neighbors are great."

He trailed kisses down her jaw and her hand on his knee crept up his thigh. He captured her lips as his touch migrated to her backside to pull her into his lap.

"Hey, lovebirds," Nathan said from the front door. "There are neighbors passing by, not to mention four pairs of eyes looking out from the front window. If you need to take things upstairs, we'll listen out for Ernest."

Jim nosed under Francesca's hair and whispered. "Not here, even if you begged me."

She giggled, straightening her dress as she stood. "Sorry, Nathan. Jim makes me a little crazed. I'm glad your mother-in-law didn't see me behave like that."

Nathan laughed and disappeared inside. Francesca went to follow, but Jim captured her right hand.

He dropped to a knee before her as his left hand fished something out of his pocket. A breathless moment later, he lifted a thin gold band before Francesca. The glow from the porch light made the tiny diamond flare with pride. It captured her heart in its simplicity as the bearer held her fascinated with his vivid gaze.

"I've had a wonderful day with you and Ernest, which followed weeks of shared adventures and increasing emotions. I want nothing more than to continue our life together so I can be there for you both without fail. Would you marry me, Francesca Wilton? It doesn't have to be soon. I'd wait forever to have you fully in a moment of shared passion."

"Jim…" She sank to the seat behind her, never looking away as the warmth surrounded her unlike any time before. Her head shifted in a partial shake as she tried to grasp the right words.

"Fran? It's not too small, is it?"

She smiled. "It's perfect. Your love is my priceless treasure."

A gasp and a few claps were heard inside the house, followed by an "it's so sweet" from Sydney. Francesca stifled an exasperated laugh at realizing their audience was as enthralled with Jim's declaration as she was.

"Then you accept me, Francesca?"

"Yes, Jim. A Christmas wedding would be romantic."

"I'd be good company that time of year with the possibility of chilly nights for me to keep you warm." The dimple creased his cheek deeper than ever when he slipped the ring on her finger, rousing a yearning for Francesca to capture the moment forever.

"You're always great company, Jim. I'll take your companionship under any condition, anytime."

THE END

Author's Note

It's been a fun ride getting to know the new characters in the Washington Square Secrets series and how they interact with old favorites, but also a challenging one—especially with the ever persistent and insightful notes from my editor, Sean Connell. He helps me get control and refocus on what's important after I let the characters run away with the story. Thanks, Boss.

Writing about the Mobile Police Department during the prohibition era proved to be a trial all its own. Years of missing records from public archives made for a lot of dead ends. At the beginning of my search in early 2023, Jada Jones of The Doy Leale McCall Rare Book and Manuscript Library at the University of South Alabama shared what the archives had for the Mobile Police Department. (There are some amazing photographs in the collection.) Thank you for your time, and to E. Lorene Flanders, executive director of USA Libraries, for getting me in touch with her.

My biggest lead came at the end of my journey in early 2024—half a year before publication and a full year after my research began. Fortunately, it left me with enough time to add in those historical details I desperately wanted to create an authentic story. Kudos to the unknown-to-me person behind the Mobile Police Department Facebook page who passed my contact information to Captain Billie L. Rowland. Captain

Rowland graciously shared his time, information (which, though slim for my requested era, was more than what public archives had), and photographs of Mobile's finest. His passion for MPD history helped me bring Officer Jim Abbott's journey to accurate life on the pages of this book. Thank you for continuing to answer my questions as they cropped up during editorial rounds after our initial meeting. Here's to hoping the MPD Museum sees new life in the future. There are many stories that deserve to be shared.

As always, special thanks to Candice Marley Conner and Jennifer Lamont for their insights into early drafts and sharing the editorial journey with me as compassionate bystanders while I struggled through multiple manuscript overhauls.

In case you can judge a book by its cover, I'm grateful to have another original Amanda Manley watercolor. Thank you for bringing my vision to life with your whimsical, Gothic vibe, once again.

Keep an eye out for the fourth—and final—book in the Washington Square Secrets series in 2025. In the meantime, check out more about Sean, Merritt, Winnie, Nathan, and others in The Malevolent Trilogy, if you haven't already.

About the Author

While experiencing the typical adventures of growing up, Carrie Dalby called several places in California home, but she's lived on the Alabama Gulf Coast since 1996. Serving two terms as president of Mobile Writers' Guild, five years as the Mobile area Local Liaison for the Society of Children's Book Writers and Illustrators, and helping coordinate the Mobile Literary Festival are some of the writing-related volunteer positions she's held. When Carrie isn't reading, writing, browsing bookstores and libraries, or homeschooling her children, she can often be found knitting or attending concerts.

Carrie writes for both teens and adults. *Fortitude* is listed as a Best Historical Book for Kids by Grateful American Foundation. The Possession Chronicles, The Malevolent Trilogy, and Washington Square Secrets are her Southern Gothic series for adults. She has also published several short stories that can be found in different anthologies as well as her short story collection *Masked Flaws and Other Stories*.

For more information, social media links, newsletter sign-up, and more, visit Carrie Dalby's website:

carriedalby.com

www.ingramcontent.com/pod-product-compliance
Lightning Source LLC
Chambersburg PA
CBHW061753190726
48289CB00007B/1931